Never Never

Book Seven
The Irish End Game Series

Susan Kiernan-Lewis

Susan Kiernan-Lewis

Never Never

San Marco Press/Atlanta
Copyright 2015

Other books by Susan Kiernan-Lewis:

Free Falling
Going Gone
Heading Home
Blind Sided
Rising Tides
Cold Comfort
Murder in the South of France
Murder à la Carte
Murder in Provence
Murder in Paris
Murder in Aix
Murder in Nice
Murder in the Latin Quarter
A Grave Mistake
Walk Trot Die
Finding Infinity
Swept Away
Carried Away
Stolen Away
Reckless
Shameless
Breathless
Heartless

1.

Sarah listened to the low-grade thrumming of the airliner as it flew overhead. To hear that familiar noise again after so many years was a reassuring flashback of the way life used to be.

"Where do ye think it's headed?" Her sister-in-law Fiona walked up to where Sarah stood in the garden—a basket at her feet and her six-month old daughter in her arms.

"My guess?" Fiona said before Sarah could reply, "London or maybe Paris. Hard to believe life goes on in the world."

Fiona reached for Sarah's baby and after a brief hesitation Sarah gave the child to her. With dark blonde hair and large blue eyes, Siobhan was an arrestingly beautiful child. Sarah's son John had been adorable as a baby, but Siobhan made people stop and stare.

"She didn't nap. *Again*," Sarah said.

"I'm told the smart ones don't," Fiona said.

"Bite your tongue."

"Speaking of the smart ones, is John in Oxford yet, do ye think?"

Sarah looked back up at the sky. She anxiously rubbed the small of her back at the thought of him so far away.

"Hours ago, I imagine," she said. "I'd give anything for just five minutes of a working Internet or a telephone. Just long enough to know he arrived safely."

Fiona gave Sarah's arm a squeeze. "In the meantime, sure you have your hands full with this little one. And before you know it, it'll be December and the lad will be back."

"I know," Sarah said. "It's right that he's focused on his studies. I don't want him worrying about me. I'd hate that."

"Of course you would."

"I assume you're here to help me bring in the veggies," Sarah said, reaching for the basket of tomatoes on the ground. "I'm counting on the truckload of mackerel Mike and Gavin promised they'd catch for dinner tonight."

"Declan wanted to go with them," Fiona said as she glanced back toward the convent. "But his headaches are bothering him again."

"I'm sorry, Fi. I wish we had a better answer for what ails him. You've used all your homeopathic stuff?"

"Aye. I think whatever's wrong is bigger than herbs and spices can handle. Oh, there's Nuala!"

From across the small stone wall enclosing the garden, Sarah saw Nuala with her two month old daughter in her arms, waving to them from the door of the convent.

"Must be time to set the table and get the gang washed up," Sarah said. She looked at the gate that led to the outside road.

The road was narrow and clogged with overhanging brush and alder trees and was only fit for horses or foot travel. Mike and Gavin had taken the Jeep they kept hidden by the main road, a good five miles walk from the convent.

Sarah knew the nunnery itself had almost no defensive features—not like the compound that they'd had to abandon in the spring—but because of its remote and concealed location, it was infinitely safer.

The monsters who'd discovered the convent earlier last spring didn't count because one of those monsters knew right where to go. For everybody else in Ireland—the convent was invisible.

"You coming then, Sarah?" Fiona called over her shoulder as she moved toward the front door with the baby.

Sarah shook herself out of her thoughts and bent to add a few more tomatoes to the basket.

"Be there in a sec," she said. She turned to look at the wrought iron gate that led to the road, and a chill crept over her skin.

Mike and Gavin should have been back by now.

*****

Hours later Sarah stood at the front door with a fussing Siobhan and looked out again into the evening. It got dark sooner every day now. Summer was definitely behind them. She strained to see in the darkness past the garden toward the gate and the road leading to the convent.

They had never been this late. And Mike knew how much she worried.

Something had happened.

Siobhan arched her back and threw her head back, smacking hard against Sarah's chin. She kicked her feet but Sarah only held her tighter.

"Siobhan, stop it," Sarah said, tasting the blood in her mouth where her teeth had bitten the inside of her lip.

"The little one is weary," a strong female voice said from behind Sarah. Mother Angelina stood with her arms outstretched for the baby. Sarah handed Siobhan over. Instantly the baby settled down and tucked her head against the Mother Superior's chest.

"I don't know what the matter is with her," Sarah said, rubbing her chin.

"She's picking up on her mother's anxiety. That's all."

"They should have been back hours ago."

"They'll be back."

"You really think so?"

"Or they won't."

"Big comfort, Mother."

"Waiting is always our hardest task."

"I just can't believe they're this late. And on the very day John left."

"You must try to relax, Sarah."

Mother Angelina wore her solid black habit straight to the floor. Its starched wimple framed her face. Her eyes were kind as she watched Sarah.

"I can't," Sarah said. "And Mike not coming home on time just proves that we need to stop leaving the convent so much. Who knows what they've run into?"

"I'm not sure it proves anything except that they're late. It's true there's much danger in the world. That's no reason not to live in the world."

"That's where you're wrong. You should see what's out there now. *Animals* hoping to kill you and take what's yours. There's *every* reason not to be out there."

"Is that what you think has happened to your husband? Someone has attempted to take what he has?"

Before Sarah could speak, she noticed that Siobhan had fallen asleep in the nun's arms. Siobhan had been pitching a fit not two minutes ago and now she was asleep.

"I don't know," Sarah said, her voice thick with discouragement.

"Sometimes real safety comes only from taking risks."

"That doesn't even make sense. I'm sorry, Mother. You're a wise woman and I have no idea how any of us would've survived without you. But safety comes from being some place where no one can find you. Trust me, I know a little something about that."

Fiona and Gavin's wife Sophia came from the back of the house and joined them by the open door.

"The other children are mostly down for the night," Fiona said. "Do you want me to take Siobhan?"

"No," Sarah said, reaching for her child. "I'll take her in." As soon as she collected the little bundle in her arms, Siobhan woke up and began to whimper.

"Any sign of them?" Sophia said. She smoothed her hand over her pregnant belly. She was due in a few weeks.

Siobhan turned toward Angelina and held out her arms to her.

"I'm happy to take her for you, Sarah," Angelina said, reaching for the baby. "She's just tired."

Sarah hesitated but Siobhan squirmed and fussed until she gave her up.

"Thanks, Mother," Sarah said, her heart plummeting as she saw how quickly Siobhan settled down again in the nun's arms.

Speaking softly to the child, Mother Angelina went into the convent leaving the three women on the wide stone porch.

"Don't worry, Sarah," Fiona said as she gave Sarah's shoulder a squeeze. "They'll be back."

"Of course they will," Sophia said. "They have to be."

Sarah wondered how Sophia had survived the last five years with such impossible optimism. As her eyes dropped to the severed ring finger on the girl's left hand, she was reminded that Sophia knew treachery and betrayal only too well.

"I just can't imagine why they're not here," Sarah said. The anxiety was growing in her chest like a living thing, threatening to overflow.

"There could be any number of perfectly good reasons," Fiona said as she looked out into the darkness.

Sarah winced at the fact that Fiona— who had lived through hell last winter, lost a baby and gained a husband who couldn't remember who she was half the time—was giving *her* comfort. She took a long breath.

"I'm never letting that man out of my sight again," Sarah said. The other two laughed.

"So young John will be back at Christmas, eh?" Fiona said. "I'm sorry I didn't go with you today to see him off. Declan was having one of his spells."

Ever since Declan had been shot in the head and left for dead last winter, he'd had terrible headaches and long spates of confusion and memory loss. He was a proud man, an Irish traveler with a history of living rough. Sarah knew how he struggled with his new condition. And how Fiona struggled.

"He'll be back before Christmas," Sarah said, watching the shadows in the woods past the garden gate and hoping to see one of them morph into the tall figure of her husband. "He was so excited to get back to Oxford that he *ran* to the helicopter."

"He's a smart boy," Sophia said. "If anybody should be in school, it's him."

"Well, the truth is," Fiona said, "it's a mother's lot to worry, so it is." She turned to Sophia and smiled. "As you'll learn soon enough."

Sophia laughed. "I can't wait," she said, rubbing her large belly. "Gavin wants me to hurry and pop this one out so we can leave."

Sarah let out a snort of frustration. "*Why* Gavin and Mike think we should leave the convent is beyond me! We're safe here. I don't understand it at all."

"Mike's not convinced we're safe here," Fiona said.

Sarah turned on her. "Are you on his side? Have you not had a big enough dose of what the outside world can dole out?"

Fiona narrowed her eyes. "Sure I have, Sarah Donovan," she said testily. "But before you regale us with how safe this place is, may I remind you of the blood bath that occurred on nearly the very spot you're standing?"

"That's not fair," Sarah said. "You know Mac and his gang would never have found us if not for the fact that Sinead Branigan lived here at one time."

"Mac" MacClenny had attacked the convent last spring. Of the three surviving assailants, one had been allowed to leave after a brief period of incarceration and one was executed for crimes committed against the women in the camp. Mac himself had been pardoned and now lived at the convent.

"I ken that your idea of safety is being well hidden," Fiona said. "But we need to be well *defended*."

"That's impossible," Sarah said. "Need I remind *you*, Fiona, about the time the Garda came to the compound and took everyone in it? There's no way we can defend ourselves against an army."

"Not in a convent, anyway," Sophia said meekly.

Sarah turned to her. "You, too?"

Sophia shrugged. "I trust Gavin. He says the convent is not our home forever."

Sarah turned away. "He's been listening to Mike."

"As a good son should."

Just then Sarah noticed a movement in the distant darkness and her heart pounded with excitement.

A tall form appeared at the edge of the garden. Sarah recognized the sloping hat and stooped shoulders. It was only Mac doing his nightly perimeter check. He did it several times an evening before retiring to the shed at the north end of the garden. While she knew he carried a gun, she also knew it wouldn't be of much use against a serious attack.

She shook herself out of the thought. They were safe here. Nobody knew where the convent was. There was no easy way to get to the nunnery. It was *leaving* the convent that caused problems.

As evidenced by their vigil on the front porch tonight.

It was nine hours since Mike and Gavin had taken the Jeep to go fishing off the coast of Rosslare—just thirty minutes north of them. Even with the overgrown roads and the portion of the trail they had to travel on foot, nine hours was too long. Nine hours meant something had happened.

Something bad.

2.

The water pummeled Mike's face like a personal vendetta.

Even with the precious seconds he'd had to jump free of the dinghy, all control was ripped from his hands as the explosion of water ruptured in front of him when the airliner hit.

He was being dragged down to the darkest depths of the Irish Sea, his arms and legs thrashing to fight the suction of the vortex. Panic filled him. He didn't know if he was up or down, if he was swimming in the direction of the surface or the bottom.

His lungs burned as he tried to combat the fear that was freezing his joints. Something hard slammed into his side spinning him end over end in torturously slow circles. He only had a moment to pray for Sarah, Gavin and the baby before his head broke the surface. He sucked in gasps of breath.

"Da!"

Thank you, God. Mike's eyes were blurred and stinging, blinding him to all but the sunlight overhead. He felt hands tugging his arm and he twisted his head in Gavin's direction.

"Da! You're bleeding!"

"Get to the shore," Mike gasped, his eyesight clearing just enough to make out Gavin's face. "Swim to..." He swallowed more water as a large wave swamped him. The water turned black around them. It was thick with debris, with oil.

Gavin released him and began to swim for the shore. One hundred meters, no more. Mike's limbs were heavy and when his feet touched something soft but solid that shouldn't be there fear race up his spine. He turned in the direction toward shore behind Gavin.

The solid form beneath his feet fell away. Mike focused on his strokes. Water filled his mouth and nose but he didn't stop to cough or retch. He plunged on through the water until he saw Gavin reach the beach and collapse. The sight gave Mike the strength he needed. His boy was safe. Now he just had to join him. The further he swam from the roiling vortex the less the water fought him.

He knew he was tiring, but the shore was close now. His waterlogged boots were like twin weights anchoring him to the seabed. He hadn't thought to kick them free. He dog paddled closer to the shore. His calf muscles spasmed violently. Suddenly, he felt the shelf under his feet. Two more hard strokes and he was standing. Five more steps and the water was to his waist.

The air was silent. No cries for help. Just the lapping sound of debris and junk scraping the shore.

Finally he fell forward to crawl the rest of the way out of the water. He collapsed next to Gavin, trembling and breathless.

"Da," Gavin said in a whisper. "What happened?"

Before Mike could answer, Gavin make a strangling sound and scrambled to his feet. The surf surged an object onto the beach next to Mike. When he turned to look, he saw it was a woman's body. Headless.

Mike recoiled and dragged himself to his feet. He saw the airliner's fuselage protruding from the center of the

Irish Sea where they'd been fishing. The surrounding water was thick with debris. And bodies.

Mike blinked several times to clear his vision, then turned to follow Gavin into the woods. The terrain dropped away when he hit the first line of trees and he stumbled. Gavin was already standing by the Jeep.

Mike staggered the last few yards to the vehicle. Gavin stood with his back against the Jeep staring over Mike's shoulder.

The sky was dark with fluttering debris as pieces of the airliner's cabin rained down on them.

"Should we...do something...?" Gavin asked.

"Nay," Mike rasped, leaning against the car. "There'll be no survivors."

"I didn't hear an explosion. Did you?"

Mike turned and felt the solid comfort of the Jeep against his back as he leaned into it, his legs shaking from his swim.

"No."

"The engines were going one minute and the next..." Gavin shook his head. "It just fell out of the sky."

"Are ye all right, lad? Can you drive? "

Gavin nodded but he seemed unable to tear his eyes away from the sight of the detritus of everyday life onboard a transatlantic airline now scattered to the winds.

"Should we...see if there's anything to salvage?" Gavin asked tentatively.

"Nay, lad." Mike watched the dark form of a body bobbing alongside the visible part of the wing of the airliner. They would do better to get back to the nunnery as soon as possible. "Let's go. We can't do anything here."

As Gavin turned from the terrible sight, Mike put a hand on his shoulder. With so much death suddenly surrounding them—of people who were drinking cocktails and watching movies just minutes ago—it felt vital to feel the solid flesh and bone of his lad.

Gavin looked at him. "You okay, Da?"

"Aye," Mike said gruffly, turning away before Gavin could see the emotion in his eyes. He jerked open the passenger's side door and fell into the seat. The sun from the September day had ebbed away leaving only the chill of the coming autumn.

Gavin got in the driver's seat and inserted the key in the ignition.

"We lost our tackle," he said. "And all our catch."

Mike closed his eyes. "We'll find more."

The sound of the ignition clicking filled the Jeep's interior.

"It won't start," Gavin said. He turned the key again. Nothing. Mike looked again in the direction of where the airliner went down.

Oh, shit.

3.

Master Sergeant Padraig Hurley stood on the parade grounds on the army base outside of Dublin city limits and watched the troops file past him. A line of three vehicles moved to where the truck depot was located behind the first barracks. It was eighteen hundred hours with most of his men expecting to be dismissed to the mess hall. He watched them go through their drill with heavy limbs and sluggish paces.

As his men passed, he even noticed scowls and disgruntled glances in his direction.

It hadn't been this way five years ago. Then, before the EMP, Hurley had the power to make their lives a living hell on this earth. That power had commanded respect and immediate obedience.

Now, over the years a full third of his troops had slunk off into the night with Hurley's superiors telling him there was nothing they could do about it—not until Ireland could rebuild, not until Ireland's allies could give them a hand, not until Ireland was on its feet again.

And in the meantime, Master Sergeant Hurley was practically leading a volunteer army.

Frustrated, he blew his whistle and watched the men come to a gradual stop. Nothing crisp about it. A few even stood with their weight shifted to one leg, their shoulders sagging, their heads twisting around to grin at a friend.

"Dismissed!" he barked, feeling an irrational urge to lift his weapon and mow down the first line of men in front of him.

Think that would get their attention? Think they might be able to hold ranks for longer than fifteen minutes then?

He watched them wander toward the barracks and the mess tent. He felt the sharpness in the air of the coming autumn and his eye again caught the line of Jeeps past the parade ground.

Only for some reason they weren't moving anymore.

****

From where she stood waiting on the front steps of the convent Sarah finally saw the two men emerge from the shadows.

"Mike!"

"Aye, it's us," he called, his voice thick with exhaustion.

She ran down the steps and into the darkness. They met in the middle of the garden path. Her arms went around his waist. His clothes were wet. She pulled back as Gavin edged past them heading for the front door.

"What happened? Why are you so late? Why are you wet?"

"Sure, I'll tell you everything, Sarah," Mike said, "only I'm starving and frozen to the bone."

"Did you fall in? Why are you wet?"

Mother Angelina met them at the door and lifted a lantern to peer into Mike's face.

"You've returned," she said. "Sister Monica is preparing a late meal. You'll need a bandage."

"Thank you, Mother," Mike said. In the lantern light, Sarah could see that his face was ashen and his shoulders sagged with weariness. In a flash, she realized they must have walked from Rosslare.

"Mike, the Jeep...."

"You're not going to let me even sit down first?"

Noises came from down the long stone hall. Sophia, disheveled and groggy, was pulling on a robe and following Gavin to the dining room. As they entered, one of the nuns was building up the fire in the fireplace. Both Mike and Gavin went to stand near it and held out their hands.

Another nun appeared with a stack of blankets and laid them in front of the fire.

"You'll be needing to take off those wet things," she said brusquely. They didn't hesitate although Sophia turned her back as her husband and father-in-law stripped in front of the fire before they were wrapped in blankets. Chairs were pushed to the fireplace where the two now sat. Sarah knelt near Mike's chair and took his hand. It was like ice.

Sister Monica handed both men steaming mugs of tea and returned to the kitchen. Fiona and Declan appeared in the doorway.

Sarah waited while Mike and Gavin warmed themselves and ate. Sister Monica stitched and bandaged a cut over Mike's eye.

"You have our curiosity," Mother Angelina said with a smile. "If you are ready to tell your tale?"

"How did you fall in the water?" Sarah asked. "*Both* of you?"

"We didn't fall in," Gavin said. He sat with one arm draped around Sophia's shoulders. He looked tired, his eyes were glassy and vacant.

"We jumped," Mike said as Sister Monica added a long draught of whiskey to his third cup of hot tea. "Did you happen to see the airliner that flew over this afternoon?"

Sarah frowned. "I heard it. Why? Did it drop something?"

"You could say that."

"It fell out of the sky, so it did," Gavin said to his wife. "The engines went silent and it just...fell."

"Almost on top of us," Mike added.

Sarah felt her heart beginning to pound in her throat.

"We jumped in the water to avoid getting hit."

"How can a plane just fall?" Fiona asked. "I've never heard of that."

"Mother of God pray for us," Mother Angelina murmured. Sarah looked at her and then back at Mike.

There's nothing to worry about. It's all over and they're alive.

"There were many bodies?" Angelina asked quietly.

"Aye, Mother. Many."

The room was silent except for the hushed prayers of the Sisters and the crackle of the wood in the fireplace. Sarah noticed that Mac had entered the room and now stood by the door listening.

"You walked back, didn't you?" Sarah asked, feeling a ball of hard panic sitting in her throat.

"The Jeep's kaput," Mike said wearily.

"Why? How?" Declan asked. His words were slightly slurred.

"We tried to start it," Gavin said. "It wouldn't turn over."

"The battery?" Sarah asked. Mike looked at her but didn't answer.

"Jaysus, Joseph and Mary!" Fiona gasped. "You think it's another EMP, don't you?"

"I fear it might be," Mike said.

As soon as his words left his mouth Sarah felt the floor drop away and her vision waver. She stood up, her hands on the arm of his chair for support.

"Sarah, lass…"

"Oh my God," she said, her eyes on the fire. The room and the people in it dropped away.

John.

Susan Kiernan-Lewis

4.

Mike stood in the washroom the next morning dripping from the ice cold water he'd just splashed on his face. He didn't need a mirror to tell him he looked rough.

Sarah had held all the questions he knew she was brimming with until he'd had a night's sleep. When he awoke this morning, she was already gone. Off tending to Siobhan most likely. He grabbed a towel and gingerly rubbed his face, mindful of the bandage.

He knew her first thought when she heard about the airliner was of John. He'd fretted about that very thing on the walk back to the convent. But in the end, it was what it was. The lad was either safe in the UK. Or he wasn't.

Deep in his thoughts, he didn't notice that Sarah had walked up and was standing at the washroom door with the baby in her arms. Looking at her, he could see she'd lost all her pregnancy weight. Her jeans even looked a little loose. He dropped the towel in the stone basin in front of him.

"We'll get him back," he said. "I swear we will."

She moved to him and he took Siobhan from her. The child's beauty always amazed him. Where she got that translucent pink skin and the wide blue eyes was beyond him. He kissed her, prompting a giggle.

"Your Da's scratchy this morning, eh, Siobhan?" he said with a laugh. When he looked at Sarah, his smile fell away.

"How?" she said, her arms crossed. "*How* will we get him back? Are we going to the UK? Or are we going to wait for him to come back here?"

"I don't know."

"Because it's just something people say, isn't it? 'We'll get him back.' Only you don't have a plan of how to do that. What if we leave and he's heading back here? You know John."

Mike sighed. "Aye, I do. The lad will come here. That's certain."

"So we *won't* get him back, is what you're saying. We'll stay and wait and hope he shows up."

"Sarah…"

"Do you think he made it there safely?"

"The plane came down hours after he should have landed in Oxford."

She chewed her lip and he knew he hadn't told her anything she hadn't already told herself.

"Have you had breakfast yet?" he asked, shifting Siobhan to his other arm and reaching for his shirt. It was cold. Either winter was going to be particularly brutal this year or just long as hell.

"Siobhan ate," Sarah said.

They moved into the sunshine and Mike blinked at the glare.

"How's your head?" she asked.

"Fine. I asked Declan to gather everyone."

"Fiona told me. What are you going to say?"

"Just that we suspect there was another EMP."

"How does that affect them?" Sarah said as they walked to the main house. "We've been essentially living without electricity for the last four and a half years. It's not like their lives will change."

"This second EMP, if that's what it was, changes everything," Mike said, pausing on the doorstep to the convent. He handed the child back to Sarah while he buttoned his shirt. "It evens the playing field. Whatever edge the Garda or Dublin or even the UK had is gone now. There are no lights *anywhere* now. No vehicles and no communications. We've all gone back to square one."

"What do you think people will do?"

"No telling. But if the Dubliners leave the city—which is likely—to look for food or to take what they need—we need to be ready."

"Is that necessary? They can't find us here."

"We need a place we can defend. A fortress."

"Not this castle idea of yours again." Sarah rolled her eyes.

"Aye, that's it exactly. A castle. With the ocean behind us and high on a bluff where we can see what's coming. Nobody will be able to scale the walls or burn us out."

"Ever hear of a siege?"

"Not when there's grazing and crops and a water source inside the castle."

Sarah looked uncertainly around her. He knew she felt safe here. The blackbirds sang and flew over the little garden plot that had comfortably fed the entire convent—nearly seventy people—all summer long.

"Likely Dublin and the other main cities will react at first by looting themselves," Mike said, "but they'll soon get hungry enough to come into the countryside."

Her face was screwed into a mask of confusion. "*Who* are you talking about?"

"The opportunists, the provisional government, the army. And it's people like us they'll look to take from. We'll need to move quickly."

Sarah put a hand on Mike's arm as if to prevent him from entering the front door. Siobhan began to fuss in her arms and he took the baby from her.

"You just got through telling me the only way to find John again is to wait for him to come back *here*."

"Listen, Sarah…"

"*No.*" Her face was flushed. "He's coming back *here*. You know he is. If…if he can."

"Sarah, lass, listen to me…"

"No! I'm not leaving without him. You can do what you want." She pulled Siobhan out of his arms, causing the child to give a startled shriek, and stomped into the convent.

******

The dining room was the biggest room in the nunnery. Since Sarah and Mike and the people of the compound had come, everyone took their meals together in this room.

Fiona thought she would never get tired of seeing their whole community around the table like one big happy family. Her two little girls sat to her left on a long wooden bench. They were inseparable and Fiona was glad for that. Both of them had seen some terrible things in their young lives. It was good that they had each other.

Declan sat on her right. Solemn, silent and still. Nothing like the man she'd once known and loved. The man who had led his gypsy family with humor and bravery. Now his hands shook and there were times when he looked at her with uncertainty.

Breakfast had been over for an hour but the air buzzed with anticipation. She hoped Mike wasn't planning on breaking the news to everyone about the EMP as some sort of surprise since she was pretty sure everyone already knew.

When Sarah came into the room—a squirming, fighting Siobhan in her arms—her face was dark with frustration. A few steps later, Mike entered to cheers and applause from the gathered men and women. He went to the head of the table and held out his arms for quiet. Fiona noticed he did not look in Sarah's direction. Sophia—so big she looked like she'd deliver any moment—lumbered over to Sarah to relieve her of Siobhan. The child settled down quickly.

Fiona knew that everyone here had cause to trust and respect her brother. From the men he'd rescued from the work camp in Dublin last spring to the women he'd brought home safely from the rape camp—herself included. She felt a movement on her right and placed a calming hand on Declan's knee. He'd even found her dear Declan and brought him back from the grave. Almost literally.

"Well, sure you'll have all heard the big news by now," Mike said in a loud voice. Instantly, the talking ceased and all eyes regarded him.

"Is it true then?" Terry Donaghue called out. A thin, wiry man, it had taken Terry many months to regain his strength. He sat with his wife, Jill, and their two sons, Tommy and Darby.

"We won't know for sure until the evening news," Mike said to general laughter. "But I think it's a fair guess."

"Did you leave the Jeep in the woods?" Tommy asked.

"Aye and I'll be asking you and Gavin to return to it and strip it of anything that might be of use to us," Mike said.

"What does it mean for us?" Liddy O'Malley asked. In her late thirties, Liddy was impregnated by rape last winter and delivered a beautiful baby girl in mid summer. Because her husband Davey refused to accept the child, Mike had asked him to leave the community.

"Good question, Liddy," Mike said. "I'd say it means good news and bad news for us."

"What's the good news?" Tommy called out to more laughter.

Mike grinned. "It means we're all working from the same playbook now, to use a phrase from our American allies."

"Some allies!" Regan called out. "They never did shite for us when the first EMP went off." She turned to look at Sarah. "No offense, Sarah."

Fiona couldn't see Sarah's face. Regan was a handful—and mostly trouble—but she was also brave and had withstood more than most so the group was inclined to be forgiving.

"In any case," Mike said, giving Regan an annoyed look, "the good news is we're all in the same boat now.".

"And the bad news?" Terry's wife Jill raised her hand as she spoke.

"We need to leave." Mike said. He gave a slight bow to Mother Angelina who sat closest to him at the table.

"Sure all of the Sisters are welcome to come with us, so they are. And we'll never be able to thank them enough for the sanctuary they gave us. I hope to return the favor some day."

Mother Angelina smiled. Mike glanced over to where Mac stood by the door and nodded to him, the invitation offered. Mac's shoulders relaxed and he nodded back.

"And go where?" Nuala O'Connell asked. She was sitting with her two young boys and her newborn daughter in her lap. Nuala knew full well where Mike wanted them all to go. Fiona wondered if Mike had asked Nuala to ask the question.

"To Disney World!" a young boy shouted. The group laughed and Terry tousled his son's hair with a grin.

"That's the shot, lad," Mike said with a laugh. "Sure we're going to Cinderella's Castle, so we are…where we'll be safe and where no one can ever take what's ours ever again."

The group applauded along with a few whistles that Fiona thought came from Gavin and Tommy.

"It's ten days walk from here," Mike said, rubbing his hands together as he clearly warmed to his subject. Fiona wouldn't be surprised if he'd totally forgotten Sarah was glowering in the audience.

"Maybe a little more. Northwest and on the coast. It's called Henredon Castle and before the Crisis it was used as a tourist attraction back in the day but it was in good shape. A classic example of a Norman fortress. Built in 1175."

"How do you know there's nobody living in it?" someone asked.

"I don't, do I?"

Heads turned and Fiona knew it was Sarah. The tension crackled in the air between her and Mike.

"Ten days is a long way to walk with screaming babies and women who've just delivered," Sarah said, her voice cold but firm. "Not to mention lugging all our worldly belongings behind us. And what exactly do you suggest we do if we get there and the place is already inhabited? Have you thought about that?"

"We do what everyone has done throughout history," Mike said with a shrug, turning to face his audience. "We *take* it."

Susan Kiernan-Lewis

5.

Sarah couldn't believe what she was hearing. Was Mike really standing up there telling everyone they were going to storm an effing castle? Had they all lost their minds? She looked around the dining hall to see the laughter and the excitement spread from person to person. Almost everyone there had a child or baby on their laps. It was insane to think any of them were going anywhere—let alone to attack some castle!

"It's exciting, is it not, Sarah?" Nuala said as she led her boys past. "Living in a castle?" She shifted her newborn in her arms. It was hard to imagine how difficult life was for Nuala—three children and no husband. And yet, her eyes sparkled with excitement.

Madness.

Mike sat down and two of the nuns appeared on either side of him to serve him his breakfast.

He already looks like the lord of the manor, Sarah thought. *Throw in a jester and a knight or two, and he's done.* There were enough people crowding around Mike as he ate that Sarah knew she'd have to wait to finish her discussion with him.

They were not leaving. Or at least *Sarah* was not leaving and she couldn't imagine Mike would leave without her. *Would he?*

Things had been tense between them all summer. Ever since the baby was born. Mike had spent more and more time with the men—which was unusual. She tried to imagine the last time they'd had an intimate exchange and it surprised her that she couldn't remember.

It was true she'd been busy most of the summer getting John ready to go in the fall, and then helping the nuns with the harvesting, the weaving, the baking. With so many more people to care for, it had been a lot of extra work. And of course, there was Siobhan. She wasn't an easy baby.

Not at all like John had been.

Sarah felt a splinter of unease invade her gut and she forced thoughts of her son away. *It doesn't help.*

Sophia and Siobhan left the hall with another of the young mothers. Fiona joined them, Declan shuffling silently behind her like a recalcitrant teenager. Poor Declan. He'd been such a force before the accident. Sarah felt a flush of guilt for only thinking of herself when Fiona and Declan had so much more ongoing daily pain.

One of the young women who'd come with Fiona from the rape camp sat down next to Sarah. Jenny had not been impregnated—although not for lack of trying on the bastards whose job it was to get her with child—and now she was waiting to be returned home.

"How are you, Jenny?" Sarah asked, her eyes still on Mike as he spoke with his men and some of the women.

"I'm grand, so I am," Jenny said. "Just waiting for Regan and Jaz to get back, ye ken?"

Jaz and Regan had decided to bring the kidnapped women from the rape camp back home—those that wanted to go. Two women who'd delivered their babies earlier in the summer had opted to stay with Mike and Sarah's group but most of the others were anxious to go home. Jaz and Regan left with a young woman the same day John went to the UK. The same day the second EMP went off. They were traveling by pony cart so the EMP shouldn't affect their journey. At least Sarah prayed not.

"Are you next on the list?" Sarah asked.

Jenny nodded. "I haven't seen me mum in two years. She probably thinks I'm dead."

"What a happy day that will be for both of you. Your reunion."

"Oh, aye," Jenny said with a frown. "Only I was wondering...since I never got preggers, do ye think I should tell her the truth of it? Me mum, I mean."

"You mean about the...forced..."

"The rapes, aye," Jenny said. "It'll upset her something brutal."

"I imagine it would." *Only I cannot imagine. I don't want to imagine.*

An image of little Siobhan flashed into Sarah's mind and she felt sweat beading up on her forehead.

"Are ye all right, Missus?"

Sarah's stomach lurched and she turned to catch a glimpse of Siobhan even though she knew the baby was safe with Sophia.

What is wrong with me?

"Just a little warm in here," Sarah said.

Mike stood up and she got eye contact with him. He nodded toward the door.

"Listen, Jenny. I need to go. I'm sure whatever you decide to do will be fine. Your mother will just be happy to have you back safe and sound."

Sarah hurried toward the door where she met Mike. He put a hand on her shoulder but addressed the people following him out the door.

"I'll be having a private word with me wife now," he said. "You all know what you need to do. So start packing. If the weather's decent, we'll leave by the end of the week."

"How? On horseback?" Tommy asked.

"We have three wagons and eight horses," Mike said, turning and exiting the room.

"Will we stop at the compound on the way?" Liddy asked.

"Aye. And load up what we can. Mind you, we'll be back before winter sets in for anything we've left behind." He gave a meaningful look to Sarah. She knew his words were meant to reassure her.

They didn't.

She walked ahead of him down the stone lined hallway. The convent had six rooms off the center aisle. She, Mike and Siobhan slept in the far room across from Mother Superior's office. She walked there now, waited for him to cross the threshold and then pulled the door behind him.

"What was all that crap about taking the castle? Were you serious?" She stood with her hands on her hips. She knew she looked the very picture of a strident fishwife but she couldn't help herself.

"Just worst case scenario, Sarah."

"But you said *nobody* could take the castle!"

Mike ran a hand through his hair and went to the bed where he sat down gingerly. A dark bruise was visible on his jaw from his time in the water yesterday.

Sarah knew she was being unreasonable. He'd just had a horrifying experience—escaping near death--and had the stitches and contusions to prove it.

"Aye. And nobody *can* take it—unless you trust the wrong people."

"You mean trick them. Tell them anything to get them to lower the drawbridge so we can blast 'em?"

"While I generally appreciate your American approach to things, Sarah, there'll be no need to *blast* anyone. I'm dead sure we can work something out."

"What if they don't want to share their castle with us?"

"They won't have a say in the matter. Don't fash yourself, Sarah. The place might well be uninhabited. Castles are cold drafty places."

"So now we're the bad guys?"

He looked at her with surprise. "How can ye say that?"

"Attacking a castle? Taking it from people who were there first?"

"Sure they can stay," he said, massaging his knee. "If they behave themselves."

"Do you *hear* yourself?"

"Look, Sarah, I ken that history isn't your strong point but in this part of the world there are three ways to come into possession of a property. Either ye buy it, inherit it or ye take it. And they're all equally valid."

"That's abominable. And it's not even a rationale."

"Duly noted."

The fury built up inside her until she thought she might slap him—even as bruised as he was. He was doing his usual steamrolling decision-making for the whole community and nobody but Sarah seemed to mind.

But she did mind. She minded very much. Before she could decide if words would have any further affect on him, there was a loud rap on the door. Sarah jumped at the sound.

The door opened and Fiona stuck her head in.

"Oy," she said with an elfin grin. "If you two can table the battle for a few hours, I think your son needs you, Mike."

Mike stared uncomprehending at Fiona.

"You're about to become a Granddad, ye old berk!" Fiona said gleefully.

******

Hurley stood in his room—twenty by twenty with a single bed shoved against the wall and a metal table that served as dresser and nightstand.

It had been a full week since the second EMP—or what the higher ups were *calling* the second EMP. All the lights were gone. All the vehicles were nonfunctioning. The stoves and what paltry communications technology they'd cobbled together in the last five years—all of it was gone and they were right back where they started.

He glanced at his watch. 0700 hours.

You'd think having lived through this once they'd have a plan for how to move forward.

You'd think that if you'd never spent an hour in the army.

Oh, there were meetings—always in the daytime since even after a week they were running out of candles and kerosene—but no answers beyond *wait for someone to come find us.*

Would it be the US? Everyone in Ireland seemed to have a relative living somewhere in the States but chances were good the Yanks were the *reason* they were all back in the Dark Ages 2.0.

Hurley tightened his tie and left his quarters.

There were no meetings today. The officers had decided to wait for rescue to come in whatever form it would. Hurley wasn't surprised at all. In fact, he was counting on their passivity.

The guard on the outside of the noncommissioned bachelors quarters turned to watch Hurley emerge.

"Morning, Sergeant," the guard said.

Hurley would have preferred he not speak but a part of him was relieved there was a guard posted at all.

Today was the day it was all going to get real. He could cut this poor blighter some slack.

"You're in F squad, Corporal?"

"Aye, sir."

"We're not in the navy, Corporal.'"

"Yes, Sergeant."

"Gather your squad with rifles and bayonets and meet me at the parade grounds at 0730 hours."

He enjoyed the look of shock on the man's face but instantly reprimanded himself. He'd fallen into sloppy habits himself and appreciating the surprised reaction from others was one he would need to break.

"Yes, Sergeant," the Corporal said before turning and disappearing into the dark.

Hurley glanced at the officer's quarters, a long squat building on the far side of the parade grounds. There were no lights on, but even when they had electricity just seven days earlier there wouldn't have been anyone up at this hour.

All of that was about to change in a serious way.

The sound of a rifle shot sounded from outside the camp. Hurley frowned. Civilians didn't have firearms—not unless they attacked a soldier and took theirs. He heard men's laughter and then another gunshot. He touched the gun in his shoulder holster and went in the direction of the voices.

He ran down the front of the darkened mess tent and past the building used as Garda Sochia headquarters. A cluster of soldiers stood by the front gate beside the large form of a dead animal on the ground.

"Attention!" Hurley bellowed. Five of the six men snapped to attention as he approached. The sixth man grinned and put his hands on his hips as if the rules didn't apply to him. On the ground lay a black bear.

Without thinking, Hurley pulled his gun from his holster and shot the grinning soldier. The man's mouth dropped open in shock as he clutched his stomach and sank to his knees.

Hurley turned to the other five. "What's going on here?"

No one spoke. Hurley walked to the bear and nudged it with his boot. He looked at the men and saw one of them licking his lips nervously.

"We...we killed a bear, Sergeant."

Hurley holstered his gun and glanced at the man he'd shot. He wasn't dead but it probably wouldn't be long. He pointed to one of the men.

"You. Carry this man to the clinic and then report to the parade grounds. Where's your rifle?"

"In...in my barracks, Sergeant."

"Get it." Hurley turned to the other four men. "How did this bear get here?"

"The zoo, Sergeant," one of the men said. "They've been roaming free all week."

"Roaming free?" Hurley looked at the camp gate and then down at the bear.

This was a sign as sure as anything could be.

For as long as Hurley could remember he'd dreamed of life in a military regiment. But even fifteen years in the Garda had not fulfilled that particular yearning in him. In the readings he'd done as a kid, he knew the one true army —the paragon above all others—had been the imperial Roman army.

After a lifetime of ridicule for what he knew to be true, it looked like Padraig Hurley was finally in a position to realize his dream.

"You four," he said, "round up whatever man eating zoo animals you can. Tigers, lions, whatever will do the most danger to our city. Do you understand?"

"Yes, Sergeant!"

"Where should we...how should we collect them, Sergeant?"

Hurley forced himself not to smile. Experiencing the pleasure of his own hubris was clearly another habit he would need to break.

"Bring them however you can...wheel them in cages, drag them in chains...but bring them *alive* to the Dublin amphitheater."

"The...opera house? Downtown?"

"That's right. What squad do you four belong?"

"G Squad, Sergeant."

"Go gather your squad," Hurley said. "Then report back here."

He turned on his heel to redirect F Squad waiting at the parade grounds to join G in the hunt for the zoo animals. Waking the officers could wait.

After all, what kind of resurgent Roman army could there be without tossing a few superior officers to a hungry lion or two?

Susan Kiernan-Lewis

6.

The journey to the castle began on the coldest day of the year so far. Barely into the first week of October and two weeks after Gavin and Sophia's baby daughter Maggie was born, the little nunnery awoke to frost in the garden that refused to melt as the morning wore on.

Six men, fourteen women and thirteen children—most of them infants—left the convent on foot, pulling a sled of provisions, their backpacks loaded. The nuns had decided not to leave, at least for the time being. Sarah only agreed to go because she knew the nuns would be here if John came back.

As she watched Mike, a toddler in each arm and easily the tallest man in the group, line everyone up in the garden, it occurred to her that he might well have asked the nuns to stay behind knowing it would comfort Sarah.

No, strike that. Knowing it was his only chance to get me to leave.

Terry, Kevin and Declan led the horses while Gavin and Tommy rode. The sled held the harnesses for the horses for when they got to the wagons hidden on the far side of the woods. Their first leg of the trip would be on foot through the thick forest, which was one of the main reasons why nobody easily discovered the nunnery. There was no road that led to it. On foot or horseback were the only ways to the convent's front gate.

Sarah held Sophia's newborn. The infant had pale red hair and dimples. She was good-natured and already slept through the night. Mike held Siobhan. He said it was because she was so much heavier but Sarah suspected it was because if Sarah carried her, Siobhan would cry. The fact that Mike and everyone else knew that Sarah's own baby hated her weighed heavily on her.

How can a child not want its own mother? John was never like this as a baby. Was there something wrong with Siobhan?

Sarah knew it was more likely it was something having to do with *her*.

Children and dogs, her mother used to tell her. *They know good people from bad. They just do.*

"Sarah?"

Sarah turned to see Mother Angelina standing beside her, her eyes probing Sarah as if she would have all her secrets. Mac stood behind the nun. Sarah knew Mac felt that Angelina's personal protection—and indeed the safety of the whole convent—was his life's job. In part this was because he'd shot and killed the young man Angelina had raised and thought of as a son, but in greater part it was because Mac was a basically good person who'd done some terrible things and was trying to find his way back to redemption.

"I wouldn't leave without saying goodbye," Sarah said.

"I know," Angelina said. "And I'll keep your lad safe until you come for him."

Tears filled Sarah's eyes. She glanced at Mac and he nodded solemnly.

"Aye," he said. "With me life."

"Thank you."

Angelina hugged Sarah and caressed the sleeping baby's cheek. "We'll see you soon," she said. "And I'm sure I won't even recognize this little one when we do."

"It's time, Sarah," Mike called. His words felt like a rope pulling her from all that was good and safe. Her face must have shown her feelings because Angelina kissed her cheek.

"All will be well, Sarah. With God's help. I know it."

Sarah nodded and then turned away. She was the last one to leave the garden. An image of John playing ball with Gavin on the north side of the garden wall came to her. It had been a sunny day and their laughter had carried up and over the highest apple trees in the grove.

She couldn't help but feel that every step she took from this place was the biggest mistake she'd ever made.

****

Fiona settled her two little girls in the back of the wagon. She and Nuala would take turns driving the horses although before the Crisis Nuala admitted she'd never even ridden a horse. Nuala's boys played in the back of the wagon with Fiona's girls and three other children from the camp and one of the young unwed mothers from the rape camp.

"Now play nicely," Nuala said to the children as she handed out sandwiches they'd packed before they'd left the nunnery.

"When will we get there, Mummy?" Maeve asked, her worried face looking out at the fringe of trees and onto the pasture they would soon cross.

For Fiona, it was still too soon to look at little Maeve and not think of how her brave mother had died— needlessly, in pain and in terror. Fiona knew the other women in the camp had forgiven Mac, the foreman of the rape camp, but she still couldn't. She was sure that was a serious character flaw on her part and she prayed nightly to overcome the deficit. And then she'd watch Maeve do something new for the first time—a new word or master a simple game—and she'd be reminded that Bridget, the child's mother, would never see it.

"Soon enough," Fiona said. "Eat your lunch and then nap if you can." She turned to Nuala who held her baby in her arms and shook the reins to drive the team forward. After Mike and the other men had harnessed up the horses to the wagons, they'd ridden on ahead to reach the old compound. Fiona had a shotgun at her feet and the other three wagons were right behind her. The day was brisk but sunny, a perfect day for the beginning of a journey, she thought.

"Your sister-in-law's none too happy about any of this, is she?" Nuala asked as she looked in the direction of Sarah's wagon.

That was an understatement. Everyone in the group knew how Sarah felt. And when she and Mike were at odds with each other, everyone felt that too. A part of Fiona couldn't blame Sarah. She herself would hate leaving the nunnery if that was the only place her child knew to return to.

Life was so uncertain these days. It was all very well to say the nuns would tell John where they'd all gone when he arrived back—*if* he arrived—but a lot could happen between Oxford and the coast of Ireland.

"Sure Sarah is tougher than all of us," Fiona said. "She'll sort it out."

Now that they were free of the woods, Fiona could feel the warmth of the sun shining down on them. It felt good on her back through her jacket. They'd brought all the wool blankets they could carry and the four wagons were full of babies and children tucked warmly within.

"It's heartbreaking, so it is, to hear that baby cry every time Sarah touches it, and she its own mother," Nuala said.

"Now Nuala O'Connell, I'll not have you gossiping about Sarah, so mind your tongue."

"Whisht, it's just what everyone's saying."

"I don't care what they're saying. I don't have to hear it." Fiona knew she was being sharper than she needed to be. Nuala's hurt silence told her that. Of course Fiona knew what people were saying. Hadn't she seen the very same thing over and over again with her own eyes? Something was wrong with Sarah and even her little lass sensed it.

Fiona clucked to the horses and brought them into a trot. The pastures on both sides of the road were brown and barren as they passed.

But whatever was wrong, Fiona could only pray it wasn't because Sarah was right about not leaving.

Susan Kiernan-Lewis

7.

The pastures they passed were bleak and colorless. Sarah remembered picking sloe berries near here at the beginning of summer. She could hear Liddy and Mary laughing together in the back of the wagon.

After what those two endured last winter, it was a miracle they could ever laugh again, Sarah thought. They were sisters, and close. Both had given birth to babies of rape and Liddy had lost her husband because he couldn't deal with it all.

And yet there they were, tweaking their babies' cheeks and giggling over nonsense as if the world hadn't erupted last winter and swallowed them up, changing their lives forever. So many of the other women rescued from the rape camp had similar experiences—and yet today here they were looking forward to their new home with excitement and anticipation.

How was that possible?

Many of the rescued women were without husbands. Mike had taken it upon himself to look after the ones who had children and had encouraged Sarah and Fiona to reach out to the childless women. There were fourteen women and thirteen children and babies. And only six men.

Twenty in total. Not an unwieldy number as communities went. A little unbalanced, unfortunately, gender wise. It wasn't just that the men were stronger and could do a longer day's work, but most of the women had newborn babies at their breasts.

The word *vulnerable* came to mind, Sarah thought grimly.

It had only been three weeks since they'd last visited the compound. The day John had flown away to Oxford. As Sarah drove her wagon to line up with the others, she felt a shiver slide down her spine at the memory. She shook the feeling away. She knew she'd relive that day when she saw the compound again and she was determined not to dwell on it.

John was gone. He'd be back at Christmas. If not sooner. Oxford wasn't that far from the Irish coast. *Even if he's on foot. But if he can manage to get his hands on a horse, he could already be at the coast—*

"All right then, Sarah?"

She looked up to see Mike trot over on his big bay. They hadn't spoken much in the days of preparation for the trip and she was surprised to see him now. The men and some of the women were already dragging supplies out the front gate of the compound

"Fine," she said but couldn't force a smile. *He's getting what he wants. He doesn't get the cherry on top too.*

Mike came alongside the wagon. Sophia sat next to Sarah with her newborn in her arms. Siobhan was in the back with four more children and two women.

"It's a good time for everyone to hop out and stretch their legs," he said, nodding to the back of the wagon where the children began to scramble out. "Not for long, mind," he called to them.

Sarah stared at the compound gate. She'd seen it more than a few times since Mac's gang had lit it on fire but the feeling of loss was always the same. Archie had died in the gravel on the main compound pathway last spring. Every time she thought of him it hurt like a razor blade to her insides.

Some things never get better with time.

Sarah knew they couldn't bring too much this trip. The four wagons were already stuffed to the limit with people and essentials. Once they were settled they would have to come back to retrieve everything else.

"How much are we bringing?" she asked.

"We'll leave the baby chairs and encyclopedias for now." Mike laughed but Sarah didn't join in. It was true she'd brought many useless things back from America last year. And the raid by the Garda last winter had stripped the place of most of their armory except for a few hidden guns and ammunition. What was left—basic medicine, iron cookware, disposable diapers, several cases of wine and whisky and even Coca-Cola, along with water purification devices, seeds, sugar, and peanut butter—would all eventually come with them to the new place.

Sophia handed Sarah the baby while she climbed down and stretched the kinks out of her back. Sarah used the distraction to focus on little Maggie until Mike moved to the back of the wagon. Someone handed Siobhan up to him and he rode away with her through the compound gates. As she watched him leave, she felt some of her tension leave too.

From where she sat in the wagon, Sarah could see the winding road that led to the gate, flanked on one side by thick woods, and on the other by the rolling pasture where they used to keep their sheep and goats. Where the flock was now was anybody's guess.

The pasture was bordered on the road side by a low sloping knee wall. Beyond it a half mile by horseback was the little cottage where she and David and John had lived. She gazed in that direction. David was buried in the pasture

near where he was killed. Mike and John had put up a
marker. *David Woodson Loving husband and father.*
Sarah's eyes burned with unshed tears and Maggie began to
cry.

So much had happened in the five years since she'd
come to Ireland. So much loss.

"Shall I take her, Sarah?" Sophia said as she walked
over. She shielded her eyes from the sun as she looked up
at Sarah.

"You might want to gather up the others," Sarah said,
shaking herself out of her mood. "I see Mike coming back
with a load for our wagon. He'll be wanting to leave soon."

Sophia held out her arms for the baby and Sarah
handed her down.

"I'll get the rest of them," Sophia called over her
shoulder as she walked into the compound.

Mike rode up with Siobhan and directed a crew of
three men carrying a stack of crates to put them in the back
of Sarah's wagon. Siobhan's face was lit up with glee, her
pudgy little hands gripping Mike's large hand that held her
firmly on his lap and her hair shining in the sunlight.

So she does know how to laugh, Sarah thought, a rueful
smile tugging at her lips.

"Did you eat something?" Mike asked Sarah as he
transferred Siobhan to her. Immediately the baby began to
squirm and reach for Mike.

Kind of hard to compete with a horsey-back ride, Sarah
thought. But she knew that wasn't the whole problem.

"We did," she said. "Are we about ready to leave?"

"Aye, nearly. If we can get twenty miles down the
road, I'll feel good about it. We'll have a hot meal tonight
when we stop."

Sarah nodded and Mike, after the briefest of
hesitations, turned away. Twenty minutes later, all the

wagons were loaded and headed back down the road. Sarah couldn't resist a backward glance at the compound, their Ameriland.

So much had happened there over the years and so much good had been hoped for. And just like everything else, it was gone now too.

****

Mike did another headcount as he rode from the tail of their wagon train to the lead. Everyone was in good spirits —well, most everyone—and the weather was holding so far, please God. He didn't have any illusions that they'd make the entire trip without some of it in a downpour but he was grateful that they could start out with adventure in their hearts and dry socks in their boots.

The road was empty. They hadn't seen another sign of life since they'd left the convent. Mike looked up at the sky as he realized they had at least four more hours before they'd need to find a place to stop for the night. The wagons were in good shape, the kiddies alternately singing or sleeping, the women all holding up as usual and doing what needed doing.

Every time he rode by Sarah's wagon, she made a point of not looking at him. As long as he'd known her he'd never known her to be this mad this long. Not even when he'd gone and got himself engaged to Aideen Malone. In fact, as Mike recalled, they'd very nearly come to blows then but as anybody with sense will tell you, wanting to wring someone's neck didn't mean you didn't care.

The way Sarah was treating him now—not looking at him, hardly speaking to him—was a thousand times worse than if she'd thrown a frying pan or taken a broom to him.

Make that a million times worse.

Mike knew well enough that it wasn't just leaving John behind that bothered her. And it wasn't just that the baby screamed every time Sarah touched her. Siobhan's birth had instilled a fear in Sarah that she hadn't had before. It was an irrational fear that some things just couldn't be made safe no matter where you went or how hard you tried.

"Mike?" Declan rode up to him, his eyes wide and startled. Mike had worried Declan didn't have the balance to ride a horse but he hadn't the heart to tell him to ride in the wagon.

"Everything okay?" Mike asked.

"I'll catch up with you," Declan said. "I need to go into the woods for a bit. All right?"

It killed Mike to hear his friend ask permission to go take a leak in the woods. "Sure, Dec. We can wait. We have time."

"Nay, I won't be long." Declan slid off his horse and looked around holding his reins as if unsure what to do with them. Mike held out his hand and Declan handed the reins to him, grinning with embarrassment. He turned and entered the woods.

Fiona's wagon pulled up beside Mike.

"Where's Declan going?" she asked as she watched her husband's retreating back.

"Going to take a piss if that's all right with his missus," Mike said with a raised eyebrow.

"Oh, go on with the pair of ye," Fiona said with annoyance and snapped the reins on the back of her horse.

Mike turned and led Declan's horse toward the head of the group.

"Oy! Gavin!" he called to his son. Gavin turned from the lead where he rode side by side with Tommy and trotted back to his father.

"I need one of ye to take up the rear. I want to get as many kilometers under our belts as we can while we still have daylight."

Gavin nodded and trotted to the last wagon. Mike noted it was Sarah's wagon.

Fifteen minutes later Declan still hadn't reappeared. Annoyed with himself for not tying Declan's horse to a bush back where they'd left him, Mike took Gavin's place at the back and sent the lad down the road to find his uncle.

A nervous sensation crept up Mike's spine as he watched Gavin disappear. Why had he let Declan go off by himself? The poor bastard was probably stumbling around lost in the woods. It was all well and good to treat Declan as if nothing had happened and he wasn't changed, but dammit, that wasn't the truth.

Mike alternately turned in his saddle to watch the road behind him to catch a glimpse of either Gavin or Declan, or stare at Sarah's ramrod straight back as she drove her wagon and pretended Mike wasn't riding behind her.

He'd get it sorted out once they were settled at the new place. *Plenty of time for dealing with all this shite then.* And who knows? Maybe she'd be over it by then. Maybe things would be back to normal.

Sarah stopped her wagon. When Mike looked up to see why he saw that all the wagons were stopped. She twisted around in her seat to look at him. The sudden cessation of movement seemed to wake up the little ones who'd been napping and now Mike heard whimpers and whines erupting from most of the wagons.

Up ahead, he saw Fiona was standing on the seat of her wagon, her hands on her hips. Hoping she'd set the brake first, Mike trotted up to talk with her.

"Where's Declan?" she demanded. "He's been gone too long."

"No worries, Fi. I sent Gavin back to collect him."

She nodded as if this information was exactly what she already knew, handed the reins to Nuala, and climbed down from the wagon.

"Now, Fiona," Mike said with exasperation. "This isn't necessary…"

Fiona grabbed the reins of Declan's horse from Mike's hands and mounted up. Not bothering to adjust the stirrup lengths, she pulled both leathers up and crossed them in front of her on the saddle, turned the horse's head and put him into a canter back the way they'd come.

A part of Mike knew she was right. Declan had been gone too long.

"Mike," Nuala said from the wagon. "I can't drive this thing *and* hold the baby too."

"The brake's on," Mike said. "Just sit tight." He trotted to the end of the line of wagons.

Sarah was standing up in her wagon now. "Where did Fiona go? What's going on?"

"Declan might have gotten disoriented in the woods. Fiona's gone to find him."

"You shouldn't have let him go alone."

She was right but Mike felt his defenses shoot up.

"Would ye have me hold his knob for him, Sarah?"

She flushed at his language but didn't back down. "I'm just surprised you thought he could handle peeing by himself."

"I'll not row with you here," he growled.

A couple men from the other wagons walked up to Mike.

"What do you want us to do?" one of them asked.

Surely the worst that could have happened was that Declan was lost? Was it possible he was hurt?

Mike looked down the road as if he could somehow *will* the three to appear.

"Terry, take over," he said finally to the oldest of the men. "Keep everyone in the wagons. Do *not* move from this spot, ye ken?"

"Aye."

"I'll be back." Mike put his horse into a fast trot down the road. The further he rode, the more amazed he was that the wagon train had travelled so far in fifteen minutes. He figured he should be able to see Fiona and Gavin around the next bend in the road. He took the turn faster than he should've and felt his horse's hooves slide on the slippery leaves, losing traction with the road.

Mike's heart beat in his throat as he loosened the reins, trying to let the animal sort himself out and gather control again. His horse found his footing just as Mike saw Gavin and Fiona's horses standing in the middle of the road.

Both riderless.

Susan Kiernan-Lewis

8.

Mike swung down from saddle, his heart hammering in his chest, his agitated breathing so loud he couldn't hear any other sound. When he got closer he saw the reins of Fiona's horse were tied to a bush. Gavin's horse had pulled free. He peered into the woods and tried to hear voices. The perspiration beaded up on his forehead.

There. A woman's voice, light and snatched away on the breeze. Mike tied Gavin's horse and his own to a sapling, then plunged into the woods.

"Fi! Gavin!" he called. "Where are you?"

He stopped and leaned again a birch tree to listen.

"Da! We're over here!"

Thank the saints. Mike jogged in the direction of Gavin's voice. The branches whipped back and slapped him in the face. There was no path through here but now he could see bushes bent and broken along the way.

He saw them in the clearing. Two figures. His throat tightened.

There should be three figures.

Fiona stood next to Gavin, her hand over her mouth. Declan lay on the ground, his eyes blinking up at the sky.

"What happened?" Mike said as he reached them. He knelt by Declan and touched his hand. Declan turned to look at him. It was then Mike saw the blood-drenched rag held against Declan's chest. "Jaysus! What happened?"

"Two blokes," Declan wheezed, closing his eyes.

"Where? In the woods?"

Declan's face whitened and he nodded.

"We need to get him back to the wagon," Fiona said.

Mike braced himself against a tree for leverage and pulled Declan into his arms. Gavin helped lift from underneath until Mike had a decent grip.

"Just clear the way for me," Mike grunted. Fiona bent back the bushes in front of him.

"He said he got turned around," Gavin said. "The bastards must have watched him go in the woods. They hit him, then went friggin' mental when he didn't have anything of value on him."

Mike focused on getting Declan out of the woods without dropping him.

"Took...took me *sgian-dubh*," Declan gasped. "The one you gave me, Mike. I tried to...I tried to..."

"He tried to get it back," Fiona said briskly. "So they used it on him." She glanced at Mike but her eyes went to her husband's wound.

God! Were they in the woods this far?

"I'll get the horses," Gavin said as he sprinted away.

Mike's arms were screaming from Declan's weight. The last thing he wanted to do was fall to his knees but he wasn't entirely sure he could make it all the way to the road.

"Stop and rest, Mike," Fiona said.

"Just clear me a path," he panted, his sweat cooling on his skin, his legs on fire with every step.

Up ahead he saw Gavin mounted up. He heard the sound of rain hitting the forest treetops but none had yet to fall on them.

"We're there, Mike," Fiona said, putting her hands under Declan's body. Even that little help made a difference and Mike knew he had the strength to make it the rest of the way.

"I'm so sorry, Mike," Declan said, tears beginning to stream down his face. "So, so sorry."

Gavin rode into the ditch and through the first line of trees. Mike felt him grab Declan under his arms and pull him slowly into his lap on the horse while Fiona pushed. Declan groaned. The sudden loss of weight on his arms made Mike stumble and he put a hand out to steady himself against Gavin's horse.

"Ye got 'im, Gav?" he asked breathlessly.

"Aye, good and solid. Meet you at the wagons." Gavin turned his horse down the road. By the time Mike emerged from the woods Fiona was already mounted and trotting after them.

Mike looked around, wondering if the blackguards who'd stabbed Dec were still around. The road was silent except for the fading clip-clop of Gavin and Fiona's horses and the patter of the rain on the road.

While he hadn't had time to get a close look at Declan's injuries, he could tell by the amount of blood down the front of him that it wasn't good.

Not good at all.

******

Sarah was the first to see Gavin ride up with Declan's limp body in his arms. The gossip had spread like a prairie fire up and down the little wagon train.

Everyone knew Declan had gotten lost. The fact that they'd brought him back was not a consolation to Sarah. She *assumed* they'd find him.

In what condition was the question.

Fiona cantered to Sarah's wagon and dismounted, tossing her reins to one of the women in the back.

"What do you need, Fi?" Sarah called.

"Some place to lay him," Fi said as she ran to the back of the wagon and began helping the children out of it.

Sarah wrapped the reins around the brake and jumped down from the seat. By the time she reached Fiona, Mike had arrived and was easing Declan out of Gavin's arms and onto the ground.

There was so much blood down the front of Declan it looked like his chest had exploded.

No way, Sarah thought, as she watched Declan feebly try to sit up. *No way he'll survive this.*

Fiona was all business now. She climbed into the back of the wagon to lay out bedding. Several of the other people in the group had walked from the front of the line.

"Move back. Give him room," Mike said. He and Gavin slid a blanket under Declan and lifted him up between them and onto the wagon. Sarah saw that Mike's shirt was nearly as bloody as Declan's. She'd hear all about it later. The woods were full of murderers and cutthroats. The wonder wasn't that one of their party was attacked but that it hadn't happened sooner.

Sarah climbed into the wagon with Fiona and pried the first aid kit out from behind the driver's seat where she'd packed it. Siobhan watched the goings on from the comforting arms of one of the compound women. Sarah knelt next to Declan and squeezed his hand.

"Hey, Dec," she said, forcing herself not to grimace at how white he looked. He squeezed her hand in return.

"I got the bleeding stopped," Fiona said breathlessly. "It's why it took us so long."

Sarah peeled away the wadded up sweatshirt Fi had used for padding on Declan's chest. *The bleeding had definitely stopped, thank God. And the wound itself looked shallow enough.*

"Hand me that bandage, will you?"

So why does he look like he's at death's door?

"Is this the only injury?" Sarah asked.

Fiona looked at her, her eyes showing panic.

"You think there has to be another explanation for why he looks like this?" she asked.

Sarah glanced up at Gavin where he sat on his horse. The patch across the front of his jeans where he'd held Declan was bright red.

Shit.

Sarah slid a hand between the blanket and Declan's back. His eyes fluttered back into his head and he moaned.

"Help me move him to his side."

"It's his front where he's hurt," Fiona said but she pulled on Declan's arm as Sarah shifted his hip toward her.

He lay in a pool of gore.

"Oh, Sarah," Fiona whispered. "Oh, please do something."

"Okay, calm down," Sarah said, her mind racing. This was well beyond her experience level.

He'd lost a lot of blood—was still losing a lot of blood—from the back wound. She reached for another wad of padding. It wasn't clean but it would have to do. She had to stop the bleeding. She'd worry about infection later. She bound the padding to his back and tied it securely with a cloth belt. Declan had passed out which Sarah hoped wasn't a bad sign. But it probably wasn't good.

"Did you talk to him?" Sarah asked.

Fiona's eyes brimmed with tears as she stared at Declan's face in repose.

"He said two men stabbed him with his own knife."

"Just the once?"

"I...he didn't mention more than one time."

"Okay. I want to clean it and see how bad it is but I need to wash up for that. Stay here."

"Sarah, sure you can fix him, can't you?"

Sarah hesitated. She tried to remember a single other time when Fiona had looked or sounded this helpless. In point of fact, Fiona was usually considered the compound healer. She had an encyclopedic understanding of medicinal herbs and concoctions and kept a good supply for most occasions.

But broken bones, bullet holes and stab wounds were a whole different thing.

Sarah glanced at Declan and then back at Fiona. What did she want her to say? A lie? What did Fiona think was going to happen when she'd backed her brother so vigorously about leaving the convent?

Is it possible she is really surprised?

"Stay with him," Sarah said jumping down.

An hour later, Sarah had cleaned Declan's wound the best she could. Fiona had some herbs in her homeopathic medicine chest for fighting infections and, even better, Sarah still had a decent supply of antibiotics. Now that the back wound had stopped bleeding, they needed to keep him quiet and hydrated until they could return to the convent. Sister Alphonse was a registered nurse.

Mike had set up camp in the middle of the road so they didn't even have to move the wagon that Declan was in. The other wagons were shifted off the road and two small campfires built at either end of the makeshift campsite. The mood in camp was somber.

It had rained early that afternoon but not long and not hard. Mike gave orders not to unpack the tents, which suited Sarah just fine. The sooner they got on the way back to the convent, the better.

Nuala O'Connell kept Fiona's little girls with her so that Fiona could stay with Declan. She would spend most of the long night trying to get beef broth and water into him, and checking his bandages and his pulse.

Sarah went to the larger campfire where she knew she'd find Mike. If there was ever a time she wanted to hear him say the words *I was wrong*, this was it.

The relief of knowing the whole mad caper was over—and had ended almost exactly as Sarah knew it would—helped ease the chronic anxiety that lived in her gut.

We're going back and that's all that matters.

When she walked up Mike stood from where he was seated by the fire.

"You look done in," he said grimly, making room for her to sit. "Come, eat."

Sarah looked around the campfire. Gavin and Sophia sat opposite them, their little one asleep in Sophia's arms. Several of the women they'd liberated from the rape camp last spring also sat around the fire.

"Siobhan's with Mary and Kev," Mike said, handing Sarah a plate of roasted rabbit.

"Great," Sarah said absently. She bit into the meat and realized she was ravenous.

"How is he?" Mike asked.

"Not good. But Sister Alphonse will know what to do."

"Sarah…"

"How is he, Sarah?" Sophia called from across the fire.

"I said a prayer for him."

"That'll help," Sarah said with a smile. She looked at Mike. "And on our first day out."

"I know. It's my fault."

He looked haggard and Sarah felt her heart soften toward him. She saw his guilt and his misery. It was true that Declan wouldn't be laying in the back of a horse wagon fighting for his life if it hadn't been for Mike's insistence that they go looking for something better. But at least Mike saw that.

"Don't blame yourself too much," she said laying a hand on his knee. As soon as she felt his leg, firm and hard under her hand, she realized it had been a long time since they'd touched. "I'm sure Sister Alphonse can fix him up."

"Sarah," he said, his shoulders sagging.

She reached out to touch his face.

"We're not going back," he said wearily.

Her hand froze. *Would he really joke at a time like this? Or had he totally lost his mind?*

"Of course we're going back," she said, edging away from him, her food forgotten. "How can you even say that?"

"Sarah…" He looked at her helplessly and then glanced at the wagon behind her with Fiona and Declan in it. "We have to go forward. There's no future for us back there."

"Well, there might be a future for *Declan* back there," Sarah said loudly.

"Lower your voice. Fiona's upset enough as it is."

"You mean you don't want Fiona switching to *my* side which you know she'll do once she realizes you're crazy enough to want to go on."

"Fiona agrees with me."

Sarah jumped to her feet. "I don't believe it! You'd sacrifice your best friend for this obsession of yours about a stupid castle?"

"Don't be dramatic," Mike said between gritted teeth. "Declan is his own man." But his eyes flitted again to the wagon. Sarah saw the indecision there. The guilt.

"You know very well he isn't any more! And now look where we are!"

"I admit it!" Mike said angrily. "I was wrong to let him go off on his own. I made a mistake. I won't make it again."

"You won't get the chance again. He'll be lucky to pass gas on his own now, let alone take a walk in the woods."

"You've made your point, Sarah. I accept the blame for what happened."

"And you'll go ahead and do what you want anyway."

"As long as I believe it's the right thing for those who follow me, aye."

"Maybe that's the key phrase."

"Be mindful of what you say, Sarah."

"Why? Because words have power? How about actions, Mike?" She turned and stomped away from the warmth of the campfire, her mind buzzing with disbelief. They weren't going back. *Unbelievable.*

Sarah felt her fury drumming in her chest as she walked away from the wagons where the road stretched back toward the nunnery.

She couldn't leave. Not yet anyway. Not without Siobhan. She just needed to walk and wear down the anger and the hurt.

The sounds of camp receded and Sarah felt a drape of calmness descend on her the further she got from the noise. She stopped, closed her eyes and took a long cleansing breath.

When she opened her eyes, she felt a little better. She looked longingly down the dark road as it bent around a far corner on its way back to the convent and imagined walking down that road in the sunshine with Siobhan in her arms.

She promised herself she would. Soon. If Mike couldn't see the dangers ahead it was up to her to save Siobhan. And John. Just thinking it made her feel calmer.

Suddenly the noise from camp amplified. She turned to look back. When she did, the noise softened. Confused, she turned again the road to the convent and instantly saw the true source of the sound.

People morphed out of the darkness. Heading toward her.

9.

Things were shaping up nicely and it had only taken the wholesale slaughter of a little less than one hundred men to affect it.

Hurley strode to the first tier of the Dublin opera house. It smelled like a dung heap and no surprise. While the lions lived comfortably on the stage and orchestra pit in the ancient indoor amphitheater, cleaning up after them was out of the question.

One of the younger Centurions had the idea that mercy might be shown to any sacrifice who was able to clean a section of the lions' den and stay alive for five minutes. Unfortunately, after the first week once all the politicians and officers were tossed to the lions, the beasts were always fairly hungry.

Hurley had known terror was the fastest way to wake up his lackluster troops and that had been absolutely proven in the past three weeks. While it was true he was only one man and could easily be overpowered, none of his men appeared to think in those terms. It confirmed what he'd always known.

They wanted to be led.

The sloppiness of the work of the Garda in the last five years was gone. It was gone as fast as it took for the mortal screams of Hurley's commanding officer to fade and everyone else who held a rank above corporal.

Hurley had quickly organized the men into three legions and renamed the Garda the Imperial Irish Army, noting of course that there was no emperor or nonmilitary leader of any kind in Ireland. It didn't matter. If the outside world ever came calling again—whether to offer aid or ask for it—they could deal with Padraig Hurley, Centurion Commander.

He surveyed the malodorous amphitheater. His men had created barriers from the stage to prevent the animals—or their victims—from escaping. The lions paced the filthy stage now, their paws clogged with feces and blood.

They would need to find more lion food soon.

The Centurion, James Brady, appeared by his side. Hurley estimated that the young man was still in his teens but he was keen and had difficulty seeing gray areas.

The perfect soldier.

"Why don't I have tigers, Brady?" Hurley asked without turning his gaze from the lion pit.

"I'm told the lions stayed together so they were easily caught but the tigers are loners and so they escaped."

Hurley glanced at the boy. "Who told you this?"

Brady didn't even blink. "Centurion Murphy, Commander."

"And was Murphy one of the ones who went out to capture them?"

"Yes, Commander."

Hurley nodded. "Gather the men. They'll want to see what happens when a centurion doesn't properly obey orders."

"Yes, Commander."

10.

After stomping around for a few minutes and trying not to put his fist through a tree, Mike was astonished to see Sarah come running back to the campfire with a grin on her face.

He thought for a moment he was bloody hallucinating.

Behind Sarah was a crowd of people led by a dilapidated pony cart painted with big yellow flowers and driven by none other than Jaz and Regan.

Mike had to admit, their timing was spot on.

The pair parked the cart in the middle of the road and descended on everyone with laughter and squeals of delight. Mike even saw Jaz give her ex-love Tommy a fairly X-rated kiss on the mouth before running over to the women who were next in line to be returned to their homes.

They could not have shown up at a better time.

Even Fiona was smiling from where she sat with Declan. The two girls brought a rush of enthusiasm and sunshine with them that they all badly needed. They also brought a small group of gypsies they'd met on the road.

Sarah quickly organized food for everyone and Mike broke out the whiskey. It wasn't often they got newcomers and it was always a big deal.

Newcomers meant news.

"Cor, I'm that sorry about poor Declan," Regan said as she tore into leftovers of roasted rabbit. "Mind you, it's dangerous out there, so it is." She and Jaz exchanged a look that made Mike frown. Obviously the two had had a close call somewhere along the line. He wasn't sure he wanted to know the details.

"Did Meggie's mum cry when she saw her?" One of the women asked.

"Did she ever," Jaz said with a laugh. "I felt like Lazarus, so I did."

"Nay," Regan said. "Lazarus is the one who got raised from the dead. Ye felt like Christ, in fact. He did the raising."

"Isn't that blasphemy?" Sophia said.

"Not when these two do it," Mike said with a grin. He turned to the three gypsy men. They were not long out of their teens and their memory of life before the first EMP would be hazy at best. "What news?" he asked.

The skinny young man known as Digger took a long draught of Mike's whiskey and wiped his mouth with the back of a dirty hand.

"Talk is it weren't an EMP," he said.

Mike was stunned. *Was that possible?*

"What else could it be?"

"Nobody knows for sure but they're saying maybe a massive solar flare. If it was an EMP nobody knows who or why since we're all off the grid now."

"Even the UK?" Sarah asked, her face stitched with anxiety.

"Oh, aye. The continent too. Me and Gareth heard stories of cars trapped in the Chunnel."

"That's terrible," Sophia said, biting her lip and looking at Gavin with worry. The baby whimpered in her arms.

"They heard that London and Paris are in total chaos," Regan said gleefully. "There's full-on riots in the streets. Digger met a bloke straight from Cardiff who said London is tearing itself apart."

Mike glanced at Sarah. She looked stricken. Of course she would be thinking of young John.

God, what a mess.

"Well, solar flare or not," Mike said, "we're all in the same boat now."

"Aye, that's the truth," Digger said, reaching for the whiskey again.

"Will you be coming on with us?" Mike asked. With two-thirds of his party women and children, he could use a little more manpower.

"Nay, thank ye kindly," Gareth said. "A berth for the night under one of your wagons and we'll be off in the morning."

Mike wasn't really surprised. Not for nothing were the gypsies called Irish Travelers.

"And you two?" he said to Regan and Jaz.

"We'll take Jenny and Moira in the morning," Regan said. "Their families are only about forty kilometers apart. And Jenny has the bairn."

"Can that old pony trap of yours handle four people?" Mike asked as he squinted at the little wagon with yellow flowers painted on the side of it.

"It's grand," Jaz said. "It's all we need, me and Regan."

These two really are two peas, Mike thought wryly. Outcasts and misfits, but good girls through and through. He was glad there was a job for them that fit them so well. He couldn't remember a time when Regan looked this happy.

"Well, it's a grand thing you're doing," Mike said. "So it is." His eyes strayed to Sarah. Although her face was impassive, he chose to believe she felt as he did—sorry for the fight and for the distance between them. He smiled and she nodded.

****

Sarah was exhausted by the time they got everyone bedded down. Even the babies—as soon as most of them were asleep, one would start to cry and get the others going again. It was going to be a long nine more days to get to wherever it is they were going.

She was sure that once they arrived, Mike would see the folly of it all. Sarah hated to have to go through the lengthy trek just to turn around and go back—especially at the cost of Declan's life—but if that's what it took, it would be on Mike's head.

"Sarah?"

She turned to see Regan wrapped in a blanket and sitting by the fire. Jaz had disappeared into the woods with Tommy and the rest of their party was already asleep. Mike was making one of his endless circuits around the wagon train. Even if Mike did lay down before dawn, he'd be up a few hundred times in the meantime making sure everything was secure. Gavin and two of the other men were taking turns keeping watch throughout the night.

Sarah sat down next to Regan, the heat from the fire comforting on her legs. It wasn't until she sat that she felt the exhaustion she'd kept at bay all day finally tug at her.

"Hey, sweetie," Sarah said. "I'm so glad you caught up with us. I couldn't believe it when I saw you coming down the road."

"I know. You should have seen the look on your face," Regan said, grinning.

"Is everything okay?"

Regan laughed. "You always know, don't you? Must be a mum thing. It's like you can read minds."

"Some minds," Sarah said with a smile. "Was everything okay when you found Meggie's home for her?"

"Oh, aye, it was grand. But it got me to worrying, you know?"

"About what?"

"Well, Meggie didn't have a rape baby to parade around at her mum's so she could play it however she wanted."

"What did she tell her mother about where she was for the past two years?"

"Oh, she told her the truth right enough. And it was fine." Regan's eyes shone with emotion. "It was wonderful to see them, Sarah. Reminded me so much of Mum. I really miss her."

"I know. Me, too."

"And it made me feel good that I could help Meggie find her mum. I can't remember ever feeling that good."

"I can imagine."

"But what about next time? Or the time after that?"

"What do you mean?"

"Well, what if one of 'em won't want them home after what's happened to them?"

"You mean like how Liddy's husband couldn't bear her after she had little Roisin?"

"Aye. What do we do?"

"You'll talk it over with the girls. Ask them what they want to do if their families won't have them back. They know they're always welcome with us, right?"

"Aye."

"Well, that's all you can do, Regan. You can't make people not suck."

Regan laughed.

"You and Jaz get along well," Sarah said.

"Oh, cracking, aye. She's grand." Regan's eyes closed sleepily and Sarah leaned over and kissed her on the cheek.

"Good night, sweetie. Your mother and father would be so proud."

*****

The next morning, Jaz and Regan and their group were in the wagon or walking beside it, ready to leave. Sarah made sure they all had lunches for the day and the girls were convinced they'd be at their first village before dinnertime.

Declan had worsened in the night and Mike decided they'd stay another night.

For all the good it would do, Sarah thought. *Declan needs a doctor.*

As she and the rest of their group waved off Jaz and Regan in their gaily painted little wagon, the pony tossing its head impatiently, Sarah reminded herself that the girls had a gun and neither was afraid to use it.

She said a quick prayer for their safety.

When they had gone, Sarah caught a glimpse of Siobhan in one of the other wagons and a stab of guilt pierced her. It wasn't that she'd forgotten about the child in the last few hours—she knew where she was and that she was well taken care of—it was that she hadn't felt, not once, the urge to go and be with her.

What is wrong with me? Is this some kind of postpartum crap? Or is this just that I have a job to do and there are others—a village come to that—to mind Siobhan while she's small?

No sooner was the thought in her head when she remembered Mike on his horse earlier that morning with Siobhan in his arms. He had been busy checking on everyone. And he definitely had time for his little lass.

No, there's no excuse for it, Sarah thought as she remembered the vision of Mike and Siobhan moving down the line of wagons. She'd heard Mike call out to one of the men and his wife had responded in a high-pitched sing-songy voice to Siobhan.

How normal. How very normal.

Sarah's guts churned at the thought of even approaching Siobhan. Her anxiety ratcheted up in direct portion to her proximity to the child. And somehow, when Siobhan was out of sight—while she was never out of mind—the terror and the panic lessened.

Sarah had fallen asleep next to Mike last night but had no memory of him lying next to her. It was possible he'd never come to bed. They hadn't spoken since their fight. Maybe that was best. Maybe talking would just make it worse.

After all, neither of them had changed how they felt about things.

Sarah walked to her wagon to see if Fiona needed to be spelled with Declan and she thought of the anti-anxiety medications she'd been on back in Jacksonville.

God, if I thought I had things to fret about back then, I wasn't even on the same planet when it comes to worry compared to now. What she wouldn't give for *one* of those little yellow tablets this morning. Just something to take the edge off the constant fear.

The fact was she had so much to lose now. She had John and Siobhan and Mike. And the world steadily tried to kill each of them in a different way nearly every day.

Nuala stood by the campfire with her baby in her arms. Fiona's little girls were playing in the dirt at her feet and her two boys were by her side. She was scolding the older boy who was looking at his feet shamefaced.

"Hey, Nuala," Sarah said. She looked at the boy. "Hi, Dennis. Or is it Damian?"

The boy looked up at her through his fringe of hair, his blue eyes bright and clear.

"Dennis," he said.

"Off you go now," Nuala said, shifting her baby to her other hip. "You too, Damian."

Both boys scampered off. Dennis immediately shoved his younger brother as they went.

"Mind yourselves, you lot," Nuala called after them in a warning voice.

"Everything okay?" Sarah asked.

Nuala grimaced. "Just lads being lads," she said. "Denny tried to roast Damian's shoes in the fire."

Sarah's eyes followed the boys until they disappeared into the woods. The very woods where Declan was knifed yesterday.

"Should they be in the woods?"

"Oh, sure you'll not keep lads out of mischief, Sarah. And you with a lad of your own all the way in the UK."

"Don't remind me."

"They're a handful and no mistake," Nuala said good-naturedly.

Sarah couldn't believe Nuala let them take off like that —boys or not. Nuala had three children—five counting the care of Fiona's two—with no husband to help and yet she looked as calm and happy as if she had a nanny helping her with all the nappy folding.

Why is she not sick with anxiety about their safety?

"Are ye all right, Sarah? You look a little peaked."

"I'm fine," Sarah said.

"You worry too much," Nuala said. "So you do. You can't change the world or keep them safe every minute. Why just this morning little Maeve was playing too close to the fire and didn't she come this close to falling in?"

"But she didn't?"

"Nay, her guardian angel was on duty. And she'll know better next time."

I guess third-degree burns are a small price to pay for such life lessons, Sarah thought, but she made herself nod as if in agreement.

Susan Kiernan-Lewis

11.

Mike sat his horse and looked down the road. He'd swapped little Siobhan for a cup of tea and now warmed his fingers against the cup and watched the steam rise up and join the mist of the morning.

Day four on the road and they'd gone approximately twenty kilometers, give or take. At this rate, it would be faster to crawl to the coast.

Should they have turned around for poor Dec? Mike shook his head as if to clear it. He couldn't explain the feeling—the inexplicable urge—to get somewhere safe as fast as possible.

Something was coming. That's all he knew. And they had to be secure when it did.

How could he explain that to Sarah?

"I can't explain why but I just feel in my gut that if we wait it might be too late?"

The *last* thing he wanted to do was give her one more reason to freak out over possible doomsday scenarios. She was already remapping the whole definition of irrational worry.

Except of course her fears weren't irrational at all.

At least Declan was improving, thank God. They'd resumed their journey yesterday and he appeared to be holding steady.

But why is it Mike couldn't look his own sister in the eye? *Is it because deep down I know what Sarah said is true? I'm willing to sacrifice Declan for my own commitment to this castle idea?*

Obsession, she called it.

He looked over his shoulder but knew he wouldn't see her from where he was. In fact, he'd seen damn little of her in the last couple of days and he was sure that was deliberate.

Probably just as well.

He had to believe that once they were settled and she began to feel safe again, she'd revert back to the Sarah he knew—the stubborn but fearless Sarah he'd fallen in love with.

He turned his head at the sound of horse hooves to see Gavin and Tommy approaching.

"Ready to move out, Da?" Gavin called.

"Before breakfast?" Mike asked, surprised.

"Thought you were in a hurry," Tommy said.

"Aye, so I am," Mike said, dumping the contents of his tea cup and tossing it to Gavin. "Take the rear, Gav. Is your lass with Sarah?"

"Aye. In the last wagon," Gavin said as he turned his horse toward the back of the wagon train.

Mike had moved the wagon with Fiona and Declan in it to the middle of the pack and assigned Kevin to drive it. Kev knew horses and would be able to avoid the frequent obstacles in the road better than anyone else.

As he moved back down to check the line of wagons, Mike thought that if he had one prayer, it would be that Declan would strengthen.

He had to believe all of this was worth the risk.

*****

Fiona felt the wagon begin to move. She hadn't realized she'd dozed off. When she opened her eyes she saw that someone had left a fried egg biscuit for her breakfast and a cup of no longer hot tea.

Declan groaned but didn't open his eyes. She put a hand on his knee and he settled.

For the millionth time since she'd climbed into the wagon she wondered if she was doing the right thing. Mike seemed so sure that going forward was best for all of them, including Declan. But she well knew how stubborn her brother could be.

Declan was at least no worse. Sarah's antibiotics and pain medications had eased him, and his back wound showed no sign of infection.

No, going forward was the right thing to do. Declan would be the first to agree—if he was in any mind to even know what was going on. *Which he wasn't.*

The morning mist still hung in the air but it was better than yesterday when they'd ridden for nearly half the morning before a strong gale had finally relented. There had been so much moisture in the air that the rocks in the road were slick and slippery.

Fiona knew this part of the country although she'd had little reason to visit it in the last five years. The pastures on both sides of the road—long fallow and unused—were brown with bright patches of purple here and there of late blooming heather. There wasn't a tree in sight.

She ate her sandwich and drank the tea, grateful for the weak sun filtering through the cloud cover. They were lucky the weather had cooperated. October usually meant rain and fog.

She looked at Declan and her heart contracted painfully. The last time she'd seen him whole and well was ten months ago—the day the Garda had come to Ameriland. After an agonizing separation where she didn't know if he was alive or dead, he'd been miraculously returned to her—changed forever.

She closed her eyes and felt the sun's wavering rays on her upturned face.

There was a better life coming. She had to believe that.

Hours later, Fiona felt the temperature drop noticeably. She'd dozed again and the chill woke her. Reflexively, she put a hand on Declan. He was sleeping peacefully and for that she was grateful.

The sun was no longer visible through the clouds, the rays no longer in evidence. Shivering, she pulled a blanket around herself and tucked in Declan's cover. She felt the wagon stop.

"How's he doing, then, Fiona?" Kevin asked as he twisted around in the driver's seat.

"He's good. Is it lunch we're stopping for then?"

"For the night I imagine. It's well past five. Had a good kip, did you?"

"I guess I must have." Had she really slept the day away? She stood up in the wagon and saw Sarah walking down the line of wagons toward her. Her face was directed downward as if she was memorizing the ground, her expression set in concentration. Within seconds, she was at the wagon and pulling herself on board.

"Hey, Fi. How's he doing?"

"He's grand, Sarah. Sleeping for now."

Kevin dismounted from the wagon and walked away. Already the other people in the group were setting up campfires and starting dinner. Fiona caught a glimpse of Mike on horseback down the line. He held Siobhan in one arm as he rode.

"I brought more Percocet. How are *you* doing?" Sarah asked.

"I'm grand, Sarah, so I am," Fiona said carefully. She knew Sarah felt betrayed by her decision not to return to the convent. "And yourself?"

"You know this is all a mistake, right?"

"I know *you* think so."

"Fine. Be that way. I just hope Declan doesn't end up paying the price."

"Because blaming a loved one for that would be a terrible burden," Fiona said coolly, her hands gripping the blanket as she felt the tension creep into them.

Sarah ignored her. She gently turned Declan to check his bandage and then tucked his blanket back.

"We need to start getting something in him besides broth and tea."

"Sure I do know there's evil in the world, Sarah."

"You more than most, I imagine."

"And then there's just bad luck. Accidents happen."

"You can make them happen less if you plan for them."

"Except sometimes the best laid plans will still have you mopping up an unforeseen mess."

"Your point, Fi?"

"We can't see the future."

"Have you been dipping into Declan's pain meds?"

Fiona felt her anger and helplessness course through her.

"I'm just trying to say that sometimes the *fear* of a thing is worse than the actual thing."

"That's idiotic." Sarah nodded at Declan. "Is the fear of Declan getting stabbed worse than the fact?"

"Of course not. It's just that I see you reacting to everything like the world will blow up in your face any minute and—"

"First, I don't think I'm reacting to *everything* like that but thanks for the globalization and, second, there's every reason to believe that this world *will* self-destruct with almost no provocation and if you don't think so, well you're just deluded."

Sarah stood up and swung one leg over the side of wagon to leave.

"No, forget delusions," she said. "With a disabled and twice-stabbed husband laying right in front of you, you're either a fool or a liar."

*****

Sarah's hands were still shaking by the time she arrived at the first campfire. Sophia and some of the other women were feeding sticks into the blaze while Gavin field dressed a dozen rabbits. The sight of the bloody carcasses turned Sarah's stomach. Seeing their little paws outstretched over their heads brought her an instant memory of a puppy she once had in childhood.

Now we eat the cute little animals we used to think of as pets.

"Oh, Sarah," Sophia said, looking up from her work. "Looking for Mike?"

Sarah swallowed down her revulsion and rubbed her hands against her jeans to make them stop shaking.

"He and the bairn are doing a final circuit before tea," Gavin said.

Sarah nodded her thanks and turned away before the insanity of calling a dinner of bloody trapped rabbits in the middle of a darkened country road *tea* made her burst into hysterical laughter. She took a long breath and walked away, hoping the exercise would help settle her mind.

Up ahead, she saw Mike on foot next to his horse talking with Terry and his wife Jill. Sure enough, Siobhan was in Mike's arms. She was kicking her legs but not in any effort to get down but clearly just because it felt good.

Was Mother Angelina right? Was Siobhan picking up on Sarah's anxiety? Is *that* why she cried every time Sarah touched her?

She heard a burst of laughter coming from the group and imagined how comforting that must be for Siobhan—the sound of her daddy's laughter, the ease and comfort of his strong arms around her.

Had she really called Fiona a liar? When the poor woman had spent the last three days and nights worrying about her desperately hurt husband?

What is the matter with me?

Vowing to return later and apologize to Fiona, Sarah straightened her shoulders and quickened her pace to catch up with Mike and Siobhan.

I can do this. By God, if I can shoot three marauding gypsies threatening my child, I can do this. But the very memory of the day she stood with John—no more than nine years old—and faced down men who would harm him only served to weaken her. As fast as a viper's strike, the image was replaced by one of John as she'd last seen him. Nearly fifteen years old, his face open and trusting and hopeful with anticipation of the future before him—and how all of that got thrown into doubt and fear when the second EMP blew.

"Well, hello, there," Mike said as she reached him. "Come to fetch us in?" He smiled but Sarah saw the question behind his eyes. They had issues to resolve and ends to tie up.

She held out her arms to the baby. "Hello, little one," she said. "I've missed you so much."

Siobhan blinked at the sight of Sarah's outstretched arms and then turned and laid her cheek on Mike's chest as if shy.

"She's just tired," Mike said.

And that, Sarah thought. *People constantly making excuses for when Siobhan turns away from me. Pitying me because my own child doesn't want me.*

Sarah forced the thought away. She put a hand on Siobhan's hair.

"I'm not surprised," she said. "It's been a long day. Uncle Gavin is getting dinner together." She looked at Mike. "I guess it's working in our favor that we weren't able to get her any stuffed bunny rabbits before now."

Mike gave her a perplexed look but smiled. They both walked back toward the camp. Sarah gave his horse a pat on the neck and remembered a time not that long ago when she'd been afraid of horses.

The memory gave her hope.

12.

The days of the journey to the castle passed in gentle repetition of the ones that came before. Declan got slowly stronger and by the seventh day was sitting up part of the time on the driver's bench with Kevin. Some days they found meat and some days they didn't. But nobody ever went to bed hungry and there was a routine to their days.

Sarah made her peace with Fiona and even with Mike to a certain extent. They didn't talk about their differences and Sarah wasn't sure they ever would. She tried not to think any further than the day she was living although in the back of her mind she *knew* she would be traveling back down this road within weeks. Either with Mike or alone, she would return to the convent and by God and all that was holy, she would find John there waiting for her.

It was this thought that allowed her to take each day as it came. It allowed her to let out the long breath she'd been holding and relax into the rhythm of her days on the road. She even found herself laughing a few times and there was a look every now and then that Mike gave her—deeply loving and caring—that reminded her of how things used to be.

Even Siobhan had relented her policy of screaming her head off when Sarah tried to hold her. Some nights around the campfire as all the mothers were trying to get the babies to sleep and someone was strumming a guitar, Mike would hand a sleepy Siobhan off to Sarah and the child wouldn't immediately protest. Once, when Mike gave Siobhan to

Sophia so he could answer the call of nature, the baby had turned fretfully until she saw Sarah.

And held out her chubby little arms.

That moment had kept Sarah going for a very long time. While there was no doubt Siobhan preferred Mike, Sarah could see she was quickly becoming the preferred number two. And she would happily take it.

The closer they got to their journey's end, there was a palpable feeling of excitement that built with each day. Now, as they got closer—within three days Mike promised —he would spend a few minutes each night talking about the wonders of the place. He'd describe the moat that encircled the castle and the four crenellated towers that gave it its imposing presence—easily visible from miles away—like a mythical citadel rising out of the mist.

In fact, after more than a week on the road and no more mishaps to mar the experience, Sarah found herself looking forward to at least seeing the castle. Perhaps Mike and Fiona were right. Their futures were before them, not behind. Except for going back to collect John, Sarah was happy to believe that the castle might be a very good place for them to be.

If nobody else was there first.

And if it truly could keep them safe.

By late in the day on the eighth day, Sarah was willing to believe that their main trials were behind them. As she set the brake on the wagon to mark the fact that they were done traveling for the day, she watched the sun descend on the horizon in a glory of reds and yellows. It felt good to go forward, knowing the goal was reachable now. Sophia sat beside her with little Maggie in her lap. Siobhan rode in the back with several other children and two women.

As Mike trotted up on his horse, he appeared to Sarah like he'd lost weight. His face—even in mid-October—was tan. His horse, a steady Percheron crossbreed named Buck, shied at the wagon and Mike sorted him out with annoyance.

"What's his problem?" Sarah asked, frowning. Buck wasn't green and he'd seen everything there was to be afraid of many times over in the last five years.

"They're all edgy today," Mike said. "Everyone here all right?"

"Of course. Is Gavin out hunting? It's been two days and no meat."

"He's well aware. Aye, he's out."

"Will we use the tents tonight? It's getting colder."

Mike nodded but Sarah knew it cost him. They were so close now that he begrudged the extra time it took to take the tents down in the morning. He probably had it calculated to the quarter hour exactly how much the luxury cost him in figuring his arrival time.

"Kev and Terry are in charge of that. Can you get started on a campfire?"

"Sure." She gave him a smile. "You know one of the benefits of a tent is the little extra privacy is affords."

He frowned and then his face cleared as he got her meaning. "Oh, aye?"

"Just saying."

He grinned and Sarah realized she couldn't remember the last time he looked that gleeful.

The night was the coldest yet but Gavin had been lucky and killed a deer so a festive atmosphere prevailed at both campfires during dinner. The children seemed to pick up on their parents' optimism because there was no crying or whining to dampen the mood.

While he was hunting, Gavin had even found an unexpected spring not far from the campsite and there was talk among the women about visiting it in the morning to do a round of much needed laundry or even take a quick bath.

That night after dinner, as cold as it was, Sarah kept the tent flap open so she could watch the campfire while Mike finished his rounds. He would take one of the watches later in the early morning but for now she waited for him with a very sleepy, contented baby in her arms.

Sarah kissed Siobhan's cheek and the baby yawned, her fight to stay awake being lost by the moment. By the time Sarah tucked Siobhan into her own bed, Mike was stripping off his outer clothes and boots. There were no quips, no comments, no hesitations. They'd never had such a breech between them before and whoever was wrong or right mattered not all to either of them.

"I'm sorry," Sarah said as she opened her arms to him and felt his strong arms lift her and bring her to him.

"Me, too," he said, kissing her deeply. "Let's never fight like that again."

"Deal."

As Sarah closed her eyes, the comfort and security of her husband solid beside her, his snores a gentle reminder of his presence and his strength, it did flit through her mind that as lovely as it was to be back on track with him, it was a little easier to say *let's don't argue* when *you* were the one who got your way.

The next morning, Mike was gone when Sarah awoke. As she gathered up Siobhan and made her way to the cookfire, she kept an eye out for Fiona and her two little ones. Doing a quick wash up in the spring would make the next two travel days infinitely more bearable and Sarah wasn't going to miss it if she could help it.

When Sarah approached the campfire, the sisters Mary and Liddy were putting together a cold breakfast for the children. The men had already begun taking the tents down. That meant Mike was pushing everyone to hurry, Sarah thought.

"Is no one up for the walk to the spring Gavin found?" she asked.

"Too cold!" Sophia said, bundled up in a shawl and a jacket.

One of the women put her mug of tea down and held her arms open to Sarah. "I'll take the bairn if you're keen, Sarah," she said.

Sarah hesitated but when Siobhan automatically held her arms out for Jill to take her, that decided it.

"Does nobody else want to come with me?"

Fiona walked up. "Cor, no, you masochist," she said with a laugh. "But give me a moment and I'll give you one of Ciara's shirts if you don't mind? I've got soap, too."

"Oh! Sarah, would you mind?" Sophia asked, turning to rummage around in the pile of clothing where her tent used to be.

Sarah grinned.

"Okay, but you'll have to hold Mike back from leaving without me," she said. "I won't be long.

*****

Mike grimaced as he looked at the broken axel on the lead wagon. Kevin said he'd tried to lead the horse backward in it to put on the harness and the fool animal reared and kicked the shite out of the wagon braces holding the axle in place. It was just bad luck the way the horse's hooves had hit which smashed the one part of the wagon besides the wheel that was not negotiable as far as being necessary.

"I don't know what got into her," Kevin said, holding the halter on the horse. "Mares, you know."

"She doesn't usually act the maggot," Mike said, eyeing the animal.

"Not usually," Kevin said. "T'is true."

"We'll have to double up. Damn, I hate to."

"Will we need to leave the load?"

"What do you think? We're stuffed to the gills as it is."

There was no answer for it and no sense biting Kev's head off. Mike admitted begrudgingly he should be glad they'd had so few problems up to now. Once they were settled, he'd think about coming back and trying to fix the axle. On the other hand, once they were settled, why would they even need the wagon? The whole point was that they wouldn't be on the move again.

It was cold this morning and growing colder every morning. Mike knew he should've started out months ago —in the height of summer—not when autumn was upon them. But he also knew he had to wait for John to go first. As hard as it was to convince Sarah to come, it would've been impossible before September. And then Sophia had the baby...

"Da!"

Mike looked up and felt the weariness settle between his shoulder blades at the sound of his son's voice.

Bloody hell, there better not be another problem...

*****

The mist seemed to come from nowhere. One minute Sarah was walking through a well-lighted patch of gorse in the general direction of the spring Gavin had given her directions to and the next minute she felt like she was on a movie set with clouds of dry ice billowing around her legs.

She held the bag of laundry she'd collected from the others and quickened her steps. She probably didn't have time for more than just a couple of soapy swishes in the spring and maybe a good face washing. She could hear the camp breaking up and it gave her comfort. Not that she was afraid. She carried her dirk and it was broad daylight. Plus, if she could hear the camp, then they would have no trouble hearing her if she needed them.

For the first time in months—maybe even since Siobhan was born—Sarah felt her heart lift. Since nothing else about her life had changed it must be her own determination to take the bull by the proverbial antlers and get a grip.

That's really all you needed to do. Self-talk can defeat you or it can empower you.

That was true back in Jacksonville in the ad agency she'd worked in—with all its jealousies and politics—and it was true in the backwoods of post-apocalyptic Ireland. It was something she would do well to remember.

Sometimes the things that are true are true no matter what.

As she picked her way through the fog, she registered the uptick in her mood. Everything was going to turn out the way it should. They'd find the castle. They'd move in and set up a new community. It would be safe and secure. She and Mike would bring John there and they'd all be together. *Snip snap. And Bob is your uncle.*

Her reconnection with Mike last night had been brief and tentative. But it was a start. Sarah knew if she was really going to forgive him for bulldozing her about this whole castle idea, she needed to be open to the new life he envisioned for them there and stop imagining all the ways it could go wrong.

She smiled when she thought of the moment last night when the only sounds in the tent had been the breathing of those she loved most in the world. And then the sting came slowly but surely when she reminded herself that she had no idea where John was breathing. Or even if.

Stop! The word screamed out in her head as the devastating thought formed. She counted to five and then felt her mood steady out. Thought stopping was a technique she'd learned years ago when negative self-talk had threatened to torpedo her confidence. Eventually, she'd abandoned the practice since taking a pill took so much less effort but as that was no longer an option.

She'd only been walking for a few minutes when the ground began to feel spongy underfoot. She must be close. Just past a thin stand of trees, she saw a narrow ditch clogged with bramble and ferns. Ferns meant water. She picked up her pace and noticed the mist was thickening.

That also made sense if there was a spring nearby, she reasoned. At the tree stand, she grabbed a sapling and pulled it aside. The spring was small and relatively silent. The water was bluish green except for the white foam of the tiny waterfall tumbling over rocks slick with moss.

Just looking at it lifted her heart. How she wished she had time for a long soak. She moved toward the spring and stopped. A feeling began at the base of her spine and crept up her neck. Her fingers went numb.

A low growl was coming from the depths of the mist.

13.

The yellow eyes appeared out of the mist like a disembodied nightmare.

Instinctively, Sarah stumbled backward and watched the animal advance steadily through the gloom.

She could smell its fur as it emerged from the fog, growing larger with each heartbeat.

Black stripes against mustard-colored fur.

Impossible. Not...possible.

The animal gathered its powerful haunches under it as it watched her. And prepared to spring.

Sarah turned. Without looking where she was going, driven only by terror, she plunged across the high grass. She gulped in a gasp of air against the panic that overwhelmed her.

A tall rockface towered before her. She skidded to a stop, falling to one knee. She placed her hands against it. Even though she was shivering, her muscles burned. She couldn't hear anything but the sound of her own heart thundering in her ears.

It couldn't be. It's not possible. It's not real.

She turned around. The tiger stood fifteen feet away. Its teeth glittering white. Its eyes drilled into hers. She stared back, mesmerized.

Any second now...any second now...

Sarah felt her terror fill every pore.

Its eyes never left hers. And then, it leapt.

Sarah flung her arm over her face. At the impact, she rocked back into the stone wall, cracking her head, her hands plunging into the beast's fur. A searing pain ripped through her head until darkness took it away.

*****

Someone is making coffee and frying bacon.

Sarah felt the sensations flit through her brain but she couldn't feel her body.

It must be Nana. A sound pierced the fog of her brain.

*Siobhan is squealing...happy squeals...*the noise pulled Sarah out of her daze. *What am I doing at Nana's? What is Siobhan doing here?*

The old-fashioned kitchen materialized around her. She was standing by the counter in front of a Mr. Coffee Maker. The audio of cartoons came to her from the living room. A laugh track and high-pitched animated voices filtered through her consciousness.

"Turn the volume down."

"Aw, Mom."

*Siobhan is speaking. And watching cartoons...*Sarah moved into the hallway. Siobhan sat on the couch in the living room, a tiny kitten on her lap. And her eyes glued to the television. She broke into another squeal of laughter.

Sarah felt a sudden loneliness flow through her. Like mourning. *Someone is missing.* She watched the kitten bat playfully at Siobhan's fingers. Sarah tried to go to her, tried to enter the room but her legs wouldn't move.

Someone was calling her name.

It all feels so lonely...

Someone is missing...

*****

"Sarah," Mike said, his eyes on the long rip in her denim jacket. He shifted her in his arms, willing her to respond to him. "Open your eyes. It's all right now, love. Wake up for me, lass."

Gavin and Kevin stood next to the body of the tiger. The animal was all ribs and teeth—and not many of those.

Sarah's eyes fluttered open and the stark panic that was in them broke Mike's heart.

"Nay, lass. You're all right. The beast is dead."

"Mike!" She struggled to sit up.

"Take it slow, Sarah. There's no rush."

Gavin knelt next to them. "He's a beaut, Sarah. You should see him."

"A *tiger*?" she said. "Are you kidding me?" She turned to look at the carcass not six feet from her and put a hand on Gavin's arm as if for support. Mike felt a sliver of anger and helplessness rift through him.

She blames me for this. Of course she would.

"He was clearly starving to death," Gavin said. "I think you coulda beat him off even without us."

Sarah looked at Gavin. "How did you know I...he was...?"

"We heard you screaming," Gavin said. "Got here just as he was about to jump."

Sarah ran a shaking hand over her face. "I...I screamed?"

"Like a banshee."

"Let's get you back to the camp," Mike said. He turned to see several camp members standing on the perimeter of the clearing, their eyes huge and staring at the animal on the ground.

"Is there anyone watching our stuff or is everyone arsing around?" he growled as most of them hurried back to the wagon train. He turned back to Sarah but Gavin was already helping her to her feet.

"How?" she said, her face white and panic-stricken.

"Probably the zoos," Gavin said.

"Does this mean we need to look out for bears and lions now too?" she said.

"It means we stop assuming anything," Mike said.

"You mean like assuming the woods are safe or the roads are safe or *anywhere's* safe?"

"Sarah…" He reached out to her but she pulled away.

"He was so weak he wasn't chasing you so much as stumbling around in the woods in your general direction," he said.

She turned to face him and he was aware there were a few people standing around gawking at the tiger to get a full performance for whatever she was winding up for. He felt his stomach muscles clench in anticipation.

"You are going to brush this off as nothing just like you brushed off what happened to Declan," she said hotly. "It was a *tiger*, Mike."

He was a complete idiot and there was no two ways about that. Whatever had possessed him to downplay what she'd just been through as a way to comfort her? She was right. If she hadn't screamed or they hadn't gotten here in time, the tiger—weak or not—could have killed her.

Could well have.

The thought turned his insides to ice and for the first time since they set out, he felt a small tremor of doubt.

*****

Mike delivered Sarah to her wagon where one of the women brought her a cup of tea. Sarah noted bitterly as he left her to get the wagon train moving again that her husband wasn't going to let a little thing like his wife being attacked by a wild beast slow him down.

The mood in the wagon train was somber for the rest of the day. The babies and children were fretful which put the adults on edge. All eyes probed the surrounding woods as if wondering what else was hiding in there.

The optimism they'd all enjoyed in the hours before the tiger attack was now gone. What was left was a lingering sense of threat.

And doubt.

The world was a scary place, Sarah thought. Anything could happen at any time.

If an attack by a man-eating tiger didn't prove that, nothing did.

Susan Kiernan-Lewis

14.

Chezzie could not remember ever being this hungry.

Not even on the long journey from the convent to Dublin last year when he'd eaten grass and his own shoelaces. He sat on a park bench in St. Stephen's Green off Harcourt Street. His stomach ached so bad it felt like it was eating *him* from the inside.

There was a dead dog in the fountain. It was white with maggots. Probably jumped in there to find something to drink but the water had stopped running when the first bomb dropped. Chezzie licked his lips, his eyes on the buzzing corpse.

He wanted to. He desperately wanted to. Hell, road kill had been what kept him alive for the last three months. But then he'd gotten sick. So sick he thought it was the end of him. And he hadn't even cared.

The park wasn't a safe place to be. There used to be tents here last year when he first arrived. And shacks. There was even some order in a weird, end-of-the-world kind of way with a grilled meat kiosk and a whore tent operating for whatever you had to trade.

But that was before the second bomb dropped. Since then things were a lot worse. The whore tent was gone. The shacks with families were gone. The grilled meat kiosk. All gone.

Sometimes, when Chezzie thought back to the convent —and he worked very hard not to do that because when he did he would often start to cry in self-pity and frustration—

he'd remember the biscuits and jam the most. Twice in the last six months he'd started back down the road to the convent, the lure of the nuns' cooking and the warmth of their underground jail cell drawing him there.

And twice the sound of that bastard Donovan's warning rang in his head like a death knell—*If you ever come back we'll shoot you on sight.*

It wasn't fair. There was Mac who was the fecking leader of the rape camp! He of all of 'em should've been strung up before poor Bill was or thrown out like Chezzie. But no. Mac—the wanker who *started* it all—*he* was eating hot meals and sleeping every night in a soft bed.

Chezzie squinted skyward. There weren't even pigeons in the park any more. He wondered how people had caught them in the past. The thought of roasted bird made his mouth water and his stomach cramped painfully. He ran a shaky hand across his face. Out of the corner of his eye he saw two men skulking along Harcourt. They didn't seem to have noticed him which was strange since he was sitting out in the open.

He knew it wasn't safe here but the corner of the alley he'd called his own for the past month had been taken over by three women with knives. He wasn't sure where to go from here. The two men were crouched over and moving quickly and Chezzie watched them with interest. One of them carried something under his arm—something that moved.

Chezzie leaned forward. A dog? A chicken? Where had they gotten such a thing? He stood up without realizing he was doing it. He'd sold his body twice for food and found a sore arse a small price to pay for a full stomach. He watched the men as they stopped and looked over their shoulders. Were they being followed? Chezzie saw no one.

He began to move in their direction. The worst they could do was tell him to bugger off. Well, as he picked up his pace he realized that wasn't *at all* the worse they could do. But his hunger drove him forward.

They'd left the park perimeter now but Chezzie saw which alley they'd disappeared down. A muffled squawk coming from up ahead told him they did indeed have a chicken. From the sounds of it, maybe even two.

Where the feck did the bastards get chickens?

He found himself running now. His legs felt wobbly. But the chickens grew louder the closer he got. His panting was deafening in his own ears. He didn't know what he would do when he caught up with the men, whether he would beg them or attempt to grab one of the chickens. He just knew he had to try.

He saw them at the end of the alley. The two men stood with their heads together as they began ripping the feathers from the live birds. The animals shrieked. One of the men bit the head off his bird and Chezzie watched the blood spurt from his mouth like a macabre fountain. His friend laughed. Chezzie must have made a sound because the laugh was stolen from the man's lips as he turned and looked at Chezzie. His face hardened. He tucked his bird under his arm and pulled out a knife, facing Chezzie.

"I just want…" Chezzie said, his voice a raspy whisper that didn't even carry to the men.

"Get away, ye gowl!" the man snarled, jabbing the air with his knife.

But Chezzie could not stop coming. "I just need…" he whimpered.

A gunshot fired. The man with the knife looked at Chezzie in surprise and then down at his chest where a blossom of blood exploded. He crumpled to his knees, the chicken racing away with a terrified squawk.

Did I do that? Chezzie wondered in confusion, as he watched the chicken run toward him. He leaned down and snatched the animal up, shocked by the feel of its body— like a loose birdcage covered in feathers. He crushed the bird to his chest and swiveled to face the alley opening.

Standing there were three soldiers. All three had their guns aimed at him.

The Garda.

One of the soldiers raised his rifle to his face and fired past Chezzie's ear. Chezzie dropped the chicken. Behind him, the sound of the other man's screams echoed off the sides of the alley's stone walls.

Chezzie turned back to the soldiers and saved his own life by fainting.

The oblivion didn't last long. A hard kick to the ribs brought Chezzie back to reality. He fought to breathe against the pain, against his lungs closing down. He was so weak. His ribs hurt so bad. Chezzie's face pressed against the slimy cold cobblestones of the alley.

"Just shoot 'im," a voice said. "We got one of the chickens."

"Commander Hurley wants the citizenry brought in for the lions," another voice said. "Not shot in an empty back alley."

The soldier's words didn't make sense to Chezzie but he knew that name. Somewhere in the back of his hunger-crazed mind, he knew that name.

"On yer feet, ye gipe!"

Rough hands yanked him to his feet and he fought to stay standing.

"Cor, he smells something rotten."

"The lions won't care."

The soldiers looked at him with open disgust. One of them pointed his gun at him.

"Don't make me touch ye again," the soldier said. "I ain't had me shots. Move!"

"I...I know your commander," Chezzie stuttered, not entirely sure why he said that.

"What's that? What's he saying?"

"Hurley," Chezzie said. And hadn't he just been thinking of poor old Bill? Was God giving him a message? With the chicken and now Bill?

"He says he knows Commander Hurley," one of the soldiers said.

"Great. They can talk it over as he fights off Leo and Simba. Let's move." The soldier jabbed Chezzie in the ribs with his gun and gestured toward the mouth of the alley.

He fell twice as they walked through the deserted streets of Dublin. Chezzie had come this way not an hour earlier and had spent much of the walk attempting to avoid the thugs and murderers who lined the path.

Now it was totally devoid of people. Not a soul, not a sound.

The soldiers strode confidently through the street with Chezzie alternately lumbering and staggering between them. It took all his concentration not to fall.

Whatever would happen now was out of his hands and there was a relief in that. He didn't bother looking where they were going. It didn't matter. These men were in charge. These men would tell him what to do. And if his struggle was finally over, they would tell him that too.

They walked down Fishamble Street to the front of the Dublin opera house. A line of six soldiers stood out front but they didn't even look at him as he was led into the main lobby. The odor of blood and shit and fear hit Chezzie like a hammer as he entered. Two of the soldiers flanked him, their hands like iron vices on his arms as they dragged him to an anteroom off the cavernous lobby. He watched their eyes as they silently communicated with one another. Bizarrely, he thought he saw nervousness.

The muffled roar of a lion rattled the framed photographs on the walls of the anteroom. The fear clawed up Chezzie's spine like a living thing, grasping for his throat. He made a strangled sound and both soldiers turned to him.

So it was true. The fecking rumors were true.

Chezzie struggled against his captors, his eyes wide with terror.

"No!" he screamed. "You can't! Please, no!"

The soldiers weren't looking at him now. They were watching the door to the anteroom, their faces tense and strained.

On the rare times he'd shared a night around a burning trashcan with Dublin's night people, Chezzie had heard the stories. Scare stories that the Garda had created their own lion pit for entertainment and were throwing Dubliners into it. Stories, like all the others, designed to strike terror into the heart by night but by light of day couldn't be believed.

"I know him, I tell you," Chezzie whimpered. "Let me talk to him."

It had to be him. It couldn't *not* be him. How many times had Bill complained about his brother in the Garda? Complained about that sadistic son of a bitch living in Dublin with electricity and hot meals and nothing changed for him? A throb of doubt wheedled its way into Chezzie's fervor of fear and desperation.

The Hurley that Bill talked about was no officer. No *commander* of anything.

Chezzie drove the splinter of doubt away. It was all he had. If he was wrong he was worse than dead. Allowing these men to kill him was one thing. Being eaten piece by screaming, flailing piece by a lion every bit as hungry as Chezzie was—was beyond the worst of any of Chezzie's nightmares.

"Please," he begged. "I didn't even steal the chicken."

"Shirrup," one of the soldiers said.

The door handle began to twist and Chezzie felt a scream welling up inside him. The door opened and a large bald headed man with shoulders the width of two men and cold, dead eyes strode into the room. He was wearing a uniform, his boots polished so they looked like black mirrors. His face twisted into a grimace of revulsion.

"Please, sir..." Chezzie said, his eyes tearing up. This was his chance. His only chance.

"He says he knows you, Commander," a soldier behind Hurley said.

Hurley's face remained contorted into an expression of having to endure a bad smell.

"Not...no," Chezzie said. "Your brother. I knew your brother, Bill."

An image of fingers laying down a hand of cards on a green-felted tablecloth flashed across Chezzie's mind. Betting everything—his life and a death too terrible to imagine—on one gambit. No room for maneuvering. No second chances.

"You know Bill?"

Chezzie forced himself not to weep. In three words he took a step back from the precipice. Just a bit. Just enough.

"We worked together at...Mrs. Branigan's camp for..." Chezzie struggled for the name of the rape camp, not sure he'd ever really known.

"I know where he worked," Hurley said, his eyes narrowing, his lip finally uncurling at Chezzie's stench. "Where is my brother now?"

"Murdered," Chezzie said excitedly, "at a secret nunnery down south. I can take you there."

15.

Sarah saw the castle from twenty miles away. Around the final bend, the land stretched like a treeless tableau, creating a stark moonscape of green, flanked on the west by a thick forest, beyond which they could hear the muted roar of the sea. The road straightened out, flat as a ruler for the final distance leading to the castle.

On the eastern side of the road were fields, now dormant and unused these past five years.

What had happened to the farmers and shepherds who lived here before the bomb? Why had no one planted the fields since then?

The castled perched on the horizon like a cutout from a child's activity book. Its stark outline of storybook crenellated towers—two of them visible even from this distance—anchored the broad expanse of limestone in between. It looked ominous, wicked, haunted.

It did not look like home.

"What do you think?" Mike asked as he rode up beside her wagon. "Crackin', isn't it?"

Sarah didn't respond.

"The ocean is behind it. And there will be a stream or water of some kind nearby. Irish castles were always built by a water source."

"Cor, Mike, it's beautiful," Tommy said from the driver's seat of the wagon. "Truly it is."

"It's built up high like that so they can see anyone coming," Mike said, his eyes bright with zeal. "We're still a good distance away but if there's anyone inside, they already know we're here."

The fields gave way to the beginnings of a village on the eastern side of the road. It looked to Sarah like it had been there since the castle was built but that was hardly likely. Or if it had been there, it had long been rebuilt. Like so many of the other villages they'd seen on their trip, this one was a series of stone houses built in two rows facing the road that dissected the town. Unlike many of the other villages, this one was deserted.

At a call from behind, Mike turned away to help one of the other wagons. Tommy drove the wagon slowly through the village. Sarah shifted a sleeping Siobhan into the basket next to her on the seat while gripping the sides of the wagon as if she would be catapulted out at any minute. The closer they rode to the castle, the greater her dread grew.

It loomed. There was no other word for it. In fact, now that Sarah thought about it, the word *loomed* had to have been created just for this castle. Immense, fierce. Threatening.

The closer they got, the more massive it got and the more threatening it grew.

When they broke free of the eerie deserted village, the road bore down on the castle at its end. It was clear there could be nothing past the castle but ocean. The woods began again to their left. Sarah heard the chattering and excited exchanges from the other wagons.

Was she really the only one to see how evil the castle was? Were they actually *excited* about living in that thing? Goosebumps crept up her arms and she rubbed them away.

Tommy put the horses into a trot which jolted Siobhan awake. The baby cried sharply and Sarah jumped at the sound before pulling her out of the basket and into her lap to try to calm her. Siobhan's face turned dark red as she screamed her frustration. Sarah patted her back and bounced her on her knee. Her stomach was sour with nerves and anxiety. The look on Tommy's face showed he was so focused on the castle at the end of the road that he didn't even hear the baby's screams.

It took nearly an hour from when they'd first seen the castle before they reached it. The pastures and fields on the right side of the road diminished until there was no more grass. It occurred to Sarah that they hadn't seen a living thing—not people or animals—since they'd gotten their first glimpse of the castle, which hunched on the horizon like a malevolent beast, crouching and waiting for them.

The woods gave way to an elaborate garden area. Protected by ancient stone walls, the land was now totally overgrown but the bones of the beds and surrounding fruit trees were vaguely evident. To the right, opposite the garden and nearest to the entrance of the castle was a gigantic parking lot—nearly the size of a football field. There were two decrepit vehicles parked in it, forlornly rusting in the ocean air with their tires long since stolen.

On a small lawn a pair of wooden park benches sat facing the castle. Sarah imagined that once upon a time castle visitors would sit on the benches to eat ice cream while marveling at the castle's impressive structure. She tried to imagine how she might have felt if she'd seen this place during happier times.

The image wouldn't gel.

The place was evil and she knew that as surely as if she had documented evidence.

Dear God, we can't live here. Why can't Mike see that? She turned to glance at him as he rode up beside her. His smiling face was flushed with excitement as he looked at the castle.

Tommy stopped and the rest of the wagons moved into position beside him.

The castle featured few windows in front—small vertical slits built for defensive archery—and a larger one in the gatehouse only. The two crenellated towers flanked a massive front wall that easily measured a city block long. If it were truly square as Mike said, all four sides would be much the same: slabs of stone, ten to twenty feet thick. The other two crenellated towers in back serving as reminders that years ago attack from the seaward side had always been an option.

The castle gatehouse with its massive wooden door jutted out from the wall and was nearly three stories high. Behind it were glimpses of the portcullis—suspended from the gatehouse ceiling in a wall of jagged metal. A wide moat circled the castle and separated them from the front door.

Sarah patted Siobhan's back and tried to see if there was water in the moat.

Mike came up to her wagon and dismounted.

"Just rain water in it as far as I can see," he said. "If we can't find a water source to channel into it, we'll put sharpened stakes in the bottom."

Sarah stared at him as if he'd lost his mind.

"Tommy," Mike said. "Unhitch the team, aye? I'll want you and Gavin to do a perimeter scout of the place to see if there's an easy way in."

"Why don't you just go to the front door and knock?" Sarah asked.

Mike grinned at her and she looked away. It was one of the few words she'd spoken to him since the tiger attack.

"I think that's just what I'll do," he said.

*****

The castle was everything Mike had remembered it would be. Majestic and impregnable. Perfect. And absolutely no way in.

Well, no *easy* way in.

Mike worked with the other men to erect the tents on the grassy knoll between the gardens and the road and across from the main parking lot. He'd seen shadows flicker in the front windows so that answered *that* question. Because of where the castle was situated, whoever was inside had seen them coming and had had at least two hours to decide what they were going to do about it.

After he, Gavin and Tommy had done a circuit of the castle, Mike knew for sure what he'd only half remembered before: there was no way in. The weather looked like it would hold at least for the night but it was mid-October. They'd have to get inside soon. One freezing rain out here without decent shelter would be a hardship he would go a long way to prevent for his group of mostly babies, women and children.

As the afternoon turned into evening, Mike smelled roasting meat coming from the castle. Gavin had already spotted several chimneys working inside so whoever was in there was warm, dry, and eating a hot meal.

His tent was set in the center of the camp beside the largest campfire. He'd gather the entire community after dinner to give thanks for their safe journey and to tell them his plans for entry into the castle. He hoped Sarah would do him the honor of standing by him for this but he didn't hold out much hope that she would.

The thought of being this close to finally reaching his goal had the joy sapped from it because of her resistance.

He could only pray that time would show her he was right to bring them here.

But first, he was going to take his wife's suggestion of knocking on the front door as a literal one.

What could it hurt?

*****

Shaun stood by the gatehouse window and looked down at the little tented community on his front lawn. They were a sizable group—larger than most he'd seen. He'd watched them approach for nearly two hours. Unlike most visitors to Henredon Castle, they simply set up their tents like they were moving in. As of yet, no one had approached.

"Are they still there?" Ava asked, coming up behind him to peer out the window.

"Aye. They've put tents up."

"Why didn't they ask to come inside?" Ava was a tall woman but still several inches shorter than Shaun. She had naturally curly hair that framed her face like a picture. Shaun knew several of the other women envied Ava's curls. *Even during the end of the world,* he thought, *women will always be women.*

"That is a good question," he said.

"They're up to something." The voice, coming from behind Ava, was shrill. Shaun didn't need to turn around to know it was his sister Saoirse. Heavyset with a ruddy complexion and hair the color of dark rust, Saoirse stood watching the activity below with flaring nostrils and her fists clenched.

"I guess we'll find out," Shaun said.

"Are those children down there?" Ava said with excitement. "They have children, Shaun. Maybe they have a nurse or a doctor?"

Shaun frowned. "I thought you said Keeva was better today."

"She's poorly again this evening. I wish we had something to give her. Two ibuprofen would bring her fever right down."

Shaun looked out the window. *Would this lot likely have medicine?* After nearly five years of scrambling and scavenging, was there anyone left with intact stores? He'd long thought that someone might do very well in the black market for items like aspirin and ibuprofen. If there *was* a black market. The problem was people nowadays didn't negotiate for what they wanted. They just hit you on the head and took it.

"You can't be serious," Saoirse said with a sneer.

"Spoken like someone without a child to worry about," Ava retorted.

"There's too many of them," Saoirse said. "What if they try to take the castle? And throw us out?"

"Let's don't overdramatize," Shaun said. "They hardly look like a group who could 'take the castle.' From here they look like mostly women."

"Please, Shaun," Ava said, her eyes watching the tent community below. "Just let one or two in."

He hesitated. He hadn't kept everyone in the castle safe for the last five years by taking a lot of risks. It had been difficult and, as the only man, fairly lonely, too.

But he couldn't chance it.

"It's too dangerous," he said. "Saoirse's right about that. What if we let them in and they won't leave?"

"But they might have aspirin!"

Shaun pinched his lips together and blew out a snort of frustration but before he could respond to her, Saoirse pushed in front of Ava and peered out the window.

"A bloke is coming to the front door!"

Shaun and Ava crowded around the window. A large man was striding to the front of the castle just below where they stood at the window. With the drawbridge up, all he could do was stand and shout up to them.

"You two stand back," Shaun said, pushing Saoirse behind him. "Let's hear what he wants."

"Ask him if they have aspirin!" Ava hissed.

"Oy, the castle!" the big man shouted up. "A word, if you please."

"Yes, we see you," Shaun yelled back. He knew that didn't sound friendly but it couldn't be helped.

"We have travelled a long way and the night is cold. Will you let us in?"

He doesn't beat around the bush.

"We need to be careful about who we let in. You understand."

"Aye, but as you can see, my group is mostly women and children."

"Tell him they can come in if the men stay out," Ava said and Shaun shushed her.

"We might be willing to let the women and children come in."

The man gave a half turn as if to look at his group.

"I can't do that," he said finally.

He doesn't trust us, Shaun thought. *And why should he?*

"We have women recently delivered," the big man said. "And we have food to trade. We only ask shelter from the coming storm."

Shaun glanced at the dark skies. There were clouds to be sure but there were always clouds. This was Ireland.

Ava pinched his arm and he waved her back without turning.

"Do you have medicine of any kind?" Shaun asked.

"Aye, we do. And a healer. Is there sickness there?"

"I'll think on it and get back to you," Shaun said, stifling an absurd desire to laugh because he sounded like he was finishing a business merger at his old corporate firm. *I'll put you on the calendar and get back to you.*

"How many of you are there, if you don't mind me asking?"

"Don't tell him that!" Saoirse said in a loud whisper that surely carried to the next county.

Shaun moved away from the window without answering the man. He pulled Ava and Saoirse away too, and wondered how he ever got anything done with all the help he got from these two.

Susan Kiernan-Lewis

16.

That first night it was too cold and wet for a campfire meeting. Sarah knew Mike would be out most of the night securing the perimeter and spelling watches with the other men. She was too restless to sleep. Sophia and Gavin's tent was next to theirs but little Maggie's relentless crying negated any interest Sarah had in popping in for a visit.

Several of the unmarried mothers were sharing a tent and offered to take Siobhan for the night. Although the child was better these days, she was still happiest in the arms of her father. Sarah bundled her up and gratefully handed her over to Catriona and Hannah before making her way toward Fiona and Declan's tent.

When she reached it, she saw it was darkened but Nuala's had a lantern burning and the sound of laughter coming from it. On impulse, Sarah came to the tent flap.

"Knock, knock!" she said, as she poked her head through the opening.

"Sarah! Come in!"

Nuala had one of the larger tents and for good reason. With three children of her own, she often had another one or two for good measure. Her two boys, nine and seven, were cheerful and agreeable. The older one, Dennis, was old enough to help mind the little ones and Nuala leaned on him a good deal.

"What brings you out on this wet excuse for a night?"

The two boys sat facing each other, their legs crossed, playing with a deck of cards. Between them and watching them carefully was five-year-old Maeve, whose mother had died the spring before.

"I thought Maeve lived with Fi and Dec?"

"Aye, but she's a bit of a handful is our Maeve. Thinks she's one of the lads and as I'm used to dealing with boys, it's no problem at all. Besides, Fi has a full plate with Declan, so she does."

Maeve grinned impishly at Sarah. Nuala leaned against the center tent pole and nursed the baby. Sarah took off her cape and folded it, dry side up so she could sit on it.

"So did Himself have a talk with the castle?" Nuala said.

"He did. He was hoping to have a gathering by the campfire but the storm knocked that idea out."

"So what did they say?"

"They said the women could come in with the babies but not the men."

"And sure Himself thinks we'd be defenseless females without him and the lads to protect us?"

"Something like that."

"He does remember how we defended Ameriland against the murderin' druids just last year, doesn't he?"

Sarah frowned as if the memory was a faint one. *Did we really do that?* And she was six months pregnant at the time. And then her heart clenched. Because Archie had been alive then. And it was because of Archie that the women had able to defend the compound.

"You all right then, Sarah?"

Sarah shook her head. "I just think this is all a terrible idea, Nuala."

"What? Coming to the castle?"

"We should never have left the convent."

Nuala frowned.

"I mean, look at us!" Sarah said. "We're all cold and wet and running out of food and Declan's hurt. And if the people in that castle don't let us in, Mike has this insane idea he's going to attack it.

"Cor, he's our own Michael Collins."

"Except he isn't. And we're not fighting for any cause except our own. We don't even know what kind of weapons they have in there and you can bet they won't easily give up. I mean, you're sitting there with a baby at your breast. Feel like scaling a castle wall and going hand to hand with a bunch of people intent on killing you?"

"I am pretty tired most of the time, I admit."

"Exactly."

"So is it tent by tent you're going, Sarah, talking everyone out of whatever Mike is trying to talk them into?"

"You think I'm sabotaging him?"

"*That's* the word I was looking for."

"Fine. Back him to the hilt. Just don't come crying to me when he straps little Darcy to your back and hands you a grappling hook."

"You're a hard woman, Sarah. Remind me not to cross you."

Her cheeks burning with frustration and anger, Sarah stood up and put her cape back on. Why was she lately turning a desire for fellowship into a battle—with everyone? She managed a weak smile for the children and then turned to make her way back to her own tent, feeling the rain cold and insistent trickling down her neck as she went.

******

The next morning, the rain finally stopped but the temperature had plunged. Mike rolled over in his sleeping bag and put a hand on Sarah's hip. He felt her stiffen. Would this war between them ever end? Did she not know how much he needed her on his side now of all times?

"I'll get the fire going," he said.

By the time he'd rekindled the embers from last night's fire, he could see that most of the camp was preferring the warmth of their tents to beginning another day on a treeless lawn at the foot of a forbidding and inhospitable castle.

He wasn't sure he blamed them. They had no place to go today, no journey ahead of them, and no goal other than getting inside the castle.

When I put it like that, it makes me want to crawl back into me own tent.

What had he been thinking to do this so close to winter? And why was he so sure they could just take the castle? Arrogance! With six men and fourteen women—and half of them newly delivered? And then there was Declan. After a few days of looking like he was on the mend, Fiona told Mike last night that he seemed to be weakening.

Mike looked up at the sky as it tried to brighten with the morning. The clouds hung low, fat and grey. So, on top of everything, there was another storm coming.

Sarah emerged from the tent fully dressed with her sleeping bag pulled around her shoulders. She looked as if she hadn't slept. He tried to remember the last time he'd seen her smile.

"I spoke with Fiona last night," he said, hoping he could jumpstart a simple, marital conversation over coffee. Only without the coffee.

"I spoke to her yesterday myself," Sarah said. "Declan's worse."

Well that was a bollocks conversation starter.

"And Sophia thinks Maggie has colic," she said.

"Babies do get it."

"I'm sure you'd know all about that. Since you know everything."

"Ah, Sarah, don't start the day like this."

"Like how? Disagreeing with you, you mean?"

"You've got a tongue could cut a hedge, so you do."

"Don't you hate it when there are consequences to your actions? When you can't just disrupt everyone's lives —*endanger* everyone's lives—without some push back?"

Mike felt the frustration build in his chest. Just the sight of the castle—so close—and yet so impossible to reach, served to ignite a dormant anger. An anger that Sarah appeared to be doing her best to ignite.

"Reevaluating the reasons you came back to Ireland, are ye, Sarah?"

"Maybe I am! John's lost with no way to get back, Siobhan will grow up wild if she grows up at all and we're stuck at the base of a castle with no way in and winter just weeks away!"

"Whisht! Hold your voice down! You'll wake the camp."

"We need to go back to the convent, Mike. You *know* that's true if you'd just let your pride stop ruling you for one minute."

"Back to the convent? *That's* your answer, woman? *Fall back, run, hide, don't go forward...*"

"How is freezing to death in a tent going forward?"

She stood before him, her hands on her hips and fire in her eyes. His hands itched to touch her, to grab her and shake her. He turned away to get a grip of himself.

"Fine," she said. "So we're here. But unless you dragged us all this way so we could camp out on a barren hilltop with no shelter and no food, I'd love to know what your strategy is for getting inside the castle? Because right now it's starting to look like it's sitting and *hoping* they let us in."

"They already said they'd let the women and children in."

"Oh, so the plan is to destroy their trust by rushing them when they open the doors to us? What a prince you are, Mike. I can't imagine why people wouldn't want to follow you anywhere."

He felt the exact moment when he hit his limit and this was it.

"Is it a divorce you want then, Sarah? To be free of me once and for all?"

She stood looking at him, her mouth open and momentarily speechless when the sound of the scream split the morning air like a knife cutting through flesh.

17.

Of all the terrible things Mike had experienced in his life, the vision of that tiny body being carried dripping wet from the surf would stand as one of the single most horrifying sights.

Nuala carried the child in her arms. Her eyes were stunned and vacant as she staggered through the surf onto the beach and sank to her knees. Sarah reached them before Mike and immediately turned the little girl on her side, pushing out the seawater from her lungs and then giving her the breath of life.

Nuala stared down at little Maeve's body as Sarah worked. The child was blue. She'd been in too long. Anyone could see it was hopeless. And yet Mike's fear and hope were ratcheted up to equal levels.

How could it have happened? Why was the lass out so early in the morning? He looked around to see Fiona racing toward them from her tent. She didn't know yet who it was.

Mike saw Nuala's lads standing back. The bigger boy held the baby Darcy who was crying. Both boys stared at the dead child on the beach with large, unblinking eyes.

"Siobhan," he said out loud and then was immediately stricken by the selfishness of that single word—that he'd thought of her when she was surely safe.

"She's with Catriona," Liddy said as she came up beside Mike. She held her little lass in her arms. Mike could see she was squeezing her too tightly and the babe began to cry.

"She said she wasn't afraid of the water," Dennis said. He was Nuala's oldest lad. He stared at the body. Sarah still hadn't stopped trying to get the child to breathe.

Mike turned to him. "It wasn't your fault. It's not your job to watch her."

"But it is."

"No," Mike said firmly. "Not when you're meant to be asleep. You could do nothing to stop this."

Dennis blinked back tears and nodded but Mike had no real hope that the lad believed him.

The sound of Fiona's wails jerked his attention back to the group hovered over the child. Sarah was sitting back on her heels now, spent and done. She looked at little Maeve as if she were in shock. Fiona fell onto the girl and hugged her to her, rocking back and forth with the limp body in her arms.

Mike turned Dennis and Damian around and sent them back to their tent. He looked at Liddy.

"Gather the other women. Nuala and Fiona will need them."

Liddy nodded and hurried away from the heartbreaking scene on the beach. Mike came over to Fiona and gently pulled her to her feet and took the child from her. He kissed little Maeve's cold cheek and turned to make the long walk back to camp.

*****

Shaun looked around the dinner table at the dozen women and two children seated there. It hadn't taken long for Ava and Saoirse to spread the word about the people camped out on the front lawn.

Naturally everyone had an opinion. The table buzzed with laughter and anticipation. His sister Saoirse sat to his immediate right and his mother to his left. There was probably no one more excited about the possibility of newcomers in the castle than his mother Beryl Morrison. Before the Crisis, as docent of Henredon Castle, Beryl had given two tours a day to eager and avidly interested tourists.

If there was anything his mother loved it was talking about the castle.

"You'll let them come in of course?" she said to him now. She pushed her dinner plate away, too excited even to eat.

"I haven't decided."

"But why ever not?" Her eyes clouded and he saw the unmistakable quiver of her bottom lip. He didn't know when she began to pout when she wanted her way—it wasn't something she ever did before the bomb dropped.

"Mother, there's more to it than just inviting people over for tea. We don't know anything about them."

Ava was watching the conversation from her end of the table. Little Keeva was sitting next to her but her food was untouched and she kept her head down on her arms.

Shaun felt a pang of guilt. *Would the newcomers really be able to help the child as Ava believed?*

"I don't know why we can't have people come live with us," Beryl said. "Henredon is four acres—more than enough space for at least a hundred people. The more people we get, the more skills and commodities we would have. It only makes sense, Shaun."

He'd heard it all before. Hundreds of times before. He reached for his tankard of water and was grateful that they'd recently gone to the spring. Unless the people camping out there intended to try to put them under siege, they shouldn't have to go outside the castle for weeks.

"Remember three Christmases ago?" he said, not looking at his mother.

He heard her intake of breath and he felt a stab of guilt for reminding her.

Three Decembers ago, in the spirit of the season, they'd taken in two young men who'd come asking for food and shelter. Before the first night was over, one of the younger women of the castle had been raped and, in the process of trying to stop it, Shaun's younger brother Rodney was stabbed and killed.

While it was true that Rodney had himself been a problem—doing his own share of raping among the women —he was still family and that tragic night left them all reeling with a new legacy of fear and distrust.

"I'm just saying, perhaps it's time to reach out to the outside world again," his mother said. "Ava said they have medicine." She leaned down to touch the head of one of the two large dogs at her feet. Shaun knew she was feeding them both morsels but when they had enough food as they did at present he didn't care.

"They *said* they have medicine," Shaun said. "We don't know that they really do."

"But Keeva is still sick."

"Mother, I know." What was he to do? If he let down the drawbridge, what was to stop them from swarming the castle?

As if she were reading his mind, Beryl said, "Saoirse said they're mostly women and children."

"I didn't say that," Saoirse said sourly from the other side of Shaun. "But even if it's true, so what? It just takes one to hold a knife to your throat, woman or not."

"Can we not talk about this right now?" Shaun said in exasperation. "I said I'd think about it and I will." He looked up and watched he expectant faces of the nine other women watching him from down the table.

"You trust me to do what's best for all, do ye not?"

They murmured back their affirmatives.

"Then let me have me tucker in peace and rest assured all will be well for all of us in Henredon Castle." He turned and put a hand on his mother's arm. "All right, Mum?"

She nodded and picked up her fork, realizing she could say no more to persuade him. When he looked down the table again, he caught Ava's eye. She watched him, her eyes glittering with meaning and intent. He knew tonight, of all nights, she would come to him. He hated that it had been so long. Or that she would come tonight because she was trying to persuade him. It wasn't that he wasn't confident of her love for him.

He just wished he had something more to give her.

******

It had taken all the power of Hurley's self-discipline not to throw the sniveling bogger into the lion pit.

Hurley stood now, his limbs trembling with the effort to contain his fury, and watched as two miscreants scraped up from the bottom of one of the streets were dangled screaming over the hungry big cats. The audience seats had been removed so that all viewers must stand. He hadn't thought he'd need to force his soldiers to watch the lions at work and was surprised to discover that some of his men didn't consider the entertainment a reward for their service.

Most, however, stood and cheered as the lions made fast work of the men his soldiers had found attempting to steal from the army post.

He'd never been close to Bill. In fact he hadn't seen him in years. As far as Hurley knew Bill had been mentally deficient from childhood. He'd gotten his job at the Branigan research facility outside of Limerick because of Hurley's position with the military. Given the moron's incompetence, and without his older brother nearby to protect him, Hurley had just assumed Bill was no longer living.

But murdered?

No. Executed.

Just thinking of it made Hurley clench and unclench his fists. The screams from the pit didn't help to mitigate the mammoth outrage he felt over some bastard's arrogance in believing he had the *right* to execute a Hurley.

It was not believable.

That someone had the *balls* to execute his brother.

As if he were the law.

Hurley turned away from the carnage in the orchestra pit below and pushed through the crowd of applauding soldiers.

There was only one law in Ireland now.

He stopped at the door of the anteroom where the captive was being held. Even over the sounds of the cheering audience he could hear the man sobbing and pleading for his life. The Centurion Brady stood guard at the door and watched the captive with an impassive face.

"Bring the prisoner back to the post," Hurley said, his eyes glossy with manic fervor.

"Yes, Commander."

He would address all the men tonight at mess. But he wanted them ready. There was much to do.

"And spread the word that we will leave Dublin tomorrow at dawn."

Brady blinked. "Leave? All of us, Commander?"

"You are promoted to Camp Prefect. Close down the pits. Free the lions into the streets. They'll do a better job of watching Dublin while we're gone than leaving a contingency squad would."

"Yes sir," Brady said. "May I inquire, Commander, *where* we are to go?"

Hurley fought down the irrational urge to cut the throat of the man he'd just promoted. Instead he turned away toward the door that led to the street.

"To a secret place," he said over his shoulder, "where one man attempts to hide from his due."

Susan Kiernan-Lewis

18.

The day crawled by like a living creature, bleating and breathing, where every pulsating breath was like an odor that slipped through the fissures of the tents and infected everyone. The sadness, the hopelessness, the sudden and terrifying loss was everywhere. If Sarah's dearest wish had been to have a few more people support her in her desire to return to the convent she was shocked to realize that the support hurt nearly as bad as the rejection.

Is there anything worse than the loss of faith? What before had been a comforting blanket of group belief was now a terrifying realization that they were all in danger—they were all vulnerable—and that people really could start dying any time now.

Nuala and Fiona were slammed the hardest by Maeve's death. Both had sworn to love and protect the child after her mother was murdered in the rape camp the spring before. But it was the loss of faith in Mike that really hurt. That and the sudden—up to now not believable idea—that they were safe as long as they believed they were.

It may take a village but not if that village is sound asleep and the child is determined enough, Sarah thought.

It was the first time for the group that the death was a child and the first time it had been an easily avoidable accident.

Because clearly even our best precautions aren't enough.

The compound women were divided into two groups for the day—the group that was attempting to give comfort to Nuala and Fiona and the group watching the rest of the children. Twelve now.

Belonging to neither group Sarah sat with Declan in his tent for most of the afternoon and watched him as he flickered in and out of consciousness.

Kevin and Terry dug the grave. Tommy and Gavin were moving the horses to better pasture and laying traps in the woods. And Mike was walking around like a stunned ghost.

Scratch that. Like a detested stunned ghost.

Fiona had turned on Mike in the immediate aftermath and laid the blame for Maeve's death at his feet. Sarah couldn't defend him but she couldn't witness it either and was relieved to sit by Declan's bedside tucked away from the now rampant fear and anger.

"Is the fear worse than the reality *now*?" Sarah said under her breath as she watched the activity of the camp though the door of the tent. The day had turned cold and grey. Rain wasn't far off. It never was.

Worry wouldn't have prevented it. Mother Angelina's voice spoke clearly in Sarah's head.

That is flat bullshit, Sarah thought. *Worry would have kept Maeve away from the water. It would have tied her to her bed and kept her from leaving the tent.*

You can't keep them safe by holding them in your arms, Mother Angelina's voice came again. *It doesn't work that way.*

Tell that to Fiona, Sarah thought as she glimpsed her sister in law through the gap in the tent flap, her shoulders heaving with sobs, as one of the compound women embraced her and tried to comfort her.

Tell that to anyone who's feared the worst and then experienced it.

*****

Mike had never felt more ostracized from his own people in his life. Right when they needed his leadership the most, they were shutting him out.

He didn't blame them.

He stood by the cold campfire beside his tent and stared up at the castle walls.

What was I thinking? In the whole obsessed, maniacal trek here from the convent—two nearly deadly attacks and one broken axel ago—what was my plan for taking this fecking castle?

He felt a wave of dejection wash over him. How is it that he, of all people, had no real vision of how he'd do that? Had he assumed it would be empty? Or that they'd be reasonable people eager to add to their population? Maybe he was just pushing against Sarah? If she hadn't been so against the idea would he have been more moderate about doing it?

Whatever his reasoning had been, the fact was the group was falling apart and it was his fault. The temperatures were dropping and they were sitting on a barren piece of land with no protection beyond the flimsy tents they'd brought with them. As if on cue he heard a sudden whooshing sound as a violent blast of wind tore down a tent and pulled it across the campground. He made a step toward it before he saw Kevin and Terry running toward it.

In the mood everyone was in at the moment he wasn't entirely sure they wouldn't rather sleep out in the open with no shelter at all than accept help from him.

He glanced at Fiona and Declan's tent and felt his heart plunge. Sarah was in there keeping an eye on Declan, who was weakening by the hour according to Fiona.

Everything about this campaign had turned to shite in a hurry.

"Mike?"

He turned to see Sophia standing by his tent. She held little Maggie—not four weeks old with cheeks chapped and red—wrapped tightly in a blanket.

"Aye, lass," he said wearily. It occurred to him that she was possibly the only person here who didn't outright hate him at the moment, although he wasn't entirely sure about that.

"They sent me to ask you when we'll get inside," she said, her eyes moving to the looming structure of the castle. She shivered.

That was another thing. He'd stupidly set up camp at the castle's base so even at the height of any day with full sunshine, they were all plunged in perennial shade and cold.

"Only we're all freezing out here," she said, "and I wouldn't ask except for the children."

He felt a harbinger of disaster tingling over his shoulders.

"I know, lass," he said helplessly and then turned around with a start as he saw her eyes widen as she looked at the castle. The man was back at the window. At the same moment Mike felt the first drops of rain on his face.

Please God, have him let us in. Please for the love of these people who trusted me and for the children...

Mike hurried to stand beneath the window. The man was alone this time.

"Hello to you," Mike called. "Can you help us then?"

Even from this distance Mike could see the answer in the man's face. Mike's heart plummeted before he even heard the words.

"I'm very sorry but you'll need to keep moving. You have nothing we need."

Susan Kiernan-Lewis

19.

As they gathered the next morning to lay little Maeve to rest on the barren hilltop, it began to snow. Sarah stood shivering next to Mike, grateful for his size as a windbreak, if not for the comfort of his presence. He held Siobhan snuggled inside his coat, the wind pulling at his long hair from every direction as the snow fell in fat lazy flakes.

Sarah glanced up at the castle and wondered if they were watching. She wondered if they saw that the people camped out on their doorstep had had a death. As she watched three plumes of fireplace smoke rise in the air over the castle, she wondered if they cared.

Fiona and Nuala's sobs were the only sounds in the camp and Sarah tried to imagine a more forlorn picture than all of them huddled together in grief and misery.

Mike had said little since the accident and Sarah knew he blamed himself. If what Nuala said about Maeve was true, the child would've found another way to kill herself—even back at the convent. Sarah's sane and rational self knew that.

But that wasn't the self who was in control these days.

All the young mothers stood in a line well back from the grave. Even so it was too close for comfort for all of them. After the words over the grave were spoken—and not by Mike for a change which also heralded a new attitude among the group—the women turned from the snowy hilltop while the men filled in the hole.

The snow was coming down harder now and while the younger children ran back to camp trying to catch the flakes on their tongues, Sarah knew the day would be cold and wet now with no fires to warm them. Before she could turn toward her tent, she saw Fiona, alone now that Declan was bedridden, heading for Mike.

"Fiona—" Mike began, reaching out with a hand to touch his sister's shoulder.

"We need to go back," Fiona said. "We can't stay here! Surely even you can see that now."

Mike sucked in a quick breath. "I...we can't, Fi. It's too late."

"It's not too late! It's only too late if we don't leave right now!"

Two other women, both holding babies, came up behind Fiona, their faces ruddy with the cold, their noses streaming.

"Fiona," Mike said. "The snow...we can't put everyone in open wagons and—"

"Well you should have thought of that!" Fiona said shrilly. "We need to get back to the convent as soon as possible."

Sarah frowned. Even *she* knew leaving now was crazy. She glanced at Nuala who was coming to join the group. Nuala looked truly devastated. Her eyes were red and there was a downward slope to her shoulders.

"We'll get inside the castle, so we will," Mike said firmly.

"Is it today or are you waiting for the spring rains first? Because in case you hadn't noticed it's fecking snowing! We're all going to die out here, starting with the bairns first."

Fiona's face was a mask of outrage and desperate fear. Sarah knew it was because she blamed herself for not keeping Maeve safe. Her eyes darted from Sarah to Mike before landing on Sarah's face.

"Are you happy?" Fiona said fiercely. "Sure you were right all along."

"Fiona, whisht," Nuala said softly. "It's not Sarah's fault. Nor nobody's. It were an accident."

Fiona jerked away from Nuala's hand on her shoulder. "Is that what you'll say when it's Darcy next?" she said nodding at the baby in Nuala's arms. "Or Dennis or Damian?"

"Stop it, Fi," Mike said gruffly. "You're making it worse."

"Am I now?" Fiona said, jabbing a finger at Mike's chest. "Not. Fecking. Possible."

Siobhan squirmed in Mike's arms and begin to cry at the sight of her aunt's angry red face. Fiona stomped back to her tent. Nuala and the other women followed her and Mike let out a frustrated sound and handed Siobhan, now crying fitfully, to Sarah.

"Where are you going?" she asked as she struggled with the unhappy baby.

"Fiona got one thing right," he said as he turned to walk away. "I reckon you're happy now."

Sarah stood alone for a moment and then walked back toward her tent.

I would've been a whole lot happier if someone had listened to me before it was too late, she thought with fury. *How am I to be blamed because I called it?*

"Shush, Siobhan," she said in as soothing a voice as she could manage. The baby was wearing two layers of wool and two layers of cotton undergarments but the wind cut right through both of them on the hill. She hurried her steps. The snow might make a fire impossible for now, she thought with dismay, but at least they could get in out of the wind.

Everyone seemed to have the same idea. By the time Sarah reached her tent, she didn't see anyone else out but she did hear whining and crying children coming from nearly every tent.

What good is being right when nobody believes you and then when they finally do, they hate you for it?

She tucked Siobhan into her baby bed and piled more blankets on her. The child had eaten just before the walk up the hill and so Sarah had every hope that sleep wasn't far off—even cranky and cold. She rubbed the baby's hands and kissed her rosy cheeks until she was sure she was warm. Although it was the last thing she felt like doing, she curled up next to Siobhan and began to sing to her. With her repertoire of lullabies limited to one and that only a brief stanza, Sarah sang snatches of her favorite slow songs over and over again; "I Will," by the Beatles, and "Yesterday."

And while she sang and watched Siobhan's eyes grow heavy, her mind whirled with thoughts and visions and spates of ebbing and surging fear.

It was true they'd lost faith in Mike and who could blame them? But now it didn't matter *how* they got in this situation—and honestly he hadn't held a gun to anyone's head—it only mattered that *they needed to get inside that castle.*

The first person who would die if they tried to return to the convent would be Declan. From there it would take the smallest of the little ones, probably starting with Mike's own granddaughter, Maggie, who was barely a month old.

No, they had to get inside that stupid castle and it didn't matter *what* she'd wanted so desperately before.

This is where they were *now.*

As far as *storming* the castle went, was she really the only one to see that the only way in was to be let in? Mike's fantasies of taking the castle aside, the whole reason he *wanted* this castle was because it couldn't be breached. Certainly not by fourteen women and a handful of men with nary a catapult in sight.

Siobhan gave a last sigh and gave up her fight to stay awake and Sarah felt a tremor of relief pulse through her shoulders. On top of everything else she still wasn't relaxed when she was with Siobhan. It was better, but not there yet by a long shot.

She leaned her head against a stack of blankets near Siobhan's bed and glimpsed movement through the crack in the tent flap of more snow falling. At this rate, no campfires will be the least of their worries. The tents will be collapsing with the weight of the stuff by dinnertime.

She looked at Siobhan's peacefully sleeping face. *She trusts us to make sure she's warm and has enough to eat. She's not worried about that. She trusts we'll take care of her.* And while it might be true what Mother Angelina said that no matter how much you loved them you can't hold them tight enough to keep them safe, at this stage you definitely could.

An hour later the snow had covered the campsites in a thick blanket of white. Sarah noticed that some of the women had brushed the snow off their tents but unless they planned on staying up all night—or it stopped snowing—that wasn't a longterm fix. There weren't very many people out but Sarah knew cabin fever was even worse in a tent and it wouldn't be long before someone trapped inside with children would venture out.

It was her good luck that it was Sophia.

"Sophia!" she called in a loud whisper.

Sophia turned to peek into Sarah's tent. "Oh, I think it's warmer in here than in our tent," she said.

"Where's Maggie?" Sarah patted a spot on the blanket next to her.

"Catriona is giving me a break, thank the saints."

"Where's Gavin then?"

"With Mike, I think. Do you mind if I lie down for a moment? I'm so tired."

"Not at all. If you'll stay with Siobhan—she should sleep for at least another hour—I need to do something."

"Mmmph," Sophia said as she wrapped up in a blanket next to the baby and closed her eyes.

Sarah pulled on her coat and left the tent. Nuala was in the garden with her baby watching her two boys kick a ball in the snow.

"Hey, Nuala. You seen Mike?"

Nuala gave Sarah a glacial look before turning away again. "He's off to storm the castle," she said.

Sarah looked at the castle but didn't see anyone.

"Oceanside," Nuala said sullenly.

Sarah turned and began to jog to the back of the castle. Going around the back meant a three-minute winding pathway walk to the beach before climbing down a long line of jagged rocks to the beach. The same jagged rocks that four-year old Maeve had somehow managed to climb through in the wee hours of the morning before drowning in the surf.

Sarah was amazed at how much taller the castle was from the back. There was a whole extra tier pushing out from the ground that could not be seen from the front.

A half mile down the beach, Mike, Gavin, Terry and Tommy stared up at the castle from the other side of the moat which was full of more and larger rocks. They were armed with rifles. Mike had a large coil of rope on his shoulder that anybody could see was too short for scaling the castle.

By the time she reached them, Sarah was out of breath. She'd been riding for two weeks in a buckboard and sitting around a campsite and—except for briefly running for her life from a Bengal tiger—it had been awhile since she'd done anything remotely aerobic.

"So this is your plan?" she said.

"What do you want, Sarah?" Mike didn't look at her as she approached.

She turned to Terry and Gavin. "Your wives are looking for you."

They glanced at Mike who waved them away.

"You might as well go too, Tommy," Mike said.

Sarah waited until the men had left.

"You've lost your damned mind," she said.

"I'm surprised you felt you needed to tell me *that* in private."

"You said yourself this castle is impregnable. The only way in is to be *let* in."

"And you heard that they've politely declined our request for that."

"We need inside that castle, Mike. There are going to be more deaths if we don't get in and I think it needs to be *tonight*."

He looked at her for the first time since she arrived. "What would you have me do, Sarah?"

"We know they have a sick child in there."

He frowned but his eyes were alert, waiting.

"Tell them we have a nurse and medicines," she said.

"I already told them that."

"Tell them again. Plus you might mention we have Coca-Cola and whiskey. That guy isn't alone in there. Trust me, the mother of that sick child is talking to him *right now* about changing his mind."

"You really think so?"

"Speaking as a mother who would run you through with a saber and toss you over the parapet if it was Siobhan who was sick in there?"

"I get your point."

"Believe me. You would."

*****

Shaun sat and stared into the fireplace from the great hall. It was empty now except for himself and the two dogs who were always looking for table scraps. His mother hadn't spoken to him since he'd told the courtyard campers to move on.

Ava was still talking to him but in a way it would have been better if she wasn't. He cringed at the memory of her blistering tirade this morning. *Selfish bastard* and *coward* were two notable remnants of that interaction that still stung hours later. He couldn't blame her but it was still galling.

Didn't she know he wanted Keeva to get better too? Did she think this wasn't killing him? He had to be careful. For all their sakes. He wedged another stick in the fire and heard the words *heavy is the head that wears the crown* and grimaced. *Truer words.*

"Shaun!"

He jumped, lost in his thoughts.

Saoirse stood in the doorway. "The wankers are calling up to us again," she said.

Shite. He should have known they wouldn't just go away. And now with the snow…

"What are they saying?"

"You'd better come and hurry. They're talking about medicine and they're talking to *Ava.*"

She wouldn't dare...

But he knew she would. For Keeva's sake she damn well would. He hurried behind Saoirse to the same window on the western side of the front gatehouse. He could see Ava's form as she leaned out the window to yell down to the people below.

Was she mad? What if they had a gun or bow and arrow?

"Ava!" he barked.

She turned around to see him but didn't move from the window. "They have Cokes and whiskey, too," she said breathlessly. "Shaun, they're not even asking to come in."

"Like hell they're not," he said edging her away from the window.

The big man was back and he had a woman with him. They looked cold and a needle of guilt wedged in Shaun's gut. The woman was smiling up at him.

Don't trust them. You know you can't trust them.

"I was just telling your Missus," the big man said, "that we have a nurse and we have medicines. Ibuprofen, aspirin, antibiotics and me sister is a homeopathic genius. If you have sickness among you—"

Shaun turned and glowered at Ava. "Did you tell them we had a sick child?"

"No," she said angrily, "*you* did last night." She clapped her hands on her hips, elbows akimbo and stared him down.

He turned back to the man.

"Fine. We'll send a basket down on a rope," he said. "Put the medicines in the basket and thank you."

"Shaun!" Ava said. "They're freezing out there!"

Shaun ignored her. He saw the man's shoulders sag inside his jacket. He knew how much he wanted—needed —to get his people in the castle but it couldn't be helped. The man leaned over to hear the woman who spoke sharply to him. Finally, the man nodded.

"Aye," he said with obvious resignation. "Lower the basket."

******

Mike stood by the castle wall and watched the basket lower. For a moment he wondered what would happen if he grabbed it and jerked the bastard out the window. The problem with that plan was that the berk would surely break his neck when he fell so would be relatively useless as a bargaining chip or even more likely, would just let go of the rope altogether.

"This way we gain their trust, Mike," Sarah said. "It's a process."

"But not one that will see our lot in a nice warm castle tonight," he muttered under his breath.

"A long process," Sarah said. "But one that will work. It's a better plan than whatever hair brained idea you had about standing all the men on their shoulders and climbing up the back wall."

The basket thumped to a stop on the ground at the same moment they both heard Siobhan's unmistakable wail coming from their tent. Mike crossed the empty moat to retrieve the basket and looked in the direction of their tent but Sarah was already moving.

"I'll go," she said. "Do you need help with the medicines? They're in Declan's tent."

"Nay," Mike said, waving up to the castle to signal they had the basket. "I'll handle it."

He picked up the basket and threaded the rope through the loop, leaving it on the ground and then crossed back over the moat wondering how tricky it would be to fill the thing with water. He hurried to Fiona's tent. He knew his face might not be one his sister most wanted to see but she'd change her mind when she heard him out.

He entered the tent and saw Declan sprawled on his bed of blankets and sleeping bags. The air was stuffy and smelled of wet canvas. Fiona watched him as he entered.

"Are we leaving?" she asked dully.

"We're getting into the castle," he said.

She jumped to her feet, her eyes wide. "Are ye serious?"

"I'm serious that I need your help to make it happen."

Her body deflated and she sat back down next to Declan.

He looked around the tent. "Where's wee Ciara?"

"She's with the other kiddies. Maeve was her best friend."

"I know, Fi. Look, I'm that sorry about everything but if you can just pull it together I promise we can be sitting inside the castle in time for breakfast with Declan in a proper bed in front of a fireplace. I just need you to do as I ask and leave the questions for me to worry about."

"Questions?" She frowned. "What are you talking about?"

"I'm planning on getting us inside tonight and I'm hoping you'll see that we might have to break the rules to do that. And that it will be worth it."

"Sure why isn't Sarah here? Could it be because these rules you intend to break would be a problem for her?"

"Will you help me get everyone inside? I don't know any other way to do it without your help. And yes. Sarah would be against it."

After a glance at Declan, Fiona turned back to Mike. "Tell me what you need me to do."

Twenty minutes later, bracing against the cold, Mike left Fiona's tent and ran into Sarah who had Siobhan in her arms.

"What took you so long?" she asked. "Did you get the Cokes?"

"I'm giving them what's important first. We'll send up the other bits later."

"Why are you giving her homeopathic stuff?" Sarah asked, peering into the basket with a frown. "Why not just give her the Percocet?"

"Fi suggested this would suit them best for a sick child."

"Really? Fi said that?"

He hurried toward the base of the castle, his long legs taking him well ahead of her. By the time she reached him, breathless and shivering, he was tugging on the line and crossing back to the other side of the moat to watch the basket go up to the window.

"They'll see we can be trusted," she said, watching the basket ascend. "This will count in our favor. You'll see."

"Aye, I hope so."

The man in the window brought the basket in and waved his thanks before disappearing inside.

"Wow. Man of few words," Sarah said, squinting up at the now empty window. She looked at Mike. "But the mother will be grateful to us. I know she will."

He put a hand on her shoulder and for a change didn't feel the tension in it. If it weren't for the fact that he'd just lied to her and she'd find out sooner rather than later, he'd bother to hope it would last.

It had stopped snowing, saints be praised. Mike and the other men spent the rest of the long cold afternoon rebuilding the fires and brushing the snow from the tents. Gavin and Tommy had been successful trapping rabbits and some of the women were already roasting them on campfire spits. Even with the snow letting up, it was still a somber day. The children played under the ever-watchful eyes of their mothers and the tension was so thick in the air it felt like wading through fog just to cross the camp from one side to the other.

And all the while, Mike waited. He didn't know if he'd taken a terrible gamble or if he had nothing left to lose. He knew for sure that if his gamble failed, Sarah would never forgive him. He'd have thrown away any chance that the people in the castle would ever trust them—long process or not—and they'd never get in.

The sun hadn't climbed very high in the sky and while it didn't rain, neither did the day warm up either. Right around dinnertime, when more people were coming out of their tents to tend to their cooking and talk with each other, it happened.

The long piercing wail of a mother's lament—coming from the castle wall above.

Mike held his breath but didn't look at the castle. Behind him he felt people turning to look. The cries went on, escalating into anger and then falling in despair. He looked down and saw Sarah standing beside him.

"What did you do?"

"What I had to for the good of the community."

She stared at him for a moment and then bolted for Fiona's tent. Mike twisted around and grabbed her.

"Sarah, no!"

"You tell me or she will! What have you done?!"

Mike dragged her back to their tent, mindful of the women in the camp now openly staring at them. The fear and distrust he'd felt this morning at the funeral came back a hundred fold.

"I'll not let you go until you promise me you'll—"

"I'm not promising anything until you tell me what you've done!"

"Do you really think I'd hurt a child?" Mike shook her, his frustration pinging off him. He forced himself to let her go, afraid once he started shaking her he might have trouble stopping.

"If it meant the greater good?" she looked at him, her mouth set in a firm line.

He ran a hand through his hair and looked away.

"Fiona called it *hen's teeth* or some such thing. I don't know what herbs they are."

"Poison."

"*Nay*. Not really. Just enough to make the child feel and look sicker. That's all."

"*That's all*. Do you hear that mother's cries? What if that was Siobhan in there? She sounds like she's lost her child. Are you sure she hasn't?"

"I did what was needed."

"What you *rationalized* was needed you mean. You're a monster."

"A monster, is it?" he said heatedly. "You won't think so two months from now when there's snow on the ground and Siobhan is warm in her bed *inside the castle*."

"Oy!"

Both Mike and Sarah jerked their heads to the sound of the voice coming from the window above. Mike took Sarah's arm and pulled her to the tent.

"Stay here," he said firmly before walking away to stand beneath the window.

"Is everything fine then?" he called up to the window.

"We'll be lowering the drawbridge," the man said, his face white with alarm.

"Oh, aye?"

"If you could send the nurse in we'd be grateful."

******

All Sarah knew was that if this didn't work, they were all screwed. They'd already proven they weren't to be trusted. Any hope they'd had of forging a relationship with the people inside was gone. Sooner or later, they would find out how they had been tricked—*by using a sick child*—into letting them all inside.

It didn't bode well.

Could the people inside hurt them? Did they have weapons? If they were angry, could they attack them? The compound group was just about as vulnerable as they'd ever been. If not for the snow and the ungodly cold, they would surely have already been attacked by drifters or other thugs prowling for victims.

Sarah sat by the struggling campfire, a wool rug pulled around her shoulders and Siobhan dozing in her lap. As soon as the castle had asked for the nurse—which, of course was another lie since nobody in the group had any such qualifications—Mike had begun making preparations for Fiona to go in.

He must be desperate, sending his own sister in.

The people inside had been careful. They wouldn't lower the drawbridge until all the men had removed themselves several hundred yards away down the road. The camp women watched silently as Fiona, carrying a knapsack full of painkillers and antibiotics, walked across the wooden drawbridge and disappeared under the raised portcullis into the castle.

Sarah had a brief view of an outdoor fire pit inside and even two large dogs romping in the interior courtyard of the castle. The men began walking back as soon as the drawbridge raised up again. Sarah held Siobhan tightly and tried not to hate the people inside for not allowing them in.

Mike wouldn't come to her now. Whatever he and Fiona were up to, he wouldn't share it with Sarah, nor would he come back to finish their fight. No, he'd spend the rest of the evening and likely the night securing the camp, checking on the horses and staying well away from their tent and his furious wife.

Sarah warmed her hands by the fire and felt the exhausted aftermath of her emotional upheaval. For a few minutes today it had felt like the old Mike and Sarah. She'd felt comfortable with him. They'd plotted together—although now it was clear he had an entirely *different* plot in mind all along. But for a little bit, it had been good again.

For such a bad day—especially the way it began—she'd not even thought much of John today. Not more than she normally did anyway—wondering where he was, who was being nice to him—or not.

Wondering when she would see his dear face again.

She was surprised to look up and realize she was one of the few people still sitting outside. Siobhan should have been put to bed hours ago. She went into the tent and put the baby down and felt the exhaustion of the day claim her as she collapsed on her sleeping bag.

Hours later she was jolted awake by a thundering noise. She sat up woozily, reaching for Siobhan, fear mounting in her throat.

The terrifying echo of the sound reverberated in the air around her until she slowly realized…it was a gunshot.

And it had come from inside the castle.

20.

"The drawbridge is lowering!"

Sarah scooped up Siobhan and stumbled out of her tent into the dark and the cold. Three lanterns near the castle entranceway glowed brightly revealing the portcullis as it slowly rose. Siobhan began to cry and Sarah gathered with a group of other women at the front of the castle.

She had no trouble picking Mike out—always the largest in any group—as he stood waiting for the drawbridge to finish its descent. The interior of the castle was lighted too. Sarah gasped as she saw Fiona standing inside in stark silhouette in the middle of the gate tower archway—holding a gun to the head of a woman while two people operated the pulley system to open the gates.

Sarah's heart thudded in her chest when, in spite of herself, the first thought that burst from her was, *Thank you, God.*

The moment the drawbridge spanned the moat and touched the ground Mike and all the men swarmed across it, weapons drawn, into the interior. They'd clearly been waiting for this moment.

Sophia ran to Sarah, her wailing baby in her arms. Her breath was visible in the cold air as she spoke.

"We're going inside, Sarah!"

Sarah jostled Siobhan to quieten her. The rest of the women huddled in a shivering, animated group, their voices rising and lowering in excited levels of agitation.

Sarah could see Mike inside the castle talking to the man they'd seen from the window. Mike's gun was still in his hand. Fiona ran out of the castle and back across the drawbridge.

Did it matter how they'd pulled it off? As long as nobody died and they got inside?

"Sarah!" Sophia said. "Gavin is waving for us to come inside!"

"It must be safe then," Sarah said hurrying beside Sophia. The drawbridge couldn't have been the original one that came with the castle, Sarah thought as she and the rest of the women picked their way across it into the castle.

Once inside, she saw two women and a man held at gunpoint by Mike's men. Mike had holstered his gun and his eyes searched the group of women entering the castle.

He's looking for me, Sarah thought. She got eye contact with him.

You were right her eyes told him. He smiled tiredly before turning his attention away again.

Sarah and the rest of the women moved to the curving patch of lawn in the interior of the castle. She shook her head in amazement at how manicured and beautiful the lawn looked, like nothing looked anymore in post-EMP Ireland. She thought it odd that the castle residents hadn't paid any attention to the outside gardens but the lawn inside was meticulously maintained.

As Sarah looked up at the second floor windows that lined the castle interior, a few heads popped out to stare down at them. Terry and Tommy ran with weapons drawn into the first castle stairwell. Soon, the heads withdrew from the windows, accompanied by shrieks.

How many were in here? Sarah glanced nervously at the women around her holding babies or trying to keep little ones quiet. If they were outnumbered, could they still fight them? One thing Sarah knew now that she was inside —*she wasn't leaving.*

Within minutes, Terry and Tommy were back in the courtyard leading a small group of nine women in their robes and slippers to where Mike stood.

"Everyone in the great hall," Mike boomed out.

While it felt remarkably warmer within the castle walls than outside, it was still cold. Sarah watched as Mike and the man led the way through a wide archway toward the back of the castle. As she waited to follow, she caught a glimpse of Gavin and Fiona helping Declan walk through the front gate and then allowing him to rest while the two of them operated the pulley system to lower the portcullis and raise the drawbridge.

Sarah watched in fascination as the door closed solidly against the world and when it did a feeling of utter security and peace came over her.

Oh, my God, she thought.

I think we just captured a castle.

*****

It was everything Mike had dreamed it would be. A small village fortress complete with a cow, two goats, dozens of chickens, enough housing for a hundred people, a small working mill house, a spring—and absolutely no way for anyone to get in.

Unless they were one tricky son of a bitch.

He was sitting at the end of a massive dining table in the great hall. Now that all the excitement was dying down, he felt the weariness of the early hour and the fact that he'd not slept last night.

Amazingly, there were only fifteen people inside the castle. One Shaun Morrison, his sister Saoirse, his mother Beryl—who had also been the museum docent and gift shop manager for ten years before the Crisis—and eight women from the village with two children.

They sat now, their backs to the walls, watching Mike and the others with hatred and fear.

Shaun sat next to Mike, his hands on the table, although Mike wasn't worried. This lot didn't seem to have any weapons but even if they did, Shaun Morrison didn't strike him as the type who'd know how to use them.

"How long have you been here?" Mike asked, glancing at the compound women standing around the massive floor to ceiling stone fireplace at the far end with their children. Nuala's two lads had discovered the castle dogs and were already on the floor playing with them. He spotted Sarah, Siobhan on her hip, watching him. It wasn't like her to stand back but then, not much had been like her lately.

"You can't stay here," Shaun said tersely. His face was pinched and tense. Mike guessed him to be in his early forties. He looked lean and malnourished like all of the castle folk.

"What happened to the people in the village? We passed through and it was deserted."

"You can't hold us here!" one of the seated women shrieked out. Mike recognized her as Shaun's sister.

"Regardless of how we came to be here," Mike said to Shaun. "I'd like us to work together."

"Impossible," Shaun said, jerking his hands into his lap. Mike guessed it was to prevent Mike from seeing they were shaking. "You *sicken* one of our children, trick us…so you can come in here…you're despicable."

Mike turned to Gavin standing next to him. "You're sure this is everyone?"

"Aye."

Mike nodded. "Take Tommy and do a security sweep of the place and report back." Gavin disappeared.

"We could help each other," Mike said to Shaun. "You look like you could use a decent meal. I see you have a cow but when was the last time you had fresh greens?"

"Feck you and your fresh greens. We're doing fine without you."

"That may or may not be true but as I've been trying to tell you, that's come to an end now, so it has. You'll not be doing shite without us from now on."

"You can't just come in here and take over!"

"That's exactly what I've done and the sooner you accept it, the better it'll be for all of ye."

"Are we prisoners then?"

"That's up to you. Will ye fight us?"

The look on Shaun's face was nearly laughable. Even he must have thought the idea of fighting Mike absurd. Mike tried another tactic.

"I see you haven't planted the garden out front. How is it you've survived so long?"

Shaun looked like he wouldn't answer but pride obviously won out. It was no easy thing to have kept his group together and at least minimally healthy for five long years.

"Trading, mostly," he said reluctantly. "Some hunting."

"What do you trade?"

Shaun blushed to his roots and Mike glanced at the women seated and staring at him.

Jaysus. Henredon Castle—post-apocalyptic hoor house.

"Well, that's over now too."

"It's not like that," Shaun snarled.

"Not any more it's not." He saw Sarah heading his way, finally too curious to stay away. As untroubled as he was about Shaun's ability to hurt him, Mike still didn't like the idea of Sarah or Siobhan too close to him. The man may not be armed, but he was definitely desperate.

"On my left side, Sarah," Mike said to her as she approached. Her eyes flickered to Shaun and then sat where he'd indicated. He nearly grinned. Was this the first time she'd ever done as he'd told her to? He'd try not to get used to it.

"I'm Sarah Donovan," she said to Shaun. "In case my husband hasn't mentioned it, I'm sorry we had to do things this way and I understand why you were hesitant to let us in but you could see we had children and babies out there in the snow and the rain. Shame on you."

Her admonishing tone surprised Mike but he was glad to hear it.

Almost like the old Sarah...

Shaun stared at her. "You're American?"

"I am. So you can appreciate the damage you've done to international relations. My embassy will hear of it."

Shaun's mouth fell open and Mike laughed.

"I admit her sense of humor is peculiar," Mike said. "But likely you'll get used to it." He grinned at Sarah and received a faint smile in return.

One of the castle women stood up from the bench by the wall and tentatively approached them. Mike recognized her as Shaun's mother. He waved her toward the table.

"I just wanted to know...to ask what is to become of us," she said in a shaking voice.

"Mother..." Shaun said, standing up.

"Sit," Mike said to him calmly but coldly.

Shaun took his seat. Mike addressed the older woman.

"Ye'll not be harmed, none of ye. But we will be living with you from now on."

"Living with us?" Beryl looked from Mike to her son who was staring at his hands. "You mean in the castle?"

"Aye. And as I was just saying to your son here," Mike locked his eyes back on Shaun, "we can do it hard or easy but sure it's your decision."

"That's a threat," Shaun said, his voice low but trembling again.

"I'm grateful you can see that without me having to spell it out."

"But...but," Beryl said, taking a seat at the table as her legs seem to give out on her, "this is *our* castle."

"No, Missus," Mike said gently. "Not any more it's not."

Susan Kiernan-Lewis

21.

From where Hurley sat on his horse he could see over the crest of the knoll ahead. In the distance, easily twenty kilometers before him, the church spires towered over the houses of the village. He twisted in his saddle and watched his marching Centurions approach in two even columns. One hundred men fully armed. Rifles, handguns, hand grenades and a rocket launcher.

He was the only one mounted, as it should be. The battle would always be fought and won by the foot soldiers. His Centurions.

Two days into their mission south and the men had proven themselves worthy of his estimation. The laziness and sloth he'd witnessed in Dublin before the second EMP was gone, replaced by hard-core obedience and discipline.

He smiled as he watched them march around him and his horse as he stood in the center of the road. Just like the Roman armies did it, he thought. None of them looked him in the eye. They knew his place and they knew theirs.

Had it been the brilliance of the lion pit that had spearheaded this transformation? Or the fact that Hurley had kept the soldiers fed and working? Was it because he'd given them back their pride in themselves? Or a goal to work toward?

Whatever the reasons, in the end, he'd succeeded in reminding them—brutally in some instances—that they were men. They were men in a world that had forgotten the meaning of the word. Until Centurion Commander Padraig Hurley.

He held up his hand and heard Brady yell out, "Troops, halt!"

His men kept their eyes pointed in the direction they marched, but Hurley's Camp Prefect kept his eyes on his commander.

The men stopped. They didn't shift in their tracks or rearrange their packs. They stood like machines, facing straight ahead.

"There's a village up ahead," Hurley said. "We'll camp here tonight. For those who have earned it, you may visit the town and take what you need."

He detected movement in the ranks at his words. He didn't need to explain. They knew. They would take what a Roman army marching through the countryside would take —comfort, food and succor from the citizens. Hurley glanced at Brady and nodded.

Camp Prefect Brady barked out, "Make camp!"

The light had begun to leach from the sky as Hurley dismounted and handed his reins to the Centurion who ran to take his horse. Hurley walked to the woods and relieved himself and then watched his men set up camp.

The feeling he'd experienced four weeks ago when the second EMP had balanced out the scales was one of realization and near euphoria. It was a message from the cosmos that this was the time—*his* time—to step forward. And he'd done that without hesitation or doubt by killing thirty officers and their juniors and by throwing to the lions no fewer than fifteen politicians. Although many had escaped into the streets or countryside they wouldn't soon be back to attempt to lead the country.

Hurley had further demonstrated his benevolence and strength of purpose to his troops by setting up army sanctioned whore houses—forcibly enlisting junior administrative secretaries as well as the daughters and wives of politicians and military officers who hadn't had the brains to flee beforehand—thereby cleaning up the streets of Dublin and rewarding his Centurions all in one.

Yes, the work he'd done since taking over as Centurion Commander had been nothing less than superhuman, he thought as he watched his men erect tents and build campfires. Brady was giving instructions to a squad of armed men—likely the first wave of visitors to the unsuspecting town.

But all of that was nothing compared to his mission. A mission that ignited deep within his very soul. The pure necessity of it urged him like a drug, relentlessly driving him, feeding his fury, and abated only by images of its promised fulfillment: Michael Donovan's head on a pike.

There was nothing to compare.

******

Three days later the temperatures had dropped significantly and it had rained every day and most nights. Hurley's saddle squeaked as he rode. His horse's mane hung in bedraggled wet clumps. The days were so much shorter now and they were only making twenty-five miles a day.

He could see many of the men were limping from blisters or other foot sores. Twice he looked at Brady to see if there was a problem but received a thumbs up every time. Taking food from the villages was proving problematic as well. There was usually not enough to feed the troops and there were few hunters among their number to make up the lack.

The captive Chezzie had sworn that the convent was brimming with food—smoked pork, chickens, fresh vegetables—but that was still two days away at the rate they were marching.

The roads were potted and broken this far south. They hadn't seen anyone traveling them although it was likely anyone would be able to see them first and slip into the woods. The pastures to the south were already barren and brown even this early in the season, with no hint of anything growing and no animals grazing.

Hurley stood in the door of his tent and watched the water drip off the roof to create a puddle of mud at the entrance. It angered him that Brady or *someone* hadn't seen the likelihood of this happening and placed a plank there. It was already long past dinner and most of the Centurions were sitting in their tents playing cards or trying to sleep.

There were ten sentries set around the perimeter of the makeshift camp but even Hurley knew they weren't needed. No one in his right mind would attempt to interfere with a cadre of the Irish Imperial Army.

He leaned against the main tent pole at the entrance of his tent, a tepid cup of tea in his hand and gazed out at the banked campfires and wet tents of his troops. There was a squad out at the nearby village. With luck they'd bring back enough food to fuel the rest of the trip without having to stop and raid another village.

It took everything Hurley had not to jump on his horse and barrel down the road, leaping over all obstacles, until he arrived at the convent. He envisioned himself kicking in the door and shocking the bastard Donovan at his dinner with one of the comely nuns perched on his lap, her eyes wide with surprise.

In some scenarios, Hurley killed the bastard immediately with his blood spurting in the face of the startled nun before Hurley raped her and slit her throat too. But in others—and these were so much more satisfying— he tied Donovan up while Hurley raped and killed his family in front of him before turning to Donovan himself now apoplectic with hate and fear.

One thing these reveries taught Hurley was that waiting was key to his maximum satisfaction. He would wait for his army of one hundred strong to rest and soak their feet and take the time to raid the villages for food before the two days necessary to arrive at the convent.

Two days that stood between Hurley and complete and bloody satisfaction.

"Commander?"

Brady had materialized a few feet away from the tent. Seeing the Camp Prefect reminded Hurley of his annoyance with the tent puddle but before he could address it, the man pointed toward the village.

"A Centurion was killed, Commander, in the village."

Hurley felt his blood rise to his face.

How dare these bastards touch one of the Irish Imperial?

"How?" he managed to say as the bile bubbled up in his throat.

"A father," Brady said. "Objecting to O'Reilly's procurement of his daughter."

"And this father?" Hurley spat out, his eyes looking in the direction that Brady pointed. Even from here he could see the church spire that pinpointed the village.

"Killed immediately, Commander. And the girl. And her mother and two small brothers."

"Where is O'Reilly now?"

"We are preparing him for a morning burial, Commander."

Hurley nodded and threw the dregs of his tea on the ground.

"Prefect Brady," he said tightly.

"Yes sir?"

"Repair this threshold tonight. You will sleep naked on the ground away from the furthest campfire because I had to tell you."

"Yes sir."

"Then tomorrow, after the burial, gather ten volunteers and burn the village to the ground."

****

Chezzie's wrists were chafed and rubbed raw from the rope around them. He was unbound only long enough to do whatever disgusting work was required of him during the trek—usually digging latrine ditches—and fed only whatever scraps fell from the Centurions' plates.

During every step of every mile he asked himself if death by a lion's claws could be worse. His hell would be over by now instead of awaiting him.

Hurley had interrogated Chezzie three times so far. Once for more details on the convent and Donovan which had resulted in Hurley beating Chezzie unconscious because he had so little to offer in the way of Donovan's description.

During the second interview, Chezzie had invented as much as he dared until it became clear he was making it up. The man who guarded Chezzie by night said Chezzie's screams had echoed up and down the valley. Chezzie didn't remember that. The concussion from Hurley's throwing him headfirst into the nearest tree had given him a blissful reprieve from the memory of the beating.

Thankfully for their third conversation Hurley only cared about the details of the trail to the convent.

Unfortunately for Chezzie, the anxiety which he'd carried away from the convent the day Donovan threw him out— along with the terror of Hurley's questioning methods— combined to make him seriously doubt he knew exactly how to get to the convent.

And if he couldn't remember, Chezzie knew he'd be *begging* to be thrown to the lions.

Chezzie was kept away from the troops. But sometimes, when the men were pissing in the woods near him they would forget he was there, and he could hear them talking. It was how he learned that a few Centurions had run off.

Chezzie was amazed more hadn't. Hurley was a brutal and volatile commander. But Chezzie never heard any of his men speak ill of him. No complaints at all. If they mentioned him at all, it was with awe.

"The Commander is coming to ask you a few questions," said his guard, a young and solemn youth of nineteen, as he pulled on the rope that connected to Chezzie's bonds. Chezzie's lacerated wrists screamed in pain as the rope razored against his open wounds. He staggered to his feet. He was weak from hunger, from the trek and from his constant terror.

Hurley walked over to Chezzie. He held in his hands a large butcher knife.

"Yesterday you said we were a day's ride away," Hurley said as he loomed over Chezzie, his eyes looking like slits.

Chezzie could not tear his eyes away from the knife. He nodded numbly.

"I'm going to start cutting pieces off you until you describe exactly how we get to the convent from here. Do you understand?"

Chezzie had an image develop in his mind. It was last summer. The nuns' garden was brimming with fresh vegetables and every day was a feast. He remembered how they looked at him when he stayed with them—smiling, laughing, scolding. They didn't hate him. They took care of him. And now he was bringing this man to their door.

"How about an ear?" Hurley said. "Would losing an ear help you hear me better?"

"The path is over the next rise," Chezzie said.

"The path. What path?" Hurley said impatiently.

He wants to cut me no matter what I say.

"The path through the woods. To the convent."

The silence seemed to stretch forever. It went on until Chezzie began to think it was all a dream. Or perhaps Hurley had cut off both his ears and he couldn't hear anything.

"Bring him to the front of the line," Hurley said finally. "He can point the way to this path." He held the knife to Chezzie's head and sliced down firmly opening up his scalp until just where his left ear began. Chezzie felt the blood trickle down his cheek as the blaze of agony finally caught up with his senses.

The Camp Prefect ran up to where they were standing. He was breathless and his eyes wide.

"Commander," he said, gasping for breath. "A wagon is heading toward us."

"Indeed?" Hurley said. He cocked his bald head like an inquisitive bird attempting to hear better.

"Two women," the Prefect said, "in a pony cart with fecking flowers painted on the side. We are moving to intercept now."

Chezzie watched the two men walk away.

Flowers painted on the side of a pony cart…and as sure as day follows night driven by a feisty little gypsy girl and an angel with a scowl. Chezzie sagged to his knees, the agony of the gash on his face beginning to push through his shock.

Poor little bitches. They don't stand a chance.

Susan Kiernan-Lewis

22.

That first day in the castle was spent organizing where everyone would sleep and bringing in the tents and horses from the outside courtyard. Sarah and Fiona set up a clinic in one of the warmest rooms in the castle and moved Declan and the little girl Keeva into it so they could be treated. Nuala set up a nursery where, along with two of the compound women, she would mind all the children so their parents could work without worry.

Mike had all the castle people—except for Ava and her sick child—put in a large room with a fireplace and a narrow window overlooking the ocean. The door was locked and a guard was posted outside.

Ava was allowed to stay with her daughter in the clinic. Sarah couldn't help but wonder what life had been like for the woman before the EMP changed everything. Ava was obviously with Shaun Morrison but not married to him. Had she been married before? Keeva was at least five years old. Was Shaun her father?

Ava leaned over Keeva and pressed a cool compress to the child's forehead. Already the Ibuprofen was bringing down her fever. Like the rest of them, the child looked like she could use a square meal and her fingernails showed evidence of rickets.

"I wanted Shaun to let you in," Ava said as she watched Fiona checking on Declan in his bed.

Sarah filled a pitcher of water and brought it to the table next to Declan's bed.

"I'm sure we'll all be one big happy family before long," Sarah said. "Locking everyone in is only until we all start to trust each other."

"It's just hard on Shaun. This has been our castle for five years."

"I'm sure it'll all get sorted out," Sarah said with a reassuring smile. She *was* sure, too. Shaun didn't look at all like the obstreperous type. Sometimes the quiet ones fooled you but he didn't strike her as a guy who craved to be in charge. Now *Mike* on the other hand…

"Is Shaun your husband then?" Fiona asked as she moved away from Declan's side.

"Something like that," Ava said.

Sarah noticed she blushed. *That's odd.* Even before the Crisis nobody in Ireland thought anything of premarital sex. And they sure didn't care *now*.

Fiona smiled at Keeva but Sarah could still see the pain in her eyes and knew she was thinking of Maeve.

"She'll be fine in short order," Fiona said. "Children are resilient."

Sarah wondered if she should apologize to Ava for deliberately making Keeva sicker in order to wangle their way into the castle. As she watched Ava, she decided not to bring it up.

It is what it is. She'll either understand and forgive or she won't.

Ava kept her hand on Keeva's forehead. She looked at Sarah. "Is it just the one bairn you have then?"

Instantly, Sarah felt her stomach sour. She rubbed her hands up and down her arms as if trying to warm them.

"No," she said. "I have an older boy. He's…he's in England right now."

"England? That's a long way away."

Sarah moved to the window that overlooked the front of the castle.

"He'll be home at Christmas," she said. "You'll meet him then." She caught Fiona's eye and they exchanged a sad smile.

Baby steps, Sarah thought.

*****

That night after a hot meal of rabbit stew in the great hall, compliments of Tommy and Gavin's trapping, and a celebratory breaking out of the whiskey to mark the first night in their new home, Sarah and Siobhan made their way upstairs up the stone stairwell to the room that would be theirs from now on.

Unlike when they lived in separate cottages at the compound, in their life here in the castle there were no longer individual kitchens or living areas for each of the families. All of the women would work in the mammoth castle kitchen baking and cooking and everyone would take their meals together in the great hall.

Sarah looked around the bedroom chamber. One of the men had already dragged their bedding and belongings into the room and set up Siobhan's cot. The chamber was large and had an anteroom with a separate living room. When they returned to the compound they would fill this room with all the books that Sarah had brought back from the States the year before.

Most of the castle living chambers faced the ocean or the south side of the castle. Sarah's room was closer to the front of the castle on the south side. From the large mullioned windows, they would be able to see the gardens and all the land that stretched to the south.

Sarah was surprised that Siobhan fell to sleep as soon as Sarah put her down. She imagined that spending the day in the nursery with other children had something to do with this. It had been a big day for everyone. Sarah felt her exhaustion pull her toward the bed. She stripped off her clothes, letting them fall on the thin carpet by the large bed. She allowed herself only a moment to wonder how old the bed was before she crawled into her sleeping bag on top of it.

She had barely closed her eyes before she heard Mike enter the room. She watched him pause by Siobhan's cot and give the baby a kiss.

Surely this must be the first time in memory, Sarah thought, where Mike was able to rest knowing that everyone was safe and protected—from weather or foe.

He groaned as he sat on the bed and she reached a hand out to touch his back.

"I'm sorry I doubted you," she said quietly.

He turned in one motion and brought her into his arms. She held him close and let out a huge breath.

"Forgive me?" she said.

"Adore you," he murmured into her hair.

That night Sarah fell asleep knowing in her bones that everything was finally on track to being okay. Tonight she even knew John really would be home with them—here in the castle—for Christmas.

****

The next morning it snowed again. Sarah watched it come down from one of the long vertical windows in the great hall that faced the ocean. Fires blazed in all three of the gigantic dining hall fireplaces. She'd gotten up early, deposited Siobhan with Nuala in the nursery, and then went to the castle kitchen to work with four other women to prepare breakfast.

They'd made a rudimentary schedule of shifts the day before. After preparing breakfast, Sarah and the other women would be free of kitchen duty until dinner which they would make and clean up after.

The castle people had been brought down to dine with them. Mike was of a mind to let most of the women go back to their own rooms as they had before. He saw no threat from them. He was less sure of Shaun and his sister Saoirse. In any case, he'd prepared a brief ceremony where each of the castle people would be brought to him to swear allegiance—if not to Mike himself then at least to the idea of not attacking or disrupting the burgeoning alliance between the two groups.

Last night, before drifting off to sleep in each other's arms, he'd mentioned the idea to Sarah and she thought it was a good one. Now she watched everyone eat a robust breakfast of bacon and pancakes with maple syrup they had brought with them and hot tea with milk and sugar, which the castle people had gone without for five long years.

Sometimes it's as simple as having a decent cup of tea again, Sarah thought as she watched the smiles and conversation down the long table of both castle women and compound women together. She hoped the castle people would see that having new people among them would be good for everyone.

If this morning's breakfast was any indication, her hope was definitely being fulfilled.

Beryl Morrison, Shaun's mother, sat beside Sarah near the front of the table. Mike and most of the men had taken their breakfast on the run in the form of bacon biscuits. Because Shaun and his sister still sat at the table, Terry stood against the wall with his hand on his holster, watching them.

Gavin and Tommy flanked Beryl. Sarah could see that the older woman was pink with excitement to have their attention.

"Cor," she said as one of the compound women came to refill her teacup, "I can't remember the last time someone wanted to know about the castle." Her cheeks were pricked with color and her eyes danced.

"So there's a real murder hole in the castle?" Gavin asked. Sophia sat to his left with their baby nestled in a sling on her chest.

"Oh, aye!" Beryl said. "Right where it needs to be, too. In the ceiling of the gateway should we ever have need of it."

"How's it work exactly?" Tommy asked, his eyes bright with curiosity.

Sarah smiled. It was pretty clear that Beryl Morrison would be happy to have the compound people inside even if they *hadn't* brought tea and sugar.

Terry moved from the wall and prodded Shaun with the nose of his gun. Both Shaun and Saoirse got up and were escorted from the room. Sarah hated to see it but she knew as soon as the two agreed not to fight them that everything would be fine. She hoped Mike was planning on asking the castle people today. The sooner the better.

What would they do if any of them decided not to pledge allegiance?

Sarah glanced again at Beryl chatting happily with the two boys and telling them her castle knowledge. Sarah looked down the table to see the other castle women smiling shyly at the compound women.

They would. They just would.

An hour later, Sarah walked around the castle interior courtyard. It was still snowing but the fresh air—and the knowledge that she could tuck her feet up in front of a roaring fire whenever she wanted—gave an energizing feel to the exercise.

There was so much to do to make the castle their home —and to prepare it for defense. But before that could be done, she and Mike needed to go back to the convent to see if John had returned.

And they needed to keep going back until he did.

She noticed Kevin on the high walkway on the parapet that traversed the front of the castle. He was alone but they didn't need more than one voice to raise the alarm. Unless invaders came in motorized vehicles—impossible now— whoever came down the front drive would be seen for hours before they arrived.

Unless they came by sea.

She pulled her coat tightly around her. She would run by the nursery to see Siobhan and then go to the clinic to check on Declan. Little Keeva was much better and they'd allowed her to go back to her room with her mother before breakfast today.

As Sarah stepped into the first archway that led to the great hall, she saw most of the castle people were lined up outside the door.

That meant Mike had begun the process of formally asking their intentions. She saw that all the women were there—including Saoirse—but not Shaun, which must mean he was inside the hall with Mike.

Be sensible Mr. Morrison, Sarah thought as she walked past the waiting women. *We're stronger together than apart. I hope you see that.*

Tommy was standing next to Beryl who was still talking to him with animation and gesturing down the hall as she pointed out more features of the castle. Tommy looked up as Sarah walked by.

"Missus?" he said. "Mr. Donovan asked that you join him should I see you."

Sarah frowned but went immediately to the door and pulled it open. Inside, she saw Mike and Shaun talking at the long dining table.

"Mike? Did you need me?"

Mike waved her over. "Aye, if you would, Sarah."

She walked to them, noting that Shaun looked like he hadn't slept. She'd made that assessment at breakfast too but the fact that he'd drunk three cups of tea and eaten all his pancakes had pushed the observation from her mind.

"Hello, Mr. Morrison," she said.

"Missus Donovan," he said glumly.

"I hope we can come to a happy understanding," she said, her eyes on Mike for a hint of how things were going.

"I've merely asked your husband how he'd feel if *he'd* been tricked out of his home and then asked to offer trust to the blackguards who'd done it."

"And I've answered him," Mike said tersely, "with the fact that it hardly matters now."

Sarah looked at Shaun. "Do you need more time to think about it?"

"And in the meantime I'll be locked up in me room?"

"You can understand how we'd need to do that until we're sure of you," Sarah said. "We'd prefer not to, of course."

"It's the victor's lament, is it not?" Shaun said sarcastically. *"We don't want to rape and pillage your village, but there you are."*

"Sure nobody's saying anything about rape," Mike growled. "Or fecking pillaging."

"Look, Shaun," Sarah said. "You need more time. That's clear. You're right. We're the victors. That's a fact. You don't like it. I don't blame you. Take all the time you need." She stepped away to allow him passage.

He hesitated as if surprised she wouldn't try harder to talk him into it.

"And I'm to be locked up again?"

"Of course," Sarah said with some impatience.

He jumped to his feet and Sarah saw Mike's hand flex near his gun holster but Shaun turned on his heel and stomped to the door. A second later, Tommy peered into the room.

"Take him back and lock him up," Mike said. "Give me a few minutes before sending the next one in." Tommy nodded and withdrew.

Sarah turned to Mike. "It's just going to take time."

"You know he was running a fecking prostitution ring in here."

Sarah frowned. "Hardly a prostitution ring. Wasn't it just trading sex for goods whenever travelers showed up?"

"Oh, is that all right then, Sarah?" Mike ran a hand through his hair. "*And* he's carrying on with all the women. A fecking polygamist, he is."

"You don't know that."

"Fiona says she's sure of it and Fiona is an amazing judge of human nature."

"That's called gossip. Did you ask him?"

"No, but if he is, he'll need to stop."

"Your way or the highway?"

He gave her a look of incredulity. "A community can't survive with that sort of thing going on, Sarah. Surely you know that."

"I don't know *what* I know except we have to get Shaun to agree to be a part of our group. Have you asked yourself what you'll do if he won't?"

"He'll have to leave," he said firmly.

"Let's work to see that doesn't happen."

Suddenly the door pushed open and Sophia ran inside.

"Mike! Sarah! Come quick!" Through the open door Sarah could hear the sounds of screaming coming from somewhere in the castle.

23.

So much for all the idea that everyone was getting along.

Sarah watched Tommy pull Nuala off the woman, Saoirse. The air in the room was electric. Sarah felt her adrenalin pumping.

Was everyone in the whole damn castle just itching for a fight?

"What happened?" Mike said. "Who started this?"

Saoirse was sitting on the hard stones of the hallway flood. Her lip was bloody. Nuala shrugged off Tommy's restraining hand. Her youngest boy, Damian, stood beside her with eyes wide with fear and a puddle of urine beneath him.

"That bitch was dragging me Damian off," Nuala said, pointing at Saoirse. "I heard his screams, didn't I?"

Shaun was next to Mike in a second and pulling his sister to her feet.

"Lies!" Saoirse shrieked. "The little bastard attacked me as I was coming down the hall."

"Hush, Saoirse," Shaun said. His face was white and his lips were pressed into a tense line. He turned to face Mike and Nuala. "This is a misunderstanding."

Mike looked at the trembling child and at Nuala's face flushed with fury. One thing he knew about Nuala was that she wasn't impetuous. If she attacked Saoirse, it was for good reason.

"A misunderstanding, how?" Mike said, narrowing his eyes at Saoirse. The woman was making a big show of dusting off her jeans and sweatshirt and glaring at Nuala.

"He was giving me the evil eye!" Saoirse said as she pointed at Damian.

"Saoirse, shut up!" Shaun said in exasperation.

"Take the lad away, Nuala," Mike said. "No sense in him being subjected to any more of this bullshite." When Nuala started to speak, Mike held up his hand. "She'll be punished proper, Nuala. I promise ye."

With a last scowl at Saoirse, Nuala took Damian's hand and retreated down the hallway.

"Punished?" Shaun said. "For what? I told you, it was a misunderstanding."

Mike turned to him, a vein pulsing in his forehead.

"She attempted to harm one of the children," Mike said. "That's not allowed."

"What are you talking about?" Shaun looked at the castle women as if to appeal to them. His mother, Beryl—Saoirse's mother—stood silently and watched.

"My sister has...she suffers from mental troubles," he said.

"Feck you, Shaun!" Saoirse said, shoving her brother hard on the shoulder. "The little brat gived me the evil eye!"

Mike turned to her. "And what was your remedy for this offense? Were you going to strangle the lad? Toss him off the parapet? What?"

"Don't answer that!" Shaun said to his sister. He turned to Mike. "Look, I'm sorry this happened but she's not responsible for her actions."

"In my castle she is." Mike said.

Shaun gaped at him. "You can't punish a mentally challenged—"

"She's not mentally challenged. You said *troubled*."

"There's no difference."

"Aye, there is. Unless you're telling me your sister cannot be held accountable for her actions?"

Sarah read Shaun's face as if his thoughts were spelled out in neon. If he said she was accountable, she'd be punished. If he said she wasn't, she'd be expelled. He licked his lips.

"You have no right to dictate about anything," Shaun said.

"That's where you're wrong," Mike said. "I have the right to keep peace among my people. I'll punish any who threaten that peace."

"*We* are not your people!"

Uh-oh, Sarah thought. *Wrong thing to say.* She saw the tic relax over Mike's eye and then disappear altogether.

"It's true that neither you nor your sister has yet sworn allegiance to me or my lot," Mike said. "In my mind that makes you outsiders."

The word *outsiders* inched up Sarah's spine like a dripping piece of ice.

Outsider meant outside the castle.

"You wouldn't dare," Shaun said. "It's snowing! We have no shelter!"

"Aye, but ye do have a choice."

Shaun looked at Saoirse whose lip was curled. He glanced at the other women, including his mother, each of whom dropped their eyes to the floor.

"Swear allegiance or get out," Mike said.

"Feck you!" Saoirse snarled.

"Aye. That's one," Mike said calmly.

"You can't throw her out," Shaun said.

"All she has to do is swear allegiance—and accept her punishment for attacking one of the children."

"Feck you!" Saoirse said again. "Come on, Shaun. Let's bugger out of here. We don't need this lot."

Shaun—his mouth open in disbelief—turned to watch Saoirse walk down the hall pushing through the two lines of women as she went.

******

Sarah stared at Mike's retreating back as he and two of the compound men escorted Shaun and Saoirse to the front of castle. The snow was still coming down. They were literally being thrown out with only the coats on their backs.

Sarah ran after him and grabbed his arm.

"Mike, this is insane," she said breathlessly.

He turned toward Gavin and Terry and gestured that they were to carry on without him. All of the women, compound and castle alike, followed in a long solemn line to the front gate.

"Take a moment and get a grip. You can't send them out there."

"That's exactly what I can do, Sarah," Mike said tightly. "And you of all people should know that." He pulled her into an empty room off the hall.

"You want safety?" he said, leaning down so his nose was inches from hers. "You ruin me life for weeks—nay *months*—about staying safe and then you'd row with me when I'm trying to do just that?"

"This is draconian!"

"No, it's medieval. There's a difference. Medieval measures worked then. They'll work now."

"Really? What's next? Ear cropping? The stocks? Public whipping?"

"What would you suggest, Sarah? When laws are broken? We live in the Dark Ages again."

"Only if we decide to! We're civilized!"

"I can hardly dock her pay! Will ye wait until it's Siobhan who's hurt next time? We need laws and laws mean consequences."

"Why is it always you laying down these laws? Can't we have a different dialogue than always *your* way?"

"No, Sarah, we can't and thank you for your support. This is a fecking thankless shite of a job and I'd gladly go back to 2012 and my motorized fishing launch—"

"Back before you met me, you mean."

"Don't be putting words in me mouth." His eyes glittered meaningfully. "Or maybe I mean ideas in me head."

She knew she'd never seen him this angry with her. That had to mean he wasn't comfortable with throwing Shaun and Saoirse out but he felt backed into a corner.

"Look, Mike," she said, forcing her voice to sound calm and reasonable. "You can't throw them out in the snow."

"They had a choice."

"*Do it my way or freeze to death* is no choice!"

"We have to have laws! People have to obey them!"

"*Your* laws! Obedience to *you*! I don't care if we do live in a castle, you don't get to be king!"

Mike's face hardened and he straightened up.

"I'm done trying to make you understand," he said.

"Oh? Thinking about tossing me out too, are you?" She crossed her arms and glared at him.

He turned and left without responding. Sarah stood in the empty room listening to the pounding of her heart. *What has happened to him? Who has he become?*

The ice-cold sliver of fear that had lived in her heart ever since Siobhan was born and John had gotten on that helicopter pierced her lungs until she found herself fighting for her next breath.

24.

The morning mist didn't dissipate as Hurley had come to expect it to. It was nearly midday and still it looked like he was leading a phantom army through a fog of gloom. It was so bitter and damp riding on these high pastures that Hurley's chest rumbled with a nasty cold.

But neither the mist nor the nagging wheezing in his chest could dampen his excitement.

Today was the day.

He imagined how they must appear to anyone watching them approach—especially in the fog. He imagined how they would appear to Donovan—an avenging army materializing from the mists of hell.

Hurley smiled thinly, his army marching solemnly in two defined columns around him. Never complaining, never flagging in their forward march to their goal. To their Commander's goal.

He caught sight of a flash of color and he saw that one of his Centurions was wearing the dead gypsy girl's bandana. Hurly frowned. The man was technically out of uniform and Hurley knew he should reprimand him but he hesitated. It was a trophy from a kill and he could see the value of that.

There would be many more such trophies today. The thought triggered a buzz of excitement in his chest that ended in a fiery coughing fit. He hated demonstrating weakness in front of the men. Cursed the fecking Irish weather that made him look—even for a moment—less than he was. By the end of the day he would show his men without any doubt exactly how strong their leader was.

The rain picked up, sluicing a cold gust of air down his collar that made him shiver.

If on the other hand, he thought sourly while his frustration curdled in his empty stomach as he rode in the downpour, they *didn't* make it to the convent today, he would kill Chezzie in the slowest possible way he could think of.

If they didn't make it to the convent today they would be forced to kill and eat the pony that they'd taken when they'd captured the girls and their wagon. A flush of annoyance crept over him at the thought of the debacle the night before with the girls. For a moment, with everything seeming to go seriously sideways, it had almost felt like things had gotten out of control.

But by the morning, the marching lines were as straight as if nothing had happened. And while it was true that one of his brave Centurions had a broken jaw from his attempt to bed the gypsy and they'd ended up losing both girls as a result, they did at least gain the pony and cart. He glanced at the man wearing the bandana around his neck.

Let the crows feed on the girls' bodies in the ditch and in the woods. There was no doubt they would have been more trouble alive than they were worth.

An hour later, the rain slowed to a gentle but constant sprinkle. Even in the cold Hurley's wet saddle pad steamed from the heat of his horse. The marching men had stopped. Hurley pressed his heels into his horse's flanks and rode to the head of the column. Chezzie stood in a ditch off the main road as if attempting to slip into the woods. As Hurley approached, he saw the prisoner was still bound and tied by a long rope to his handler, but pointing to something in the woods.

The young Centurion holding the prisoner's rope turned and snapped to attention at Hurley's approach.

"Commander, sir," he said. "The prisoner has found the opening to the path through the woods."

Hurley glanced at Chezzie who stood with shoulders slumped and his eyes on the ground as though fully expecting to be shot where he stood now that his usefulness was over. The sight nearly made Hurley smile.

He twisted in his saddle and motioned for the two columns to enter the woods.

"Single file," he shouted.

He pulled his horse back to let the men go before him, congratulating himself on his self-control by not racing ahead of them. He caught the eye of the prisoner's guard. It appeared Chezzie wasn't the only one wondering if the end of the line had arrived for the prisoner.

Hurley shook his head and watched the guard turn and drag Chezzie down the path into the woods.

Plenty of time to tie up that loose end, Hurly thought. *Especially if this proves to be the wrong path. Would hate to repay the man with a quick death when leading us a merry chase requires so much more.*

He patted the neck of his horse and cleared the rumbling in his chest with a vociferous hacking before hocking up noisily onto the ground. He wiped his mouth with the back of his hand and watched his men become swallowed up by the mist and the woods. His heart was racing with expectation and excitement.

Two more miles by woodland trail.

They would arrive at the hidden convent within the hour.

Susan Kiernan-Lewis

25.

Mike sat his horse and felt the cold invade his heavy wool coat until it reached his bones. It had been five days since he'd exiled Shaun and Saoirse Morrison. During that time, he and the other men had settled the pair in an abandoned cottage and stocked them with fresh game. Someone—usually Gavin or Tommy—dropped by at least once a day to deliver fresh bread and check on them.

Some exile.

Except for the lack of security, Mike thought the pair had a pretty decent set up.

Five days, he thought to himself, since the two left and the tension in the castle had significantly lessened. Even Shaun's own mother was happier than Mike had seen her.

The woman Ava—whom Mike suspected was Shaun's common law wife—said she had never seen Beryl as happy as when she was talking with Gavin and Tommy about her beloved castle or giving them tours of the place.

Five days since they'd discovered the garage behind the gift shop break room—complete with nonfunctioning microwave ovens and a refrigerator but also two pre-1985 tractors Mike was sure would operate once they'd fetched petrol from the old compound.

Five days since they'd found another room crammed to the ceiling with an inventory of antique cross bows and assorted implements of torture.

Five days since Sarah had said more than a few words to him.

No matter how he tried to tell her that Shaun and Saoirse were happier where they were—that the whole castle was happier with them where they were—she only saw Mike as a tyrannical bastard determined to have his own way.

Deciding to give up his search for game for today, he turned his horse back toward the castle. Normally he would let the lads do all the hunting but he had needed to be out of the castle this morning. He needed the exercise and the fresh air. For a castle as big as Herndon was, it was surprisingly small quarters when you shared it with a woman who hated your guts.

Was he wrong to have thrown them out? *Is it true I'm not able to see any way but me own?* Was Sarah right that he had let his temper make the decision before his reason had had a chance to catch up? And if it was true, could he reverse it now? *Ride over to Shaun's and tell him all is forgiven, he can come back inside?*

Mike shivered and loosened the reins. The horse knew his way back to the castle stables and the warm mash that would be waiting for him there.

****

Fiona stood next to Declan where he sat on the stone bench in the interior castle courtyard. She would have loved to have taken him to the front catwalk but he wasn't ready for climbing yet. He wasn't even ready for stairs yet.

"How do ye feel?" she asked.

"For the millionth time," he responded with a fond smile, "I'm grand."

She'd tucked a wool rug over his knees and while she knew he appreciated the warmth, she also knew he was aware of how much of an invalid it made him look.

Call a spade...

It was a cold day but with no sign of rain or snow and every reason to believe the sun might shine for a few minutes though the clouds. Fiona hated that Declan had to be cooped up in that clinic. His wound had healed with no infection, thanks to Sarah's antibiotics, but he wasn't getting stronger.

They were all at the limit of their medical knowledge. For whatever reason, his recovery had stalled.

Catriona and Hannah, two women who had been in the rape camp with Fiona, emerged from the large stone archway opposite the courtyard. Both carried long bows in their arms and quivers full of arrows on their backs.

Fiona waved to them as they went to the lawn of the castle interior. Mike had set up targets there for them.

"They look like warrior princesses," Declan said softly.

Fiona turned to look at him. "Aye, they do," she said. "Mike asked for volunteers for short bows and nearly all the women volunteered."

"Odd, that," he said as if to himself.

Fiona watched him and wondered what belabored reasoning was going on behind that face. He struggled so much with the simplest mental actions these days. And even more now that his body had betrayed him as well.

"It's a blessing," she said. "Because we need the lads for work the women can't do like blacksmithing and plumbing."

Declan turned to look at her, his face impassive.

"We're having to redo the toilets," Fiona explained. "It's a lot of digging." She laughed. "When given the choice between digging a new dunny or learning to shoot a bow and arrow, every woman in the castle reached for a bow." She laughed again but Declan just watched her blankly.

He's never coming back to me, she thought. *That's the truth of it. Ciara will never know her real da and I'll never see but glimpses of the man I fell in love with.*

She reached over and took his hand. It was cold. She blinked back fierce tears. She still had him alive in front of her. She had his handsome face and the firm comfort of his touch. And that was something.

A sound from the gate tower made both her and Declan look in that direction. They'd only been in the castle less than a week but already there were defensive systems in place. She watched as Kevin waved to someone outside the castle—most likely Mike—and then give the signal to Terry who, along with his wife Jill, manipulated the pulleys to lift the portcullis and lower the drawbridge.

Fiona always found this moment chilling. After all, they were only truly vulnerable at the moment when the door was open and anyone and anything could get in. She found herself holding her breath until Mike trotted his horse through the gate and Terry labored to raise the drawbridge again.

"Impressive," Declan murmured.

She looked at him with surprise to see he was watching the whole procedure.

"Mike is having the lads add sharpened stakes to the moat," she said. "In addition to getting the moat filled up again. There'll be no one can get to us then."

"Not like before," Declan said with eyes glazed and fixed on some unseen point on the horizon.

"No," Fiona said, her voice choking on the tears she refused to let fall. "Never again like before."

******

The sight of the convent emerged from the profusion of vines and tree branches like a hidden Shangri-La. Even from the interior of the woods, Hurley could see the flat grey stone peeking out with the late afternoon sun illuminating its surface with gold and red.

If he were a religious man, he'd have to say it was a transformative moment.

But he wasn't.

Or a patient one.

The minute Hurley knew they were really on the right path, he put his horse into a trot in the tight confines of the woodland path and pushed to the head of the column. The path was just wide enough for one man on horseback or a steady single file line of one hundred armed men.

He was the first to see it as he burst out of the woods and into the clearing. In front of the medieval stone nunnery, two figures dressed in black looked up from where they worked in the garden.

Hurley tamped down the desire to laugh out loud with pure joy. He took a long controlling breath to steady his mounting exultation, then raised his rifle and shot both women where they stood.

Susan Kiernan-Lewis

26.

It wasn't possible to believe.

Of every conceivable scenario that Hurley had run through his mind in the days it took to travel to the convent —and there had been hundreds, from being given false information from the captive to taking twice as long to find the convent—it had never once occurred to him that he would arrive and *Donovan wouldn't be there*.

He clenched his jaw and stood in the small convent chapel and stared through the plain glass window to the garden area outside.

His men were bivouacked in the garden and frontcourt where they were trampling and uprooting plants in order to pound in tent stakes. As Hurley stared out the window, he watched the sun drop away outside like a blood red ball drenching the sky with gore before snuffing itself out. It was quiet outside, which surprised him. He'd made it clear to Brady that the men had the run of the place—and that included rape of the conquered.

Perversely, the men appeared to be in the process of building cook fires and settling in for the night.

True, the women were all old but Hurley hadn't thought that would be an issue. They were human, after all.

Clearly the Centurions were reacting to the fact that these women were nuns, Hurley thought as he snorted in impatience. *Good Irish lads, Roman Catholic, most of them if anything at all*. And even if they'd had no religious upbringing at all—more likely—they'd all seen enough movies to get the idea that nuns were sacred.

How can you believe that if you don't believe in God?

Clearly, he didn't know his men as well as he thought he did. Instead of angering him, which was his initial reaction, Hurley decided to be grateful for the opportunity that revealed the fact to him.

Because now he could deal with it.

The slaying of the two nuns in the garden should have sufficed to inform the head nun that he must be dealt with seriously. His dossier of intent, he thought with a smile.

She sat now, her back board-straight in the front row of the pew facing the altar. She wasn't unattractive and not all that old but Hurley felt no desire to take her.

"Where is Donovan?" he asked for the third time, not bothering to remove his gaze from the quiet activity outside the chapel window.

"I will not tell you." She spoke calmly. Her tone enraged him. *How can she not be quaking in her chair? Does she think she's untouchable? The bodies of two of her black crows lie in full view from this window!*

He looked at her and felt the fury build in his chest.

"Camp Prefect!" he called out. The chapel door swung open and Brady stuck his head in the room, his eyes going first to the nun before looking at his commander.

"Yes Commander."

"Bring in the first one." He glanced at the head nun and had the satisfaction of seeing her tense.

A plump elderly nun was pushed through the door. Brady stood behind her, his hand on her elbow. Hurley saw the women's necklace prominently on her full bosom—a wooden cross that she clutched with one hand.

"What is your name?" Hurley asked pleasantly. Unlike his own lieutenant, the woman did not look at the head nun before answering. Hurley snorted in disgust. It seemed she was intent on demonstrating that she answered to a higher authority.

"My name is Sister Ambrose," she said, her voice low but wavering. She was nervous. She was afraid.

"Tell me, Sister Ambrose, where is the man Donovan?" Hurley asked.

"I do not know."

Hurley stood up and watched both nuns stiffen at the same time.

As well they might.

He walked to where Sister Ambrose stood and turned and smiled at the head nun...

...before driving his fist into Sister Ambrose's stomach.

The nun gasped and bent over, holding her belly but Hurley grabbed her headpiece to jerk her face up. It came off in his hand, revealing a gray haired matron.

"Hold her!" he barked at Brady. The Prefect came up behind the sister and pinned her arms back.

Hurley looked at the head nun. Her eyes bulged wide with fear and horror.

"Someone needs to tell me where Donovan is," he said to her. Before she could speak, he smashed his fist into Sister Ambrose's face. He saw the head nun jump to her feet and he bellowed, "Sit back down!"

She hesitated, her eyes not on him but on the woman sagging in Brady's hands.

Hurley pulled out his handgun and held it to the head of the moaning, barely conscious woman in Brady's arms.

Before he could ask the head nun again, a sound of crashing wood came from the hallway behind Brady. The door swung open and a man filled the entranceway, his eyes going to Hurley and his gun and then to the head nun.

"Who the feck are you?" Hurley snarled.

"Mac, no!" the head nun said.

"*Mac*, is it?" Hurley said correcting his aim to the head nun. "So you're the one Donovan spared before he hung my brother. Is that right?"

The man in the doorway stepped into the room and Hurley pulled back the hammer on the gun he was aiming at the head nun.

"Not another step," Hurley said. "Or I kill her. Brady, bring Chezzie in here."

Brady dropped the nun he was holding and exited the room.

"Do you know who I am?" Hurley asked Mac.

"I don't give a shite," Mac said, his eyes on the head nun. "What do you want with us?"

"I want to know why Michael Donovan let you live. I want to know why he murdered my brother. I want to know where Donovan is right now."

"Feck you."

He noticed a silent communication between the man and the nun and felt a wave of fury race through him. *The bastard was asking her something and the head bitch was answering!*

The door swung open wider and the cretin Chezzie was ushered into the room.

"I'm...I'm sorry, Mother," Chezzie blurted out immediately. "I didn't mean to. I'm so sorry." He began to weep.

"Shirrup!" Hurley barked. He was tempted to just shoot the wanker where he stood. "Answer me! Is this the one who was shown mercy while my brother was not?"

"Your brother was a murdering rapist," Mac said. "He didn't deserve the dignity of the trial he got."

"Shut up!" Hurley screamed, now pointing his gun at Mac.

"I'm sorry, Mac," Chezzie sobbed. "I didn't know what else to do."

"We forgive you, Chezzie," the head nun said. "This is not your fault."

Screaming in rage, Hurley turned his gun on Chezzie. "Shut up! Shut up! Shut up!" he screamed, shooting Chezzie four times in the chest. The man's body jerked as each round hit. The head nun screamed.

Hurley turned the gun on her but addressed Mac, "Tell me where the feck Donovan is or I swear—"

Mac lunged across the room at him. He grabbed Hurley by the shoulders just as Hurley jammed the gun barrel into the man's stomach.

"Mac, no!" the head nun said.

Hurley pulled the trigger and felt the roar of the shot reverberate throughout his own body.

The nun ran to them still locked together and put her hands on Mac's arm as if to lead him away. But there would be no leading now.

Mac slumped to his knees, his head lolling to the side, dead before he hit the floor.

Hurley staggered backward until he hit the edge of the altar. His hands were shaking. He hadn't expected the bastard to go for him. Brady stood in the doorway, his gun in his hand, looking from his leader to the nun now on her knees on the floor.

"You have nothing to bargain with," the nun said, her voice ragged with pain as she touched Mac's bloody head. "You have nothing I want."

"Not even your life? Or the life of your people? I will kill every woman here one by one. I will burn this piece of shite convent down to the bare rocks."

She gazed serenely up at him. "And I will pray for you from the other side."

Hurley stared at her upturned face with frustration and building fury.

Another soldier appeared in the door.

"Commander!" he said. "We've found one who'll talk."

Hurley turned to see one of his soldiers prodding another nun into the room. She was elderly, her facial features sharp and bony. Her eyes went first to the nun's body on the floor, and then to Chezzie's and finally to Mac's. An involuntary groan escaped her.

"Sister Mary," the head nun said, shaking her head.

Keeping his eyes on the woman in the doorway, Hurley lifted his gun and pointed it at the head nun's head where she knelt on the floor.

"Tell me or she dies."

"*No*, Sister!" the head nun said more firmly.

Sister Mary eyes filled with tears.

"They went to Henredon Castle," she said.

******

An hour later Hurley stood at the verge of the woods until the very last Centurion had passed him. The sun had dropped and they would spend the night marching. Even if time wasn't crucial—*and it was*—he wouldn't have allowed his men to spend the night on the convent grounds. There was something about the place that unsettled them. They were hardened professional soldiers who would mindlessly obey his every order—as they'd proven in the last hour and many times before. But there was something about the convent and its occupants that shook them.

There would come a time when he would help them in the confusion they seemed to feel toward God or religion.

But now was not the time. Not when every minute counted. Not when they were so close to their goal.

Henredon Castle wasn't an hour away from Hurley's boyhood village of Ardara. Like every other school child in the area Hurley had been to the castle many times.

Having to wait for his revenge churned in his stomach like a festering poison. He told himself it would make the final justice all the sweeter. But right now the waiting felt like a corn snake trying to choke down a too large rat.

The heat from the burning buildings behind him warmed his back. Stepping into the cold interior of the woods after his Centurions felt wrong. He and his men should be rewarded for their efforts in their quest and yet it felt as if they were stepping *away* from warmth and comfort, away from the light.

Very strange.

He twisted in his saddle to look back at the convent. Every building was on fire, including the little picket fence that surrounded the garden. He could just see the stark silhouettes of the three heads perched on staffs jammed into the ground by the front door of the convent.

The criminal Mac.

The informant Chezzie.

The cowardly Centurion who had hesitated to accept the honor of lighting the torch to the place.

He swung his horse's head away from the convent.

They would reach the castle in five days.

Three if they pushed.

Susan Kiernan-Lewis

27.

Shaun looked around his new home. The fridge and cookstove—both useless—took up a third of the kitchen. The table and chairs had long been stolen and fed to some campfire somewhere, probably soon after the first EMP had gone off.

He would have liked a fireplace but he wasn't in the mood to go scouring the countryside looking for a better place. Besides, this cottage was close to the castle. It made it more convenient for the daily castle handouts he and Saoirse had become accustomed to in the last two weeks.

He sat on an upturned tree stump in front of the cottage and felt the sun's rays on his back through his jacket. Saoirse had had plenty to complain about, of course—not the least of which was the "charity" being forced on them by Donovan.

Is there something wrong with me that his handouts don't bother me?

Like so much in life, the things he resisted or dreaded the most...became his greatest gifts.

He glanced around the frontcourt of the cottage to catch a glimpse of his sister. She was usually talking so he didn't normally need to try to find her. He grimaced. *Did I say talking? Make that shrieking, complaining, and snarling at varying volume levels.*

He sighed and looked at the animal trap at his feet. Its teeth were stained rust brown with evidence of its last use. Donovan had brought it the day before.

Something about *feed a man a fish or teach him to fish. Bugger.* He supposed he was going to have to learn how to use the damn thing and hope it didn't take his arm off at the elbow in the process. He would need to break down and ask Donovan how to set it but he wasn't ready just yet to further embarrass himself in front of the man.

I still have some pride.

Besides, Donovan said he'd bring a couple of rabbits today. There was no hurry on the whole trapping thing.

He spotted Saoirse coming from the woods where she was doing God knows what. His heart felt heavy when he saw her. All his life he'd done his best to watch out for her —or watch out for whatever unlucky soul got in her way. Now that he thought about it, that was how he became master of Henredon. Well, that and the fact that it was where his mother had worked for fifteen years. But after so many years of carrying the weight of Saoirse's special needs on his shoulders, it felt like a natural progression to care for the rest of them too.

In a flash, a vision of Ava filled his mind. Beautiful, sweet Ava. Shaun was under no illusions there. If it hadn't been for the Crisis, he'd never have had a chance with her. First, because she went to university and he only aspired to. Second, because she was beautiful and in love with her husband, Danny. Poor lad. He'd had an "accident" early on and widowed Ava leaving her with little Keeva. Shaun hadn't known Danny well but he couldn't say he'd been sad to see him go.

Especially not since…well, no use thinking of that. The fact that Ava had turned to Shaun—and his bed—after Danny died was all that mattered.

"Has the bastard shown up yet?" Saoirse said, tromping heavily over to where Shaun sat. She was filthy, her hair a rats nest and her face streaked with dirt.

Whatever was she up to in there?

"Not yet."

"He's later and later. Pretty soon he'll stop coming."

"Maybe."

"If you're thinking I'll change me mind and accept whatever fiendish punishment he has in store for me—"

"No, Saoirse. I'm not thinking that."

"Good. Because I'd rather die of starvation or be torn apart by wild animals."

"I know. You've mentioned that." *Nearly every day since we came to live here.*

"It makes me want to rip her face off with me bare hands just thinking of her in there all warm of a night, laughing at us, eating hot soup…"

Shaun frowned. "Who are you talking about?"

Saoirse made a face to indicate her astonishment at his stupidity.

"That bitch Nuala, of course. It's because of her and that brat of hers that we're here."

"It's not really," he said but he knew it was an argument he'd never win. Just like every other dispute he'd ever had with Saoirse.

"Bollocks!" she said. "And you know we *have* to get back inside, Shaun. You *know* that."

"I don't know, Saoirse," he said tiredly. "What's the worse that could happen if we don't? We die of starvation, as ye say?" He nudged the trap at his feet and then jumped when it made a pinging noise. "We'll master this bastard and Bob's your uncle."

"The feck he is," she said as she turned to go into the cottage.

He was grateful when she left. Not that she'd stay inside long once Donovan showed up but he appreciated whatever brief moments of peace she gave him.

The quiet of the countryside was truly astounding. Living in the castle he'd never noticed it before. He'd spent some time looking at the stars from the catwalk and he often enjoyed an evening walk around the courtyard of an evening. But the sounds of the castle—women laughing, talking, children crying—always obliterated the perfect stillness of the countryside.

It was true that it was harder living here outside the castle walls. Even with Donovan providing them with food, he and Saoirse still had to work for every drink of water and every moment of warmth or comfort. And there was never a feeling of safety. Not even for a second.

So how was it that while he was always in a constant state of exhaustion and insecurity, he'd never felt better? He shook his head with wonder. There could be no doubt it had to do with the sudden removal of responsibility for the care of the others.

For the first time in a long time, he didn't have the weight of the world on his shoulders.

Let Donovan have the worry and stress of feeding all those people and of arbitrating their petty dramas—especially a community of all women. Let him listen to their complaints and their ungrateful whining.

If Shaun had known two weeks ago when Donovan was pressing him so hard to *pledge his allegiance* that he'd feel this way he'd have signed up in blood on the spot.

A crash from inside the cottage reminded him of why that could never have happened.

No matter how he felt or what he wanted, he'd *always* have Saoirse to take care of.

As for their mother, well, Beryl was a born teacher with a brand new audience. He had no doubt she was fine and perhaps some day they'd all be together again. But meanwhile someone had to look out for Saoirse.

He spotted Donovan coming over the rise of the adjacent pasture. Even from this distance he could see the bulging saddlebags on either side of him.

The last time Donovan came he'd brought cornbread—compliments of his American wife. It had a very strange texture and was unlike anything Shaun had ever tasted.

Shaun hoped he brought more today.

******

The afternoon sun had disappeared behind a bank of clouds by the time Mike left Shaun and Saoirse. He felt a little less guilty about leaving them today because he knew it was only a matter of time before he'd bring them back to the castle. He wondered, was it his own stubbornness that hadn't done it before now?

If you asked Sarah, she'd say yes.

The cottage was less than an hour's walk from the castle through the western woods and across two pastures. Mike had been relieved to find a place so near. Other houses had either burned to the ground or been trashed so thoroughly they were uninhabitable. Even so, the same trip to the cottage from the castle took nearly as long on horseback as on foot because there was no bridle trail through the dense woods.

Halfway into his visit today, as he was asking Shaun about his system for castle garbage removal, his crazy sister had joined them. As she'd only ever cursed Mike before, he'd found himself thinking this was a step in the right direction.

Until she squatted on the trap at Mike's feet and urinated.

Shaun pulled her away and Mike began to see the kind of stress the man was under trying to control his sister. Sarah was right about that, too. The girl wasn't mentally right and as much as Mike dreaded bringing her craziness back inside the castle, she couldn't be left out here with winter coming on.

Would Shaun come back? Would he accept Mike as leader of the castle?

Mike's horse picked its way across the pasture.

He would if he had any brains at all. That man no more knew how to set a trap than organize a rocket to orbit the moon.

Twenty minutes later, as Mike turned down the main road leading to the castle a long curl of smoke was visible high above its walls. Mike imagined all the fireplaces were likely going strong—as cold as it was—and if Gav and Tommy were as lucky hunting today as they'd been lately, all the roasting spits were probably full too. His mouth watered at the thought.

Even Sarah had relented on her *my husband is dead to me* game plan as far as he could tell and had actually smiled at one of his jokes at dinner the night before.

He wasn't sure what it would take to make her feel truly safe—probably a lot of time passing without major mishaps... *and somehow getting John back home again.*

Thinking of major mishaps, his thoughts strayed to Declan. He would always blame himself for what happened to him. He knew in his heart that he'd really lost his best friend the day he and Sarah rode away looking for the lads last fall. It had taken a long year and a longer list of tragedies, but it was clear that Declan would never be himself again. The weight of Mike's sorrow—for himself and for Fiona—pressed heavily on him.

He concentrated on the castle ahead, growing closer with every step. Even his horse seemed to hurry. Some day there would be a mill inside the castle, a storage bursting with food, and even a school for the bairns. It would be a life of ease and enjoyment, of plenty and fellowship. Already he and Terry were mapping out the planting of the garden for next spring.

Yes, it would be a good life—and, please God, the one he'd promised Sarah on their wedding day.

He saw the lanterns moving along the top of the castle wall as he approached. He hadn't expected to visit as long as he had with Shaun. As Mike watched the drawbridge descend, he caught glimpses of activity within. One woman —it looked like Catriona—was hurrying across the courtyard with a child and a long bow in her arms.

The image made Mike smile. The smell of dinner cooking filled the courtyard as he entered. A child's wail in one of the distant rooms made him think how it would likely be another five years at least before the sounds of crying babies didn't herald him home. He handed the reins to Gavin and dismounted.

"Made it back before dark," Gavin said.

"Just."

"How were the Morrisons, then?"

"I'm thinking about inviting them back in."

Gavin nodded. "Sarah said you would."

"Did she now? Where is she?"

But Gavin was already leading the horse back toward the stables.

After washing up, Mike made his way to the great hall. The fact that it had been a tourist attraction before the bomb meant this room above all others was well furnished.

The reproduction tapestries hanging on the stone walls muffled the sounds of voices and utensils clinking against metal plates.

He stopped to kiss Siobhan who was in Jill Donaghue's arms tonight. Nuala sat with her two boys and her baby. She looked tired. Probably rethinking the sanity of volunteering to head the nursery, he thought with a grin.

Gavin and Tommy sat with Beryl between them, their heads together. Sophia and little Maggie sat beside Gavin.

As Mike walked by he stopped to kiss his granddaughter and gave Sophia a reassuring squeeze before taking his place at the head of the table.

Sarah was at her place at the head of the table waiting for him and, saints be praised, she was smiling. While she hadn't moved out of their rooms during their recent cold war, she might as well have for all the contact they had. Tonight, however, it looked like detente was in the offing.

"Good visit?" she asked.

"You were right. They need to come back."

She raised her eyebrows. He dropped a hand to her knee.

"And yourself?" he asked.

"Pretty good. I spent time with Ava today. She was a paralegal before the bomb."

"Now *that's* useful," he said. One of the men handed him a platter of roasted rabbit.

"I would've thought *you'd* think so what with your fascination with laws."

He glanced at her and saw she was teasing. It had been so long he almost didn't recognize it. He put down the platter and turned in his chair to face her.

"Can I trouble you for a private conversation tonight, Sarah," he said lightly, "where every ear in the castle can't hear?"

"Secrets?"

"Just those between a man and his wife."

She turned away to accept a bowl of mashed potatoes but the hint of a smile was on her lips.

"I think that can be arranged," she said.

That night, after his rounds to make sure the sentries were awake and ready, Mike hurried to their bedroom. Siobhan was asleep and Sarah waited for him in bed. Without a word, she folded back the covers in invitation.

He dropped his clothes on the slate floor and slid into the warm bed bringing her into his arms where they held and forgave each other—again—for everything said and unsaid between them in the last several days.

The moon through the south window illuminated her face and he truly couldn't remember seeing anything as beautiful.

"I promise you're safe now, Sarah. Nobody can get in. Not without a tank or a flame thrower—and neither of those things exist in our world any more."

"I'm sorry to be such a basket case."

"Sure you're not. Not-at all."

"I'm so tired of worrying about everything, Mike. I know once I have John back, I'll be fine. Promise me we'll get him back."

"I do promise ye, Sarah. And once he *is* back, he'll not be allowed to leave. *Ever*."

Sarah laughed and Mike felt the tension in his shoulders ease at the sound of it.

"Well," she said with a yawn, "at least not until all the lights turn back on in the western hemisphere. I don't think that's too much for a mother to ask."

****

Sometime early the next morning, deep in the thickest cloud of sleep, the smell crept under the heavy wooden door of their room and slid up the sides of the bed. It stole into the room like an invisible phantasm until Mike awoke, choking and coughing.

Smoke…

28.

Sarah was on her feet with the baby in her arms before Mike was even out of bed. The smoke was thick on the floor and pooled around their feet.

"Mike!" she screamed. He leapt to his feet, looking confused in his half awake state.

"Outside!" he rasped as he snatched up his clothes from the floor. "Go to the courtyard!"

Barefoot and wearing only her nightgown, Sarah dashed out of the room and ran to the end of the stone hall. From the window at the end of the hall she could see a bonfire in the courtyard jumping and cavorting across the dry winter grass of the dead lawn.

Mike put a hand on her arm as he passed.

"The water supply is outside," he said. "Go to the courtyard. Tell everyone to—"

"Mike, the fire is *in* the courtyard," she said. Siobhan was now screaming in her arms. But he was gone.

Sarah ran down the icy stone steps of the stairwell. As soon as she came into the courtyard, the thick smoke billowed like dense fog. The moon had escaped behind the clouds and only darkness, panic and fear swirled in the courtyard.

She heard screams and could see shapes and figures as people ran out of the other building wings into the open.

"Sarah! Sarah!"

"I'm here, Sophia!" Sarah cried, trying to move in her direction. The screams of the children and the babies interlaced with the hoarse voices of the men around the stone perimeter.

How could there be so much smoke? Is it possible this is an accident?

Sarah had no time to think more. She saw Jill—clutching her little boy's hand—step out of the cloud of smoke, her face streaked with soot.

"They've got the gate open!" Jill shouted as she passed. Behind her streamed a hoard of panicked women in their nightclothes. Sarah tried to see beyond the fire in the courtyard. She remembered a large holly bush had been there. Was that what was burning? How? There'd been no lightning last night.

"Sarah!" Sophia gasped as she grabbed Sarah's arm. "We must leave! The castle is burning!"

Sarah turned toward the gate and watched the people stream out.

"It can't burn," she said as Sophia ran toward the gate. "It's made of stone."

No one heard her. Mike was shouting orders over the din. A sudden fear seized Sarah that she and Siobhan would be the only ones left inside.

She turned and ran toward the gate, feeling the warmth of the inferno recede behind her as she ran onto the wooden slats of the drawbridge and out into the coldest, darkest part of the night. She stumbled half way across and tightened her hold on Siobhan as she fell to one knee.

The sounds of horses screaming behind her shot a bolt of terror straight through Sarah.

Someone was stampeding the horses out of their stable. She looked frantically to both sides of the bridge for escape. The jump would kill her and Siobhan both.

The pounding of the horses' hooves moved through the ground like an earthquake.

Suddenly a hand from behind her pulled her to her feet. It was one of the castle women, her eyes narrowed with effort and determination. She dragged Sarah forward where they both jumped to the other side seconds before the horses crashed down the bridge and into the front court outside the castle.

"Thank you," Sarah gasped, her knees turning to jelly.

The woman didn't answer but ran to join her group. Outside was pandemonium. Most of the people had gathered in the castle parking lot. They stared at the castle as if expecting it to burst into flames.

Why did we run? Sarah thought as she stumbled to the parking lot to join the others. *The castle can't burn. Why did we panic?*

She saw Sophia next to several of the other compound women. Sarah went to her.

"Where's Gavin?" Sarah asked.

"With Mike," Sophia said. She shivered in her nightgown and held Maggie tightly.

Sarah looked around. "Fiona?" she said. "And Declan?"

"Nuala has Ciara," Sophia said. "I don't know where Fiona is."

Sarah looked back at the castle. The fireball seeming to grow larger behind the stark outline of the arched front gateway.

"I think I do," she said grimly.

****

Fiona sat in the stone room of the clinic and watched the people pour out of the castle. She glanced over at Declan, who was still asleep on his cot. There had been no point in moving him. All she could really do besides abandon him, which she wouldn't do, was prepare herself for whatever was coming.

A fire in a stone castle? She looked around and noted the wooden door, the wooden tables, and the beds with their wooden frames. But everything else was stone.

She didn't fear fire. Not like she had at the compound where a few well placed matches could—and did—see the end to everything they'd built.

No, fire wasn't their enemy at Henredon. Although why the fools running for their lives outside didn't know that— especially the castle women—she couldn't imagine.

She bent over Declan's bed and listened to his breathing and the rattling deep in his chest. She had no idea if that was good or bad. He seemed to be in no pain and when he was awake, he was usually lucid. Well, as lucid as he'd been since the attack last year.

A wave of sadness washed over Fiona at the memory of that attack. So much lost in one afternoon.

She went to the window. While the clinic didn't look out directly over the front, it did give a clear view of the northern woods beyond the gardens and the closest castle pasture. She knew that's where Mike and the men would go. The spring was there. They had yet to devise a way to have ready access to water within the castle. It seemed the group who'd lived here before hadn't even tried. They just went out every couple of weeks and dragged in enough to last them awhile.

As Fiona stood by the window, she could see the men around the spring. The clouds shifted and a strong shaft of moonlight lit up the ground below, allowing her to easily pick out Mike. She watched him gesture to the others and then saw the horses appear at a run. She caught her breath. They were panicked and one of them was headed straight up the main road like the devil was on his tail. Fortunately, the other three horses didn't follow.

What a nightmare. She turned to look at Declan and then back at the activity of the men at the spring. Mike was standing with his back to the castle, his hands on his hips.

That was when she saw the figure materialize from behind a bush. The glint of moonlight on the knife he held sent a shiver of terror though Fiona and she felt the scream building in her throat.

He was running straight for Mike.

******

Shaun couldn't believe his eyes. As the sky lightened with the coming morning, a fire raged in the interior of the castle and everybody was outside in the parking lot either screaming or running around acting crazy.

Saoirse, what have you done? he thought as he ran into the crowd of screaming people.

He'd awakened not an hour ago to an unusually quiet cottage and the dead certainty that Saoirse was gone. He didn't know when but *where* was a given.

Whatever reason Saoirse had, Shaun knew it could only mean disaster—not only to the people in the castle but for him and Saoirse too. If only the stupid girl could see that.

He hurried as fast as he could through the woods, stumbling over branches and into invisible holes and praying he didn't run into any wild animals. He had to get to Saoirse before she got to the castle. Why hadn't he listened to her threats? Why hadn't he paid more attention to her ranting?

He knew she hated Donovan and all his people. She'd told him she wanted them dead every minute of every day of the past two weeks.

Saoirse, what have you done?

Shaun knew his sister well enough to know she'd go for Donovan first—and then probably Nuala or even her child.

He ran into the crowd and two of the castle women grabbed him by the arm and squealed their pleasure at seeing him. He shook them off and, in his determination to find Saoirse, even pushed past Beryl as she attempted to throw her arms around him.

"Where's Donovan?" he shouted to two compound women standing with their babies in their arms in front of the castle. One of them pointed in the direction of the spring.

Of course. He would be getting water to put out the fire. Shaun started to run around the drawbridge when a woman stepped into his path.

Ava. With the moonlight lighting up the planes of her beautiful face and her hair wild around her shoulders, she looked like a goddess. Shaun hesitated and for one mad moment wondered if this was all a dream. A dream capped off by the appearance of this radiant creature who was the embodiment of all feminine beauty in the world.

"Shaun," she said.

He touched her arm and the dream dissolved in his hands. Keeva was standing by her mother and slapped his hand away. The child screwed up her face to cry.

"What did you do?" Ava said, her face angry and accusing.

******

Mike thought he heard a scream somehow above the cacophony that was the soundtrack for the night. Why that one scream—faint and familiar—would make him turn when all the others were just so much background noise, he would never know. He felt a hard thud against his shoulder and then a jolting pain that shot immediately into his brain.

He twisted around to see Saoirse pulling her arm back with a butcher knife in her grip. His hand shot out and grabbed her wrist as she brought her arm down for another stab. She was strong and Mike was off balance. He felt her wrist slipping out of his grip.

"You're dead!" she screamed, her eyes on his in loathing.

He stumbled backward, only having time to hold up both hands as he fell. He watched the knife rise up again and then a dark shadow shot across Saoirse's face. She yelped and dropped the knife. Gavin appeared beside Saoirse as she collapsed to her knees.

"Ye bastard!" Shaun screamed as he pushed past Gavin. "She's mentally challenged! She's not responsible for herself!"

Gavin picked up the knife and pointed it at Shaun.

"The blood on this blade is me da's," he said roughly.

Shaun looked at Mike, still lying on his back. Saoirse tried to stand but Shaun forced her to stay on her knees.

"He broke me nose!" she howled.

"Shut up, Saoirse," Shaun said.

Sarah ran up and knelt by Mike.

Mike didn't feel any pain but he knew he'd been stabbed. Was he in shock? He looked at Sarah and tried to speak.

"How bad is it, Sarah?" Gavin asked, his tone frantic.

"I don't know. Mike? How do you feel?" She had her hands under his shirt. Her probing was gentle but she needn't have bothered. If he could speak, he'd tell her that. He didn't feel any pain. He didn't feel anything.

"Not good," Sarah said shakily, drawing back a hand coated with his blood.

"It's not her fault," Shaun said, now trying to pull Saoirse to her feet and away from the group.

"Well, I'd like to know whose fault it is!" Gavin said hotly. "Da! Are ye okay, Da?"

Mike wanted to tell him not to worry but just now he was extremely tired. It occurred to him that this could all be sorted out after a wee kip. He smiled at Sarah and felt sorry for her look of concern. But she'd know soon enough that everything was fine.

And isn't that all she really needs? To know that we'll all be well and fine?

"Mike, don't close your eyes," she said urgently. "Mike, sweetheart. Stay with me, please."

But she didn't understand how tired he was and how fine they would all be. He heard the group moving around and now Saoirse was crying and Sophia too it sounded like.

Silly lasses.

The last thing he heard before he felt himself drifting away to a quiet place of no noise and infinite peace was somebody shouting.

They were yelling something that sounded like, "There's people coming!"

29.

Shaun pushed through the gathered crowd. He ran to the front of the castle and stared down the main drive. For a moment he couldn't believe what he was seeing. It looked like an army of people.

An army of people heading straight for the castle.

His bowels turned to ice as he saw the speed they were making. Gavin ran to his side.

"Who are they?" Gavin asked, panting.

"Everybody inside the castle!" Shaun screamed, waving his hands. He turned to Gavin. "They'll be here in minutes. Get everyone inside, *now!*"

Shaun ran back to where Saoirse was sitting next to Donovan. He scanned the crowd for any sign of Ava or Beryl and was relieved to see them both in the crowd of people moving back across the drawbridge.

Just not fast enough.

"What's the matter?" Sarah asked, still kneeling by Donovan. "Who is it?"

"I have no idea," Shaun said, jerking Saoirse to her feet and pushing her toward the castle. "But they'll be here in a few minutes."

Sarah jumped up. The color was gone from her cheeks as she looked in the direction of the main road.

Gavin pulled his father to a sitting position. Donovan didn't look good. His wife had staunched the blood in his wound, but he was close to being unconscious. Shaun grabbed Donovan's arm and helped Gavin get him to his feet.

"Get everyone inside," he said to Gavin as Sarah took Gavin's place at Donovan's side. "Stand by to raise the drawbridge *fast*. Get the other men, lad. Hurry!"

Shaun could hear the sounds of the oncoming army now. He staggered forward with Donovan leaning heavily on him, forcing Sarah to run beside them to catch up. He didn't have enough breath to urge her to hurry. It was all he could do to prod Donovan into moving his legs. He was a big man and right now a very slow one.

"Mike, hurry!" Sarah said desperately. "You need to move your feet!"

The first few soldiers of the army came into view just as Shaun touched foot on the edge of the drawbridge. If he stumbled now, both he and Donovan would end up in the moat. He tried to blot out the sounds of men's voices shouting behind him.

Come on ye, bastard, he mentally urged Donovan. *Move yer fecking feet!*

He could see Gavin and two other men were standing inside the gate tower on the other side of the portcullis, their hands on the pulley switches—waiting for the three of them to get inside before they attempted to raise the draw bridge.

"Stop 'em!" a voice shouted from behind them. "Get 'em before they get the drawbridge up!"

A bullet whistled by his ear and then another, both thudding into the stonewall of the castle gatehouse. Screams came from inside the castle. Shaun's legs burned as the terror propelled him across the drawbridge, dragging Donovan and his wife with him. He felt the bridge go up while they were still on it. The three men inside the castle were straining to raise it even as the portcullis descended like a giant's gaping mandible. The sickening sounds of bullets hitting the wooden drawbridge as it raised was like the soundtrack out of a horror movie.

He fell to his knees and watched Sarah crawl under the quickly closing portcullis. Hands reached out to grab Donovan and drag him inside. Shaun felt strong hands grabbing him, too, his legs finally useless, as they pulled him under the descending jaws of the portcullis. He lay trembling on the ground, his stomach roiling as he tried not to vomit. People were taking Donovan and Sarah away. He heard the groans of three men as they hauled the drawbridge up and cranked it solidly in place with the windlass—and with it the frustrated howls and gunfire of the men outside muted to a distant din.

A hand reached down to touch his shoulder and when he looked up, he saw that it was Ava. She patted his shoulder as if to say, *spit-spat! On your feet, soldier!*

If he hadn't been so weak with the distinct possibility that he was about to lose bladder control he would have laughed.

Fifteen minutes after they'd gotten the drawbridge up, Shaun climbed to the top flight of the northern crenellated tower with Gavin, Tommy and Terry. From here they could look out without danger of presenting themselves as easy targets.

What he saw took his breath away. The castle parking lot and gardens and the main drive itself for at least a quarter of a mile in every direction was covered with men moving about and setting up camp. Already a large tent had been erected front and center to the castle entrance.

He'd never been more right when he called them an army. Almost all of the men below wore at least a part of the telltale colors of the Irish National Army. They were soldiers.

Tommy turned to his father, Terry. "Da! It's them! It's the same ones as before!"

Shaun was bewildered. "You know them?"

Terry pointed at the man in the tent. The one wearing his full uniform and watching them through binoculars.

"Aye. The bastard there in front. He's the same one came for us last winter."

"*Came* for you?"

"Took us to the Dublin work camp," Terry said, licking his lips in agitation. "Took us to hell, he did. Took the women and children, too. Although their hell was at a different address."

"Da, he's the one shot Declan," Tommy said. "And Kendra."

"Jaysus God," Shaun said in a voice low with awe and dread. "What are they doing *here*?"

******

Hurley gave orders for his men to set up his tent. Seeing the castle inhabitants scurry back into the castle like so many terrified cockroaches had been a much anticipated and delightful pleasure of what was to come.

What hadn't been so delightful was the fact that his men hadn't been able to kill even a single man before the buggers escaped inside.

He would have a word with Brady about that. It was *his* responsibility to ensure that the men were sufficiently trained. And motivated. An army needed its chain of command. After all, Hurley couldn't do it all. But weak links in that chain made for disrespect among the ranks. Changes might need to be made.

Hurley stood in the late afternoon light and stared up at the castle. He imagined what terror the people inside must be feeling.

As well they should.

He had waited a long time for this and he wouldn't be rushed. He'd have his revenge—in due time. And every person in that castle who thought they were safe right now...who thought they could escape Centurion Commander Padraig Hurley...every single man, woman and child would soon know the full measure of the terror that they could only imagine right now.

Susan Kiernan-Lewis

30.

Mike opened his eyes and for a moment couldn't figure out where he was. He looked to his right to see Declan sound asleep in the bed next to his. Before he could twist his head around to look to the left, he was seized with a searing flash of pain. He took a long breath and froze all movement.

"Don't, Mike!" Sarah said. "You'll start it bleeding again."

He turned his head enough to see her standing next to his bed with her hands on his shoulder as she tried to push him back onto the bed.

"What happened?" he croaked. His shoulder was throbbing, the pain diminishing by the second but not fast enough.

"Saoirse stabbed you."

He had an image of Saoirse with knife in hand and her face twisted in a grimace of hatred.

"It wasn't a direct hit," Sarah said. "And Gavin got to you before she could try again."

He remembered now. Fiona's scream. He groaned and eased back on the bed.

"And we have company outside," Sarah said.

A motion by the stone archway made him turn his head to see Shaun enter the makeshift clinic.

"Good. You're awake," Shaun said. "We have a problem."

Mike sat up and instantly felt a landslide of pain crushing his shoulder.

"Mike, no!" Sarah said as Mike tried to get out of bed.

"Did you dope him?" Shaun asked, coming closer to peer at Mike. "I need him lucid."

"Will someone tell me what's going on?" Mike asked as he winced.

"A group of people is camped out in front of the castle," Sarah said.

Mike blinked and tried to understand what she was saying.

"Who are they?"

"Gavin said they're the same ones cleaned you out before," Shaun said, watching Mike appraisingly. "They're outfitted like they're the Irish fecking army."

"Have you spoken with them?" Mike asked.

"Mike, I'm going to give you something for the pain," Sarah said.

"Nay, Sarah. I need to know what's going on."

Shaun glanced at Declan's bed and then pulled a chair up to Mike's. "I haven't tried to talk to them," he said. "They were shooting at us when we closed the drawbridge so I know they aren't here to help us dig a new well or plant barley."

"They *shot* at us?" Mike rubbed a hand across his face and felt the muscles in his shoulder contract agonizingly when he did. "What's the status now?"

"There are about a hundred of them. Gavin says they've got what sounds like repeating rifles," Shaun said.

"Feck me," Mike swore.

"My sentiments exactly."

Mike looked at him and sighed. "I'm sorry for throwing you and your sister out. I was wrong."

"Thank you."

Mike felt like he'd been run over by a ten-ton lorry. His whole body craved sleep—and painkillers.

"You think they can get in?" Mike asked.

Shaun frowned. "I...no, I don't."

"But what?"

"I don't know how much food we have on hand."

"You're worried about a siege?"

"It's our only real vulnerability. If they're willing to wait."

Sarah spoke up. "We have food to last a week if we're careful."

"Water?"

"Same."

Shaun nodded and got to his feet.

"So I guess we pray they don't have the patience to wait us out."

****

After Shaun left, and after promising Mike she'd wake him if anything happened, Sarah gave Mike something for the pain and to help him sleep.

Everything had happened so fast that she hadn't had a chance to process how she was feeling. On the one hand, her worse fear had definitely come to life. They had sacrificed everything to get to this so-called invulnerable fortress, and now parked on their doorstep was the one thing they were vulnerable to—an army with modern weapons.

On top of that, Mike was out of commission and Sarah wasn't sure she trusted the man who was in charge.

When Fiona came in to spell her before dinnertime, she had Siobhan in her arms.

"She was asking for her Da-Da," Fiona said, handing the child to Sarah.

"Well, she'll have to settle for Number Two," Sarah said, forcing a smile and wondering if it was true children could tell when you were faking it.

"Has Declan awakened?" Fiona asked as she tucked the sheets around her husband and looked into his face.

"No, sorry. Not a peep."

"He sleeps more and more."

"Could be he's sleeping because he's mending," Sarah said.

"Could be."

"What's happening outside?" Sarah had hoped her tone would sound unconcerned but it sounded afraid even to her.

"They can't get in, Sarah," Fiona said.

"If you say so. Any idea how the fire started last night?"

Fiona frowned. "The fire?"

"Don't you think it's wildly coincidental that we all get flushed out of the castle at the very moment Saoirse is waiting for Mike with a butcher knife?"

"Are ye saying *Saoirse* started the fire? From *inside* the castle?" Fiona gave Sarah a look of disbelief.

"So you *do* think it's just a coincidence."

"I don't think anything at-tall, Sarah," Fiona said with frustration. "Except that we might want to handle one problem at a time. Right now Shaun's doing all he can until Mike's on his feet again. He's got men watching the army from all four corners of the castle. And his mother is working with Gavin and Tommy to tell them about whatever defensive capabilities the castle has."

"Pretty helpful to have the castle gift shop manager in here with us."

Fiona gave Sarah a sharp look.

"Something on your mind, Sarah?"

"Just not sure why everyone's trusting these people all of a sudden, that's all."

"What would you have us do? Throw them to the army? We're in this together now."

Sarah turned and looked at Mike. The wound, although painful, wasn't as bad as it could have been. He'd be stiff for a couple of weeks but no major tendons or muscles had been severed as far as she could see.

"You probably saved his life, Fi, when you screamed to him."

"Cor, I thought I'd die when I saw that she-bitch go for him," Fiona said, shaking her head. "Now, *Saoirse* is a worry. I'll say that and no mistake."

"Yeah. You think?"

"Go eat something, Sarah. No sense in staying here. I'll come get you when he wakes again."

Outside the wind had picked up and Sarah was reminded of how quickly the cold came to Ireland in November. She wrapped Siobhan tightly in her blanket and hurried across the courtyard to the wooden door leading to the great hall. She could smell meat roasting and a quick glance up at the sky confirmed that it was coming from the castle chimney. The dark shape of a man walked the catwalk on the front wall of the castle.

Inside the dining hall, most people were finishing up their meal. Sarah found Sophia seated next to Jill and Nuala with babies in their laps, their dinners finished.

"Sarah! How is he?" Nuala asked as Sarah came to join them.

"Sleeping for now." She looked around the dining hall. "Where is Saoirse?"

"Gavin has someone keeping an eye on her," Sophia said as she jostled little Maggie on her knee.

"Does anyone know what's going on outside?" Sarah asked.

"Gavin said they're setting up camp," Sophia said. "They look like they intend to stay a while."

Not good.

"What's our plan, do ye know, Sarah?" Nuala asked. "They can't get in, can they?"

"Sure, no," Jill said. "That's the whole point of our being here! Of course they can't get in. Right, Sarah?"

Oh, why didn't we stay at the convent?

"I think we're safe for now," Sarah said, not feeling at all safe. "Once Mike's better, we'll come up with a plan."

"Shaun has been very helpful," Nuala said, blushing slightly. "He spoke to us at dinner saying it's all under control. He has a very nice way about him."

"Where is he?" Sarah asked, craning her neck to look around the room.

"Out on the watch towers with the men," Sophia said. "He said we're to carry on as normal. Put the little ones to bed and do what we'd normally do."

Yeah, what we'd normally do with a hundred cutthroat professional soldiers camped out on our doorstep.

"Does anybody know what they want?" Jill asked.

"Gavin says they likely want to take the men back to the work mines," Sophia said.

Jill gasped and blanched at her words. Even Nuala looked solemn.

As well they might, Sarah thought.

The last time the men were taken to the mines, the women were taken too.

"Well, they're not getting in," Sarah said firmly. "So it doesn't matter why they're here."

Her words sounded hollow even to her.

"Who's on kitchen duty tonight?" she asked.

"Catriona and me," Sophia said with a sigh. She kissed little Maggie and handed her to Jill.

"I'll help you," Sarah said, "after I take Siobhan to the nursery."

The little group broke up with Sophia walking to the far wall of the dining hall where the kitchen was located and Sarah and the rest going back out the door to the castle interior.

How can we all behave as if nothing's going on? Sarah thought as she stepped outside.

There is an army right outside that door! And the bullets from their guns are still embedded in the drawbridge to prove it!

She must have been holding Siobhan too tightly because the child began to cry and Sarah looked down to soothe her.

Suddenly the dark sky above them exploded into full daylight. Somebody screamed. Sarah fought against a surge of dizziness as the ground tilted beneath her.

The searing flash of the fireball slammed against the stone wall near the door they had just walked through. Showers of sparks and embers rained down on them.

"They're firing on us!" someone screamed.

"A cannon! They have a cannon!"

Sarah ran toward the archway that led to the clinic and Mike. She felt the heat from a falling remnant of another fireball sizzle past her.

Hell itself seemed to have opened up.

****

From where Shaun stood, it looked like a shooting star. It arced gracefully from the base of the castle until it reached its full height over the courtyard. By the time it was falling inside the castle, Shaun was racing down the stone stairwells into the interior.

Already screaming had erupted across the castle in ascending levels of anguish. Even as he ran, Shaun knew the rocket launcher—or whatever it was—couldn't hurt them as long as they stayed out of the courtyard.

Why hadn't he told everyone to stay inside? *What lunatic thinks "Behave as normal" is any kind of defensive strategy?* As he ran, he thought of Ava and wondered if she was still in the dining hall.

He reached the courtyard to see pockets of fire smoldering all over the lawn—as if the fireball had splintered into separate spheres of destruction.

Jaysus! The cow—the one animal they'd kept alive for five fecking years—the one animal they had besides the useless fecking dogs—had been hit with one of the larger chunks of fire. Its carcass lay in a smoking heap directly in front of the first gate to the portcullis.

There was nobody in the courtyard, thank God. And no bodies except for the cow. He ran into the first stairwell and into the hall.

"Everyone stay inside!" he shouted. "Do ye hear me? No one is to go into the courtyard or to the dining hall!"

One of the doors wrenched open and Ava stepped into the hall.

"Ava, lass—"

"Shaun, there are still women in the kitchen," she said.

"I'll get them," he said. "Is my mother with you?"

She nodded.

"Tell her to go to the clinic." He turned and ran back downstairs and across the courtyard. Any moment he expected another fireball to come flying through the air and drop right between his shoulder blades. He ran to the dining hall.

"Oy!" he shouted. "Is anyone in here?"

Sophia and Catriona came running into the dining room from the adjoining kitchen with hands full of dishtowels and eyes wide with fear.

"I need ye to stay here until someone comes for you," he said.

"What's happened? Is anyone hurt? Are they attacking?"

"You'll be fine as long as you stay inside," he said. "I'll send someone for you when it's safe."

They nodded grimly and he bolted back outside.

Was that the first volley? Would there be more? Would they wait until the castle relaxed again? Or would they know that everyone would stay indoors now and further attacks of that kind would be wasted?

Shaun ran back through the exposed courtyard and dashed into the stairwell—the furthest one by the north watchtower.

He glanced up to see one of the compound men, and cursed the fact that they had not decided on a way to signal or communicate. Were the bastards setting up for another onslaught? Once inside, he ran to the clinic on the second floor. Mike was waking but still groggy. His mother was there too with Sarah and Fiona. A fledgling worry throbbed at the base of his skull but he couldn't put a finger on what —among everything else—it could be. All he knew was that something else was wrong and if he could just take a moment to focus his thoughts, he'd probably realize what it was.

He just didn't have that moment right now.

"What do we do now?" Sarah asked. She was holding her daughter in her arms and looked like she was going to break down any minute.

He turned to his mother.

"How do we secure the castle?" he asked bluntly. "Tell me what we should do."

Beryl stared at him with her mouth open and then glanced at the others in the room.

"Shaun," she said in a small voice. "Henredon Castle is a tourist destination. We have no defense against modern weaponry."

"Come on, Mother!" he said, feeling the fury pulse through him. "For years you've been telling me this place is fecking impregnable and now I need to know *how*!"

"It...it *is* impregnable against medieval weapons, Shaun," his mother said, her eyes filling with tears. "But against mortars or...or rocket launchers...be reasonable."

He couldn't believe what he was hearing—and who he was hearing it from. He stared at her as if she had betrayed his entire childhood.

"You are telling me that all this time it was rubbish?" he screamed. "We are fecking defenseless?"

Mike swung his feet from the bed and sat on its edge, but his shoulders flinched with the pain.

"Steady on," Mike said. "How were any of us to know we'd have to deal with assault rifles and flying incendiary bombs?"

As soon as Mike spoke, the undeveloped thought that had been nagging at Shaun jumped to the forefront of his mind like a sledgehammer pounding home.

Where was Saoirse?

****

"Commander, sir!" the private said loudly as he snapped to attention. "Permission to approach!"

Hurley frowned and looked at Brady who stood beside him in the tent. The Prefect widened his eyes as if to say he had no idea what the private wanted. Fury coursed through Hurley.

Did the imbecile know nothing? It was his job to know!

"Enter!" Hurley spat out, his eyes never leaving Brady's. The man had begun to sweat.

The tent flap opened and two soldiers entered with a homely stout woman between them. The fury welled up inside Hurley until he thought he might murder everyone in the tent in the next few minutes.

"I don't care if she shits gold bullion," he snarled at the soldiers as he pulled his gun from his shoulder holster, "how dare you bring her to me?"

"She says she knows a secret way into the castle," one of the soldiers blurted.

Hurley slid his piece back into his holster. An oily smile spread across his face.

"Does she now?"

Susan Kiernan-Lewis

31.

No one slept that night.

Mike's head was pounding and his shoulder was a dull spasm of ongoing pain, but he dragged himself off the bed. Fiona, Beryl and Sarah—holding Siobhan—had spent the night in the clinic. The three women looked at him in surprise as he moved to Declan's bedside. He found the handgun that he had instructed Shaun to place there on the table by the bed.

Satisfied, he turned to face the women, their faces alert and expectant.

"What do we do now?" Beryl asked.

Mike felt sorry for her. It wasn't her fault that the castle wasn't capable of withstanding a twenty-first century assault. She acted like she had let everyone down somehow.

"Will you stay in the clinic and help Fi with Declan?" he asked.

She flushed with relief. "Of course I will."

"Is that Dec's old handgun?" Fiona asked.

"It is. Not that I think you'll need it but I don't know what to expect from today."

He looked at Sarah.

"Will you listen to me and mind what I say, Sarah?" He didn't have the strength to fight his wife *and* the bastards outside.

She hesitated but then nodded.

"Gather the other women and take Siobhan to the nursery. Wait there until this is over."

"Shaun said there are still two women in the kitchen," Sarah said.

"They're safe enough where they are," Mike said. "No sense in crossing the courtyard if we don't have to."

Shaun opened the door and stepped inside.

"Everybody ready?" he asked, his eyes going to his mother first.

"Where are the lads?" Mike asked, wincing in pain but gratified to realize it didn't hurt has bad as it had even minutes before.

"All four men are either on the parapet or patrolling the crenellated towers," Shaun said. "Basically just watching."

"What about the girls and their longbows?" Fiona asked. "They've been practicing for weeks now."

Mike shook his head. "They'll be useless against repeating rifles. I'd rather they stay safe for now."

"How are we for guns and ammunition?" Sarah asked.

"We're fine," he said. They weren't at all fine. There was no way they could go head to head with that lot outside when it came to gun power. He saw the fear in Sarah's eyes and he hated seeing it worse than the pain in his shoulder.

This is exactly what she was afraid would happen.

He glanced at Beryl. "Do we have any kind of weaponry at all in the castle?"

She paused. "There's a trebuchet," she said.

"Isn't that for *taking* a castle?" Shaun said, his frustration pinging off him in waves.

"It's for whatever we can use it for," Mike said. "Get Gavin and Tommy to position it in the courtyard."

"What are you thinking of loading it with?" Shaun said with exasperation. "We're a little short of boiling pitch."

"The fire bomb killed the cow," Sarah said as she gazed in the direction of the courtyard. "It's at least something to throw."

"Dear God," Shaun said. "My life has turned into a Monty Python skit."

Mike grinned and saw that some of the tension had been let out of the room. He sobered and narrowed his eyes at Shaun.

"Where's your sister?" he said. Somehow he couldn't see Saoirse sitting with the rest of the women, knitting and waiting quietly for her fate to be decided by the menfolk.

"Sophia said Gavin had someone watching her," Sarah said.

"Find her."

"Aye," Shaun said, his face flushing. Mike knew the responsibility for his sister must be onerous. But now was not the time for mentally disturbed women to be roaming the castle.

As Mike left the clinic he gave Fiona a reassuring smile and motioned for everyone besides Beryl to leave. A glance out the window told him it was no longer the darkest part of the night. Dawn couldn't be far off.

******

The rest of the early morning was spent positioning the trebuchet in the courtyard and periodically looking down at the army encampment in front of the castle.

Mike placed Terry and Kev on opposite sides of the castle. Kevin watched the oceanside and Terry the front. So far, it appeared that the army was focused on getting a good night's sleep.

That's more than any of us will have, Mike thought tiredly as he braced himself for another wave of pain in his shoulder. Sarah had stitched the gash closed right after he was brought to the clinic. So long as it didn't get infected, it should mend well enough.

The trebuchet was a recent reproduction but it was still a rickety contraption. They quickly rejected the idea of loading up the smoldering, bloody cow carcass, but had little else to toss over the ramparts. Even if they had something to launch, Mike reflected, there was little hope it would do enough damage to warrant the effort.

The only real plan with any chance at all was the one that involved withstanding a siege. Mike felt a wave of hopelessness crash over him. What kind of bad luck was it that they should be attacked before they had a chance to build their stores? Sarah was right. They couldn't last long in a siege. They just weren't ready. It never occurred to him before how passive that kind of battle was. It was almost as bad as hiding and hoping nobody found you.

Almost.

Mike stood by the stone archway that led to the main courtyard and watched the sky begin to lighten. Gavin had rescued the two women from the kitchen—one of them Sophia—and delivered them upstairs to wait with the other women and the sleeping children. He stood now beside Mike and scanned the tops of the castle walls while Tommy knelt by the trebuchet, unable to give up on it. Shaun emerged from the archway on the far side of the castle.

"Did you find her?" Mike asked.

Shaun shook his head. "She's not in the castle," he said.

A shank of ice drilled into Mike's spine. "How is that possible?"

Before Shaun could answer, a voice shouted down to them from the front gate tower.

"Mike!" Terry yelled. "They're calling to us! They're ready to parlay!"

Mike pushed off the stone wall, his excitement building.

"Ask them what they want," he called up.

"Nay, Mike," Terry said, his face streaked with dirt. "The bastard says he'll only talk to Mike Donovan."

Susan Kiernan-Lewis

32.

How does the blackguard know my name?

Mike turned to go into the stairwell before climbing to the top parapet where Terry stood. Unlike where he and Shaun spoke to each other when Mike was on the outside, the parapet afforded a comforting shield against possible gunfire.

"Stay here," he said to Gavin. The lad was right on his heels. Mike winced at the first step up but the question of how the bastard outside knew him combined with his growing belief that the attack might be coming to a head blunted the pain in his shoulder.

Terry met him at the most exposed corner of the catwalk and nodded in the direction of where it was enclosed over the front gate tower.

His initial impulse was to stand unobstructed and deal with their visitors face on. But with so many soldiers and possible points of attack it would be impossible to watch them all. A sniper could too easily pick him off. He slipped into the tower and stepped to the right of the nearest loophole window. Used largely in medieval castles for archers to shoot without being seen, Mike would be able to speak from here without danger of being shot.

"I am Mike Donovan," he bellowed out the window. "Why are you here?" His heart was pounding in his chest. Seeing the army was much worse than hearing about it.

They stretched as far as he could see. It was getting less possible to believe it was all a mistake of some kind.

A large man in full army regalia materialized out of the morning mist and stood in front of the moat staring up at Mike's window. Again, Mike had to force himself not to step forward. *Pride goeth before being shot through the heart,* he reminded himself.

"My name is Centurion Commander Padraig Hurley," he said. "I am here to destroy this castle and all who cower within its walls."

Can't be clearer than that.

"You cannot fight me and win," Hurley said. "But there is another way."

"I'm listening," Mike said.

"My men and I will pack our tents and leave you in peace, not a hair touched on your good people."

"And all we have to do?"

"Not *we*, Donovan. You. All you have to do is come out and face me."

A trickle of fear burned in Mike's stomach.

"Do I know you?" he asked.

"Not at-all."

Mike watched the army begin to move about. He could only imagine how they'd fed themselves on the road. Likely at the expense of anybody they met who had something of value that could be taken from them.

"Do I have your word if I come down you won't try to come in?"

"Aye. I'm a soldier. My business is only with you," Hurley said. "You have ten minutes. If you make us go through the siege, I'll torture everyone inside including the bairns. And you'll be the last to die. Think about it." The man turned and walked into his tent.

I should have given orders to shoot him, Mike realized. *Too late now.*

He glanced at Terry who stood by the back wall staring at Mike. Mike stepped back onto the catwalk over the castle interior. Sarah was there.

"Sarah, I'm nearly sure I asked you to stay with the other women."

"You're not going out there," she said. "That is not happening."

Did he have a choice? Or any time to come up with another plan?

"You heard what the bastard said," Mike said wearily. And in that moment, he had the sickening realization that there was no way out of this. If the maniac on the other side of the wall had a beef with him and was willing to let the castle alone, then that beat sieges or whatever other desperate plan the castle had at the moment.

"You know he intends to kill everyone no matter what you do!" Sarah said.

He put a hand out and drew her to him. She felt thin as her shoulders trembled under his hand.

"We can't withstand them," he said softly.

"You said this castle was impregnable! Why the hell did we march all the way across Ireland?"

"It is. Or it would be. But with fire bomb launchers like the one this morning? Even if they don't batter down the front gate, we'll be starving within two weeks. All they have to do is wait us out."

"Then let them wait! Don't make it easy for them. We're safe in here as long as we don't open that gate. Same as before when *we* were the ones trying to get in."

He took her by the hand and led her down the stairwell to the courtyard interior. Most of the women had gathered there now with their babies in their arms and small children sleepily by their feet.

Sarah shook off his hand. "We'll post a sniper. Next time he shows himself…Bam! Head of the snake. Once we take *him* out the army will leave."

Shaun stood next to Ava as he watched Mike and Sarah emerge from the stairwell.

"Sarah," Mike said helplessly, "we don't have time for that. We have ten minutes."

"You can't go out there!" she said, her eyes wild with horror. Mike turned away. He couldn't bear to see his own fear reflected in her face.

Shaun, his face solemn, took two steps toward him.

"I swear I'll do everything to protect and care for them," he said.

"Mike, no!" But the tears in Sarah's voice told him she knew it was the only way. She was just railing against the unfairness of it.

He turned to Gavin and embraced him. Sophia ran to them with Maggie and he brought her into the hug.

"I love ye both so dearly," he said. "And God willing, I'll see ye again before the day's end." He kissed Sophia's cheek and then the baby's head. They turned away, Sophia openly sobbing.

"We love you, Mike," Nuala said as she brought Siobhan to him.

He nodded and took the baby, then turned and opened his arms to Sarah. She came stiffly to his side as if hypnotized.

"No, Mike," she murmured into his shoulder with the baby between them. "You can't leave me. You swore you never would."

"I need ye to tell Fiona goodbye for me," he said softly. "I pray I see you later…on the other side of…things." He looked at Terry. "Tell 'im I'm coming out." Terry reached out a hand to grip Mike's shoulder and then, with tears in his eyes, turned toward the stairwell.

"Raise the drawbridge," Mike said to Tommy. "Gavin and Kev, stand ready, guns aimed. If it looks like anyone is coming toward the castle while the door is open, shoot to kill." As he looked at Sarah, his eyes softened with how much he loved her and the burning guilt of how he'd let her down.

"I'm sorry," he said and kissed her. Then he turned and straightened his shoulders as the drawbridge began to lower.

****

"It's so quiet, isn't it?" Beryl said as she folded the last of the clean bandages and stacked them on the counter by the window. "I wonder if the blighters outside will give up and go away when they realize how hopeless it is."

"I pray for that," Fiona said as she helped Declan to a sitting position in his bed. He smiled at her weakly but at least seemed to know who she was. "Are ye hungry, Dec?" she asked.

"Aye," he said woozily. "Is Ciara near?"

"Sure, no," Fiona said as she settled next to him with a cup of broth. "She plays all day in the castle nursery."

"She's happy then?"

"As two clams," Fiona said, smiling bravely as she poised a spoon of broth by his lips. "I'll bring her by this evening after dinner. How's that?"

"That's grand," he said wearily and took the broth.

"He's looking much better," Beryl said shyly. "Getting stronger every day, so he is."

"I think so too," Fiona said. And she did. Declan was definitely making progress.

"Where is everyone?" he asked, looking over Fiona's shoulder.

"Working," Fiona said. "Mike was in here a few minutes ago. You slept right through it."

"What happened to him?"

Fiona glanced at Beryl who blushed and looked away. *It must be hell to constantly be apologizing for Saoirse,* Fiona thought. Although it looked as if Beryl had given up on that, allowing Shaun to carry the load of responsibility for his difficult sister.

"Nothing that wasn't easily sorted out with a well placed stitch or two," Fiona said brightly, "and some of Sarah's miracle antibiotics."

Declan gestured to the handgun laying on the side table by a pitcher of water.

"You can never be too safe," Fiona responded cryptically.

"Is there something going on?"

"Nothing to worry about." Fiona caught Beryl's eye again and the older woman shrugged sadly. No sense in upsetting Declan. He could hardly do anything about what was happening.

"I miss being…a part of things," he said wistfully.

"You will be soon enough," Fiona said. "Don't forget there's the castle toilet needs retrenching so you might want to enjoy your time off while you can."

Declan grinned and shook his head at the broth spoon. His smile faded as he regarded Fiona.

"Not what you signed on for," he said.

"Don't be daft."

"I love you, Fi." His eyes filled with tears.

"I love you too," she said, rubbing tears from her own eyes and trying to smile. She noticed Declan was distracted by a movement behind her where Beryl was working. Fiona turned to see what he was looking at and realized that Beryl was standing perfectly still by the supply closet with her face gone bone white.

"What is it, Beryl?" Fiona asked, and stood up. That was when she heard the sound. An indescribable rumbling or vibrating noise was coming from the walls. Fiona felt the tips of her fingers begin to tingle. She watched Beryl's face as the woman stared at the closed door of the closet.

Suddenly, the door burst open. Two men in camouflage filled the entranceway of the closet, their rifles pointing at shoulder height.

Beryl screamed. Instantly a belch of fire erupted from both guns and Beryl staggered backward with a fountain of blood shooting from her chest.

Fiona stared in horror as Beryl fell groaning to the floor. Another gunshot exploded in the air—this one near Fiona's face—and she saw one of the soldiers jerk spasmodically as if yanked by a rope. Blood gushed out of his neck and he dropped his rifle.

Fiona lunged for the dropped gun as more shots shattered the small room.

Susan Kiernan-Lewis

33.

Sarah stood holding Siobhan in her arms as she watched Mike move woodenly across the drawbridge. Her breath was coming in pants and she kept shaking her head.

This can't be happening.

Gavin stood next to her, swearing impotently as he held his rifle to his shoulder, his eye on his father, his finger on the trigger.

It seemed to take hours for Mike to walk the thirty feet across the drawbridge to the waiting army outside. From where she stood, Sarah couldn't see who was waiting for him. She stayed out of Gavin and Tommy's line of fire and prayed it wouldn't come to that.

True to their word, nobody rushed the castle and Kevin began cranking the windlass on the door the second Mike stepped across the moat.

"Terry!" she screamed. "Tell me where he's going!" She looked up but Terry had already run back to the front parapet. Siobhan began to whimper.

Gavin's arms sagged to his side as he held his gun. Sarah knew a part of him was sorry not to have the chance to kill the bastards. She turned and looked past him at the trebuchet in the middle of the courtyard. Tommy was slumped against it despondently.

"We can't just do nothing," she said as she ran to the trebuchet. "We can't just wait for them to kill him."

"You heard them," Tommy said as he shook his head. "It's the price for the rest of us staying safe."

Terry was back on the catwalk. Sarah looked up.

"If you get a clear shot—" she said, but Terry was already shaking his head.

"The bugger never came out of the tent and now Mike's gone inside," he said.

Sarah felt a knot of despair hardening in her stomach.

"Keep watching!" she said before turning back to Tommy.

"Do we really have *nothing*? Nothing but a damn *cow* to throw at them? Are we really this helpless?"

"We needed more time to prepare," Tommy said sadly. "We just *got* here."

Sophia and Gavin joined them. Sophia cried quietly as she held baby Maggie wrapped in a sling across her chest.

"I'm so sorry, Sarah," Sophia said. "Mike is the bravest man in all of—"

Sarah felt the anger she'd tried to repress for so long build inside her. She saw Shaun herding the other women back inside the castle wing. They trudged toward the stairwell in acceptance and dejection. *Everyone was writing Mike off and already moving on! How had this happened?*

"How did Saoirse get inside the castle?" she shouted.

"What...?" Shaun looked helplessly at the group and then walked over to them. "What are you talking about?"

"Saoirse was inside the castle last night," Sarah said. "How did she get in?"

Gavin leaned toward Shaun menacingly. "She came through the secret tunnel, didn't she?"

"I knew it!" Sarah said.

"All right, yes, but I never thought she'd come here," Shaun said, rubbing the perspiration from his face.

"Mrs. Morrison told me and Tommy about the tunnel —" Gavin began.

Muffled sounds of gunfire filled the air—five shots like a series of cars backfiring one right after another. Sarah felt her knees weaken.

Mike...

But Shaun and Gavin were already running to the first stairwell leading to the castle interior.

"It's coming from the clinic!" Shaun yelled.

******

The second soldier in the mouth of the tunnel seized up and clawed at the jamb of the door. The wound pulsated over his right eyebrow. Behind him, Fiona saw two more soldiers, their faces peering out of the darkness.

Without even looking she knew Declan had found the gun Mike left. She glanced at Beryl and knew there was nothing she could do for her. If the poor woman wasn't dead yet she soon would be.

There were no more gunshots.

Fiona snapped her head toward Declan's bed to see he was slumped backward on the bed, his gun hanging loosely from his fingers. A cold gush of dread rippled up her spine.

Noooooooo....

A moan from the dying soldier in the doorway forced Fiona's attention back to the tunnel opening. She leveled the gun in her hands at the two soldiers in the tunnel.

"Drop your rifles!" she shouted but her words sounded like a terrified squeak. The two soldiers didn't move.

"I need help!" Fiona screamed. Out of the corner of her eye she saw the puddle of blood beneath Beryl grow wider and wider. "Help me! Somebody!" Her hands felt slick with sweat as she threaded her finger around the trigger. She felt the gun shake in her hands.

Please, let him not be hurt too badly. I beg you, please...

Suddenly the door behind Fiona flew open. Her shoulders sagged with relief and she dropped the rifle to the floor and ran to Declan.

Gavin aimed his rifle at the two soldiers.

"Drop yer weapons and get the feck outta there now!" he bellowed.

The two soldiers slid their rifles across the floor and stepped over the bodies of their two comrades.

Shaun moaned and ran to his mother's body.

Fiona hovered over Declan, her hands hesitant to touch him. He lay on his bed, a bullet hole between his closed eyes.

Fiona uttered an unearthly howl of pain as she leaned over his body and snaked her arms around his bleeding head.

"No, no, no," she moaned, sobbing, her hysteria rising higher and higher to echo off the tall stone walls.

******

Mike wasn't surprised to see Hurley hadn't come out to greet him. While Mike hadn't specifically given orders to shoot him, it was understandable that the bastard might think he had. Three soldiers—their faces implacable—stood in front of the large tent that faced the castle. They carried guns but didn't aim them at him.

Why would they? It was obvious he was readily sacrificing himself.

The wound in his shoulder throbbed deeply which kept him alert against the waning affects of last night's pain medicine.

One of the soldiers stepped forward and patted Mike down. The other two shouldered their guns and glanced up at the parapet of the castle to see that they were being watched.

"The commander will see you," one of the soldiers said, jerking his head to indicate the tent entrance.

Mike was grateful he wasn't bound. At least not yet. If there was a hope in hell of getting out of all this, he'd need the use of his hands. Although even if he were to somehow overpower Hurley—with a fecking army on the threshold of the castle and no food inside to last a siege—it still wouldn't do any good in the long run.

He forced himself not to look up at the castle. He knew Sarah wasn't watching and if Gavin was, it would only weaken Mike to see him. As a soldier held the tent flap open for Mike, he walked in. There was a lantern in the center of the tent. Two of the tent corners were reinforced with transparent plastic panels that allowed the weak Irish sunlight to light the interior.

Hurley sat at a small table. He was a large man with a bulbous bald head. His well-developed arms strained inside his uniform sleeves. He appeared to be studying a map. He did not look up when Mike entered.

An unearthly fury seemed to erupt from the soles of Mike's feet that blotted out the fear, the unknown, and the gnawing agony in his shoulder.

"Is it possible I might know *now* why you are here?" Mike asked, biting off every word. One of the soldiers moved to flank him. He grabbed Mike by his shoulder. Mike flinched as the pain came alive in explosions of agony. The soldier twisted him around and jammed the butt of his rifle into Mike's stomach.

Mike gasped and sagged to his knees. The pain radiated out from his solar plexus setting his entire torso on fire.

"Get out," Hurley said. For a mad moment, Mike thought he was talking to *him*.

He grasped the side of the table and hauled himself to his feet. The soldiers disappeared out the door of the tent behind him.

"I apologize for that," Hurley said. "But my men know I don't like being interrupted at my work."

Mike would have answered if he'd had enough breath but he was still recovering from the gut-wrenching pain of the stomach blow.

He tore his eyes away from Hurley's face and looked around the tent to see if there was something—anything— that might help him fight this lunatic. So far, all he saw was a military nutcase with an agenda—and a hundred soldiers backing him up.

"You're wondering how we know each other," Hurley said, watching Mike slowly straighten as he recovered from the attack. "I visited you once before. At your fort."

So it's true. He's the bastard who attacked the compound last fall. The bastard who killed Kendra. And shot Declan.

"But where our connection truly matters," Hurley said, "is through my brother, Bill."

Mike shook his head as if to clear it.

"I'm told you hung him this last summer."

Ever since the lights were snuffed out by the first EMP five years ago Mike had killed more men than he could count. But Bill Hurley's death at his hands was one he had absolutely no qualms about. The man was an evil murdering rapist and while Mike had taken no pleasure in hanging him, he hadn't had any trouble sleeping afterward either.

How did Hurley know about it?

"Your brother was tried for the rape and murder of two of our compound women."

"So you don't deny you hung him from a tree outside the convent of Our Lady of Perpetual Sorrow?"

An ice pick of fear drilled its way into Mike's gut.

Hurley knew the name of the nunnery. A convent so secret even the Vatican had forgotten about it. A convent impossible to find unless you'd been there before.

Chezzie.

Chezzie was the only one who knew what happened that day. Chezzie was the only one who had left.

And the only one who knew the way back.

"I can see by your face that you figured it out on your own," Hurley said. "The man you let get away came back to seal all your fates. Poignant, really. And a valuable lesson to go forward with: never leave any unfinished business. That is if you had a life ahead of you to go forward with. Which you don't."

Mike forced himself not to react. He urgently needed to move, to cross his arms, to shift his feet—to control the welling sense of futility and dread building in his chest.

"You're probably wondering why I would believe the word of a liar and a felon. That's a reasonable question," Hurley said. "And it is why I had the charge confirmed by people I'm sure even you would acknowledge as credible."

Mike felt a hopeless shudder wrack his body.

The bastard's been to the convent.

"I'm not at all surprised the convent stayed untouched for so long. It wasn't at all easy to find." Hurley eyes were alive with menace. "Let's just say it's not *untouched* any longer."

Mike's heart was pounding at the thought of the kind of evil he must be in the presence of. "If you hurt them—"

Hurley lunged to his feet and knocked the table from between them, his face red with rage, spittle flinging from his lips.

"My men raped and killed every person at the convent for the crime *you* committed against my brother," Hurley said as he closed and unclosed his fists and a violent tic pulsated over his left eye. "You think you are the law? This country is *mine*. Justice and punishment are mine. And mine alone."

Mike no longer heard him. His mind was buzzing with the inability to think beyond the man's words of death and torture.

It can't be true. Even if the bastard was sick enough to do it, surely his men... Flashes of enraged, destroying armies down through history—the Celts and Vikings rampaging and killing, destroying and massacring innocent villagers—formed in Mike's mind.

His stomach roiled as his mind tried to reject the image of the convent being assaulted in this way. *Mother Angelina...the good sisters...no, it couldn't be...*

"I have waited two weeks to bring you to justice, Donovan," Hurley hissed as he drew a long knife from his belt sheath. "Two weeks to see you pay for your crimes."

Mike took a step backward. His hands were untied. He had that. Hurley was big but they were evenly matched for size. If he could somehow get the knife...hold it to his throat...use him to get past the guards without being shot in the back. If he could just...

Hurley coughed a hacking explosion that sounded like a frontal attack in its own right. The coughing seemed to escalate his fury. His face was swollen red with fury.

"Guards!" Hurley shrieked. "Secure the prisoner!"

Mike turned as two soldiers filled the door of the tent. He lashed out with a fist and felt them grab his arms. Stepping into the two soldiers, Mike tucked his head and drove it into the face of the nearest man, hearing the cartilage crunch like the sound of dry twigs underfoot.

An explosive pressure erupted behind his ear and Mike felt darkness pressing in as they dragged him to the ground. Two more soldiers stepped into the tent. One pulled a short cord of rope from his belt.

Mike saw stars glittering in his periphery as he tried to clear his vision.

"Tie him," Hurley snarled, now standing next to Mike. The soldiers tugged Mike's hands behind him and cinched them tight. Hurley grabbed Mike by the hair and jerked his head back, exposing his throat.

"We're going to hang you in full view of the castle. But first you'll accommodate me for the wait I endured by allowing your friends to hear your screams." He jabbed the tip of the knife into Mike's throat. The two soldiers stood behind Mike, holding him firmly. The pressure of the knife pressing into him erupted into an electric jolt as the blade pierced his skin. Mike gasped.

"And we won't finish until the whole world is screaming along with you."

Susan Kiernan-Lewis

34.

"Take him outside," Hurley said.

"Yes, Commander!" The four soldiers grabbed Mike by the upper arms and dragged him to the tent door. He fought to walk even if it meant he was walking to his own execution. The agony from the men yanking on his shoulder worked to clear his head.

Was there a chance? A ghost of a chance? Mike didn't look at the castle. He found himself praying Gavin wasn't watching.

Once outside, the two soldiers on either side of him hesitated.

"Tell your people if anyone fires down on us," Hurley said, "we'll kill everyone inside starting with the children."

"I have no control over what they do," Mike said, his jaws clenched tight.

"Bring him over here," Hurley said stifling another cough as he walked closely behind one of his soldiers, clearly using him as a shield against a direct shot from the castle.

The group walked twenty yards away from the front of the castle and behind a large yew tree.

Mike saw Hurley's problem and likely his soldiers did too. The bastard couldn't torture him in full view of the castle without risking being shot. But torturing him behind a bush took all the fun out of it.

Fighting to ignore the shooting pain in his shoulder and his throat, Mike pulled himself to his full height.

"Need a fecking battalion to hold me, do ye?" Mike said, his voice acidic with disdain.

"I don't need to prove meself to my men," Hurley said hotly. But he coughed again.

"Are you sure?" Mike looked at the soldier holding him. "Because from where I'm standing—"

"Shirrup, you!" the soldier—a young man in his early twenties—said to Mike, but he stole a look at Hurley.

And Hurley saw it.

"Go! All of ye!" Hurley yelled. "I'll deal with him. Anderson, you and McKinney get ready to enter the castle through the tunnel. Everyone else group at the tower gate and prepare to enter. Tell them we'll dig Donovan's heart out with a rusty spoon if they don't raise the drawbridge." He looked at Mike as he spoke and his eyes were flat.

"Yes, Commander. And once we're inside?"

Mike held Hurley's eyes and steeled himself. It didn't matter what the bastard said, he told himself. *They're just words. They're just words.*

"Kill everyone."

Mike swallowed down the bile of his fury and his fear. He pulled against his bonds behind his back but they were solid. He felt them cut into his wrists as he twisted against them.

Because he knew he couldn't wait for Hurley to make the first move, Mike was on the balls of his feet when the ground suddenly vibrated and pushed him skyward. The roar of the explosion was delayed by seconds and then obliterated by screams by the time Mike found himself splayed across a hawthorn bush ten feet from where he'd been standing. With his hands still behind him, he'd had nothing to protect his face and the sharp and jagged branches jabbed into his neck and chest.

Mike pushed himself onto his feet. The bush was coated in globs of red gore. He looked down to see where the wound was and instead saw the decapitated head of the young soldier who'd just told him to shut up.

Smoke and fire erupted in tall columns where Hurley's tent had been. A bomb? It was definitely an explosion. But coming from where? Mike saw Hurley sitting on the ground and shaking his head as if in a stupor. But unhurt.

The knife was on the ground.

Mike knew he had only a split-second where Hurley was dazed and unarmed. A moment that wouldn't come again.

He lowered his head and aimed for Hurley as the man attempted to stand. He hit him solidly smashing into the lower half of Hurley's jaw. Hurley went down with a loud thud spitting teeth. Before Mike could kick away the knife, Hurley lunged for him and wrapped his fingers around his neck.

Mike felt the thundering pain in his wounded shoulder like a hundredweight around his neck, pulling him down and smothering him against the iron necklace of Hurley's hands. He twisted his hips to flip the bastard on his back but Hurley unclenched from his neck just long enough to smash his fist into Mike's face.

Fireworks went off inside Mike's head as he absorbed the blow. His hands were trapped under him and behind his back. Hurley hit him again but Mike turned his jaw and the blow slid off his face, catching his nose instead and breaking it.

Hurley straddled him and punched him one fist over the other. The knife had to be under them or next to them. Hurley was too determined to kill him with his bare hands to worry about the knife. Not with a helpless victim under him with hands tied. Mike took two more punishing blows. He tried to move away from the punches but his thinking was getting foggy. The darkness was trying to claim him. He *wanted* the darkness to claim him. He felt the ground with his fingers, his head rocketing sidewise with the viciousness of Hurley's attack.

Mike's fingers found the blade.

Not giving himself time to react to the agony exploding in his face, Mike tightened his grip on the handle of the knife. He slashed at his bonds, feeling his wrists tearing too.

Hurley punched him again, once, twice before Mike raised his chest up and slammed him hard with his head. When Hurley recoiled, jerking backward, Mike whipped his arm out from behind him and stabbed blindly at Hurley's side. He felt the knife go in and then stop as it banged into the resistance of a rib. The man howled and scrambled away from Mike. The cut was bloody but not life-threatening. Hurley held his side and glared at Mike like a wild animal—his eyes darting from left to right as he tried to gauge Mike's movements.

"Brady!" Hurley screamed. "First Prefect! To me, *now*!"

"Everybody's too busy dying, arsehole," Mike said, his mouth full of blood. He let it drip from his lips, afraid to take his eyes off the man in front of him. The fingers holding the knife felt slick. He clutched the knife and got to his feet.

"Brady!" Hurley yelled again. Now his eyes went from Mike's face to the knife.

Somewhere on the other side of the tree at the castle, Mike heard rapid gunfire.

Were the soldiers already inside killing people?

He saw movement over Hurley's head, but forced himself not to take his eyes off him even for a second. More screams pierced the air that was punctuated with gunshots but he didn't dare turn to see what was happening at the castle.

And then he heard Sarah's voice. He knew it wasn't real but in that moment when she came to him inside his head, every fiber and electrical pulse in his body reacted.

He hesitated.

And that was all it took.

Hurley lashed out with a hard kick to his kidneys. The pain ignited in Mike's lower back. He saw the satisfaction in Hurley's eyes as Hurley threw himself at him, hitting Mike full in the chest and knocking the knife out of his hands.

Pinned beneath Hurley, Mike writhed to free himself, groping for the knife on the ground.

Hurley gave a grunt of triumph and held the knife aloft in his fist over Mike's head. His eyes were feverish with intent.

"I execute you in the name of the Imperial Irish Army and the Irish Empire!"

Mike struggled to bring his arms up to protect his throat as Hurley slammed the knife downward.

Susan Kiernan-Lewis

35.

Mike never heard the gunshot that saved his life. He felt the blade fall against his chest as it tumbled from Hurley's fingers.

Followed by Hurley's body.

Brady stood six feet away pointing a pistol at arm's length. He didn't look at Mike. His eyes were solely on his leader. Two soldiers appeared behind him. Over their shoulders Mike caught glimpses of men running, stumbling, falling. The screams and the gunshots filled the air around him but the tree blocked his view of the castle.

Brady lowered his arm and jammed the gun into his shoulder harness. He walked over and tugged Hurley's body off Mike so it lay facedown beside him.

Mike was amazed to see that Brady was really just a kid. He didn't look old enough to be out of school let alone in the army.

"Can you stand up?" Brady asked him.

Mike climbed unsteadily to his feet.

"Anderson! Jamison!" Brady shouted before turning and spitting on Hurley's body. "Grab this piece of shite!"

Brady leaned down to talk to the back of Hurley's head.

"How's the field promotion feel, Commander?" he said with a sneer. "You were in charge and now you're dead." He straightened, keeping his eyes on Hurley as he muttered to himself, "Fecking lunatic parks us out in the open to be picked off one by one."

The two soldiers lifted Hurley's body under the arms. They looked expectantly at Mike.

"After you, squire," Brady said wearily, waving toward the front of the castle. "Your lot will shoot our fecking heads off unless you go out first."

It was then that Mike realized the sounds he was hearing was a steady line of *rifle* fire *coming from the castle.*

The castle was shooting down on the men camped outside the walls with no benefit of cover. He and Hurley had been behind the only protected spot anywhere near the castle.

His heart pounded as he realized what was happening.

Head of the snake. My God, this has Sarah's name written all over it.

He stumbled out from around the tree and raised his hands to the castle.

"Don't shoot!" he called. "They're…they're leaving." He turned to glance at Brady and the young man nodded.

"Aye we fecking are. As long as we can do it without a bullet or a fecking arrow in our backs."

The two soldiers dragged Hurley's corpse to the drawbridge as it was lowering and dropped the body face down in the dirt. Mike looked up to see five figures in silhouette on the parapet—each with a rifle or long bow. One of the figures waved. Gavin.

Mike grinned which made his face ache. His right eye was already swollen shut. He turned to see the drawbridge fully open and Sarah flying across it. Toward him.

"Mike!"

She hit him solidly, nearly knocking him off his feet but then pulled back and began touching his chest, his face, and his neck. She was looking everywhere at once as she gently assessed his wounds. The fear in her face dissolved as she realized what he didn't have the breath to tell her.

He was okay.

With his last ounce of energy, he opened his arms to her and she slipped into them. His battered face was buried in her hair. And when the trembling began she held him like she would never let him go.

Which was just fine with him.

****

Sarah didn't know who was shaking more—her or Mike. As he talked with the tall soldier who walked out with him, she checked him for any injuries and found nothing serious. Forcing herself not to step on the so-called commander's body as she pulled Mike back toward the drawbridge, she signaled to Kevin to get ready to close the drawbridge behind them. She wanted the soldiers to leave immediately. But Mike was already telling the soldier they could take the time they needed to collect their dead and pull down their tents.

She looked up at the parapet and saw the men and women lined up there with bows and arrows and rifles pointed down. She could only imagine what it must have felt like for the soldiers, to be down here—completely vulnerable—while bullets and arrows rained down on them.

As soon as she and Mike were inside the castle, Mike was swarmed by their people who slapped him on the back and embraced him. She could see the pain in Mike's face with every hug, but he was grinning too.

When he finally extricated himself from the crowd to find her again, she stood waiting for him in the courtyard with Nuala and Sophia, who added their hugs and kissed him soundly before scurrying off to the dining hall and the nursery.

Mike eased himself down onto the garden bench that abutted the eastern castle wall. Three women walked past them toward the kitchens to start the afternoon meal.

Just a normal Tuesday afternoon, Sarah thought, *after everyone thought we'd all be dead for Wednesday morning.*

The men resumed their positions on the parapet and watched as the army packed up and broke down their tents.

"Tell me," Mike asked.

"Tommy had some C-4," Sarah said as she slipped a hand inside Mike's shirt. The stitches on the gash in his shoulder had pulled apart. "He found a way to put a fuse to it and we hurled that into the middle of them."

"That explains the big boom," Mike said wincing.

"And all the women who'd been practicing like maniacs with their bows and arrows all week didn't see any reason not to use them."

"Did they hit anyone?" Mike shook his head and laughed.

Sarah frowned as she slid her hand gently along his collarbone. "Maybe one guy? In the leg? But it didn't matter. We scared the crap out of them. The *soldiers* didn't know we couldn't hit a target at ten paces."

"I felt like I was looking up at the fecking Alamo," Mike said. "With everyone lined up there on the parapet."

"I think the Alamo is an unfortunate reference," Sarah said and wiped her bloody hands on her jeans. "We need to get you sponged off and bandaged up. Your nose is broken again."

"What's wrong with the clinic? There's got to be a reason we're not there right now."

Sarah sighed. "Mike…"

"What happened?"

"The bastards got inside the castle. There's a secret tunnel that comes through the clinic."

"Shite."

She squeezed his knee as she watched his face register that Fiona and Declan and Beryl had been in the clinic.

"Fiona...?"

"She's fine," Sarah said. "But Beryl, no. And Declan."

"Oh, Jaysus. I need to go to her."

"Not yet, Mike. She's pretty raw. Although it helped to get you back inside. A lot."

"What a disaster," Mike said, shaking his head.

"No," Sarah said, standing up and tugging on his sleeve to get him to his feet. "One thing today was *not* was a disaster. We repulsed an effing army today when we were totally unprepared. And while we did lose two precious members, it could have been much, much worse. We live to fight another day."

An hour later after Sarah had cleaned his cuts, loaded him up with painkillers, restitched his shoulder and bandaged his other wounds—his wrists, his throat, his broken nose, and a gash over his eye—Mike insisted on seeing Fiona and Shaun before going in to dinner.

Both she and Shaun were in the room that had been used as Shaun's cell before he'd been thrown out of the castle weeks earlier. Someone had set a line of candles on the built-in stone bookshelves in the room and a small fire burned in the hearth. The bodies of Declan and Beryl lay side by side on twin tables. Their hair was combed and hands arranged as if in prayer.

Mike put a hand on Shaun's shoulder and the man turned and nodded. Fiona stood up and went to Mike and hugged him. As he held Fiona, Sarah could hear him murmuring to her in Gaelic.

Sarah's own eyes stung with tears. It was true that Declan had been in the process of leaving them for a long time. Ever since the day he'd been taken from the compound last winter. After being shot and left for dead, he'd never fully recovered.

Her heart was broken when she remembered the Declan she had known—the gypsy king so full of life and verve who'd loved Fiona and Ciara so dearly and who had been the best of friends to her and a brother to Mike and young John.

And he would always be the man who'd saved Sarah's life years ago on a cold, wet day deep in the heart of the Welsh wilderness.

We'll remember you always, Dec, Sarah thought, wiping the tears from her eyes. *And we'll make sure little Ciara never forgets you.*

Mike and Shaun stepped outside the room and Sarah hurried to join them. She knew there was still the matter of the two soldiers in the tunnel to resolve.

"Where are they now?" Mike asked Shaun.

"One of them is injured," Sarah said. Mike gave her a baleful look but if he thought she would keep quiet, then he'd taken too many pain pills.

"As I understand it," Shaun said as they walked down the stone corridor toward the room where they'd locked up the soldiers, "these weren't the ones who shot Declan or my mother. Declan killed those two and we still have to clean up the clinic."

"There are bodies still there?"

"Aye. There were four soldiers in the tunnel. The two who opened fire on everyone in the clinic, and these two bringing up the rear."

"Mike, you can't kill them," Sarah said.

"I can't let them leave here alive knowing about the tunnel!" Mike said in frustration. He nodded to Tommy who stood outside the door. Tommy unlocked the door.

The two soldiers sat next to each other on the floor. Sarah had patched up the arm of one which had a ricochet wound from a bullet bouncing off the stone walls. They were brothers. Both stood as Mike, Shaun and Sarah entered the room.

"We can destroy the tunnel," Sarah said. "Then there's nothing to know."

"That tunnel might save our lives one day," Shaun said.

"It didn't help much today," Sarah said.

The two soldiers listened but their eyes were on Mike. And he didn't look happy.

The taller of the soldiers—the one with his arm in a sling—cleared his throat.

"Me brother and I would like to formally request prisoner of war status," he said. "We don't have family any more and if that wanker Hurley is really dead…"

Sarah noticed the younger man was missing two fingers. It occurred to her it might be the result of an instance of army "justice."

"Are you asking to live with us?" Mike said, dumbfounded.

"I…I'm really strong," the younger soldier said, "and neither me nor Frank are married. Frank here was a grammar school teacher before the bomb dropped and I'm dead clever with mechanical stuff."

"We *could* use a few more men," Sarah said. She glanced at Shaun who shrugged.

"Can't argue with that," he said.

"Are ye both mad?" Mike said. His face was flushed and Sarah wondered for a moment if perhaps she'd overdosed him. She should at least have let him have his dinner before asking him to play King Solomon.

"These bastards raped and murdered everyone at the convent!" Mike said.

In a flash, Sarah felt the ground push away from her. It felt like someone just doused the lights. All the lights in the world.

When she came to seconds later, she was on the floor with Mike kneeling beside her and everyone talking and shouting at once.

"We never! It didn't happen!"

"I swear on me life! No one touched the Sisters!"

The nausea swam up from Sarah's stomach until it lodged in her throat.

"Sarah, lass, I'm sorry," Mike said, patting her hand. His eyes were distraught with guilt. "I may be wrong about that. The lads say the nuns are fine."

"We swear it's true!" Frank said.

"Well, we'll know soon enough," Mike said gruffly over his shoulder to him. He turned back to Sarah and tried to smile reassuringly. "We'll head back there straightaway and see for ourselves."

Sarah steadied herself with a hand on the cold stone floor. Her forehead felt damp but her stomach was settling down.

Yes. They would go back to the convent. Soon. Tomorrow.

"Promise me you didn't hurt them," she said in a hoarse voice.

"We swear, missus!" Robby said. "Not a hair!" But Sarah saw a quick, guilty glance to his brother.

"What are you not saying?"

Mike helped her to her feet.

"It's just that…" Frank said as he looked at the floor.

"Out with it!" Mike barked.

"It's just…that bastard Hurley shot two of the nuns right off and then made us torch the place," Robby said. His eyes welled with tears. "And…and when me mate Denny wouldn't do it right off, the fecker shot him too."

"And stuck his…his head on a pole," Frank finished.

"Jaysus," Shaun said. "What was that? Motivation? Jaysus."

"All right," Sarah said and patted Robby on the shoulder. "It's all right. If you had nothing to do with it—"

"We swear, missus!"

"I believe you," Sarah said tiredly, feeling a throbbing ache in her temples. "Do you want to sleep on it, Mike?"

"Sleep on what?" he asked with exasperation. "About whether or not they can stay? Are ye serious?"

"You can see they're harmless."

"I don't see anything of the sort, Sarah. I'm sure some people thought that monster Hurley looked normal too."

"Oh, no, never," Frank said, shaking his head.

Robby shook his head too. "No way was that berk ever normal." He shivered.

"You can stay," Sarah said firmly.

Frank looked at Mike with wide eyes. "Squire?"

"You heard her," Mike said. "You can stay. But I'll be watching you."

"Thank you, sir! Thank you, missus!"

"Go on down to the dining hall," Sarah said. "Might as well start today being a part of things."

"No," Mike said. "First you can spend an hour filling in the tunnel." He looked at Shaun and raised his eyebrows.

Shaun nodded with resignation.

"Sure, might as well," he said, "since having it so far has only worked against us."

Susan Kiernan-Lewis

36.

The next morning brought more snow. Sarah knew she'd never forget how close they came to losing everything. And in spite of her brave words to Mike, she was sure she'd never feel safe again. The attack on the convent in many ways was the hardest blow. For so long she had believed it was the only safe place left.

The fact that the convent had been found by Hurley's lot had shaken Sarah to her core.

Frank and Robby assured them that while it was true Hurley had burned the convent and killed Mac, most of the sisters had not been harmed. She had to believe that. But even so it gave little comfort.

Her safe haven was not safe nor a haven. *Was any place?*

Most of the women stayed in the castle with the babies and children or in the kitchen baking bread and cooking up the last of the rabbits for lunch. Shaun was overseeing the sealing up of the castle tunnel by the two young soldiers. Mike spent the morning resting and regaining his strength until it was time to come together to bury their dead.

Sarah needed to walk the parking lot and step off the dormant garden. She needed to see that the army was truly gone, even if they'd left plenty of evidence of their brief occupation.

"Blimey, they're pigs!" Terry said as he and two other men sorted through the debris left behind.

The fleeing army had left mostly garbage and half-formed attempts at latrines that were surprisingly full for as brief as they'd been there.

Fiona was inside with Declan's body until it was time. Beryl and Declan would both be buried next to Maeve in the far corner of the garden—as well as the two soldiers killed in the tunnel.

As Sarah bent to pick up trash, she found herself periodically looking down the long road to see if she could spot anyone coming. The road had developed a light dusting of snow which muffled the sounds of the men and women picking up trash.

She shivered in her wool jacket and was nearly ready to come inside for a hot cup of anything when she spotted a flash of color. Squinting, she saw that it was an article of clothing on the ground. She stepped closer for a better look.

And then froze. It was a woman's scarf. And she had seen it before.

She picked up the scarf and held it in trembling hands as she remembered the last time she'd seen it—knotted around Jaz Cooper's neck. The fabric was tinged with brown stains—old blood. Sarah closed her eyes and felt a groan lift up out of her diaphragm.

God, no, please don't. It can't be.

She stood and looked around the debris field, her heart pounding as she frantically scanned the area for any more clues.

Was it really Jaz's? She looked at it again. There could be no doubt. She stuffed it in her jacket and stumbled away, her stomach roiling with nausea.

Had the girls run into the army? Is that what this meant? She twisted her head and looked at the castle. The young soldiers, Frank and Robby, would know. She stood staring at the castle but her feet refused to move.

As long as she stayed right here, didn't go inside, and didn't ask them for the truth, both Jaz and Regan lived.

She looked up at the slow moving grey clouds and the falling snow. *This day right now holds them in it alive.*

But the minute I go inside and ask...

She turned and slowly began to make her way back to the castle. A prayer over and over on her lips...

******

The fields to the south of the castle looked as devoid of life as every pasture in Ireland did in November. The creeping afternoon mist advanced steadily toward the castle.

Mike watched as the men lowered first Beryl and then Declan into the ground. Every single person, every baby and every child watched with him while the cold and wet mist slithered under jackets and wool caps. A few babies cried. A few babies were always crying.

Mike held Siobhan in one arm—his good arm—and Sarah's hand with the other.

All the people gathered into two groups—the original castle people and the compound people. Each group had lost a beloved member. Both were brought together today and unified by their grief.

Shaun stood with Saoirse at the far corner of the castle group. It had taken every ounce of Mike's self-control—and a full hour of convincing from Sarah—to forgive the woman but he had done so for Shaun's sake and the sake of their cohesion as a community. Now Saoirse stood dry-eyed and bored as her mother was laid to rest.

It seemed Saoirse had slipped away from the army after her betrayal of the castle and hid in the woods until they'd left. As Mike watched her now, he heard Sarah's words echoing in his head that forgiving Saoirse was the first step toward gaining each other's trust—something they needed to do to go forward.

Mike felt the weariness sink deep into his bones as he listened to the compound men say a few words about Declan. Fiona stood at the front of the group with little Ciara by her side.

So much sadness, Mike thought. *Is this how it's always going to be? Constantly losing the ones we love?* A stab of anger pierced him as he listened and he fought to soften it. Now was not the time for anger. Now was the time for goodbye. And for forgiveness. Sarah squeezed his hand and he glanced at her. She raised an eyebrow. She could always read his mind. He gave a slight shake of his head.

I'm fine.

At least as fine as anyone can be in this new world of ours.

Fiona stepped forward and threw a handful of dirt into the open grave. When would he see his sister smile again? Would that be any day now because of something Ciara said or did? Or would it take months for her to see the world as something besides bleak and cruel?

How many more burials would there be? He watched as the castle and compound people stepped forward one by one to drop handfuls of dirt into the graves. Frank and Robby had confirmed that Jaz and Regan had both been killed two weeks earlier by the army and their bodies left in the woods for the foxes and crows.

Sarah squeezed his hand again so he knew he must've flinched or stiffened again.

He and Gavin and Frank would go first thing in the morning to find what they could of their remains.

And then we'll do this all over again, he thought bitterly as he watched Shaun weep unashamedly for the loss of his mother.

****

That night was a muted celebration. When the drawbridge closed and all the hearths were roaring with warmth and the spits were full of roasting meats, there was an infectious feeling in the castle of comfort and safety.

Mike hated seeing the empty chair next to Fiona at dinner. He knew it was just for tonight and he appreciated the symbolic gesture. But there would be so many times in the coming days when he would feel the keen loss of his best mate. He needed whatever moments he could find where he could forget—just for a little bit—the gaping hole in his heart.

The children always served to tear the adults out of their unhappiness, Mike noticed as he watched Sarah with Siobhan on her lap. The child had settled with her somewhat and he was relieved to see it. It wasn't that Sarah was any less anxious about Siobhan's safety—*was she?*— or at least not that he could detect, but there was a noticeable resurgence of that Sarah strength that had been missing for so long. *That* was the thing he was sure Siobhan was picking up on. She was feeling safe in Sarah's arms.

Sarah had taken the news of Regan's death hard. Not unlike their dearest adopted daughter Papin, Mike thought with sadness, Regan had been a trial for everyone from day one. But also like Papin she'd evolved into a strong-willed young woman whom both Mike and Sarah had been proud of. In some ways, the loss of Regan hurt worse than Declan's because Regan was young and vibrant.

She was like a strong Ireland enduring unimaginable hardships and coming out on the other side.

Except of course she hadn't.

Shaun stood and raised his hands for silence in the dining hall. Sarah looked questioningly at Mike but he shrugged.

"I'd like to say a few words," Shaun said, "on this sad but happy day for all of us at Henredon Castle." He looked at Mike from across the room and Mike gave a slight nod of affirmation.

"Not to put aside our grief or make small of that because we have all lost important people today," Shaun said, his voice wavering with emotion. "But we did an incredible thing as a community yesterday. We came together—castle and compound people alike—and we did the impossible. We fought against an army and won."

Shaun held up a glass of wine in Mike's direction. "I for one am happy to belong to this community and I pledge wholeheartedly my support and loyalty to Mike Donovan and to all the good people of Henredon Castle."

The hall erupted in cheers and shouts of "Hear! Hear!" Mike lifted his glass to Shaun.

Well, at least that's settled, he thought. *And all it took was a broken nose, two fractured ribs, seven deaths, getting stabbed, and a cow blown all to shite.* But he smiled tiredly and lifted his glass again and again to all the people who turned and toasted him.

And when he caught Sarah's sad eyes he could see she was thinking pretty much the same thing.

37.

The following weeks in Henredon Castle passed in a steady routine as people healed and reached out to each other in new friendships. Life fell into a pattern of work and play that soon felt as if they'd always been together.

Mike and Gavin and Tommy went out with Frank early the morning after the burials and returned the next evening late with Jaz's body. They had searched the surrounding woods for Regan but found no clear trace of her remains.

Because of that, Sarah chose to believe—until the months passed and Regan never returned—that she was somehow still alive. She knew Mike didn't hold out hope but Sarah found no point in believing otherwise.

Not until she was forced to.

Early in what was Thanksgiving week back in the States, Sarah found herself standing on the parapet and looking down the long road that led to the rest of Ireland and the world. The snow from the last several days had finally stuck for good and now everywhere she looked she saw an undulating blanket of white with an occasional brown branch or stubby bush sticking out. She tried to imagine how it would feel to see American military Jeeps driving down that road and then wondered, *To what purpose? To take me back home? Is that what I want?*

What she really liked to imagine when she looked down that road was the image of John coming home, his backpack on his back and a staff in his hand.

Coming home for Thanksgiving.

When Sarah thought of all the Thanksgivings she'd shared with John—all the happy smells of bustling kitchens —succulent turkeys and dressings, the pumpkin and fruit pies—she remembered him when he was little, wearing colorful paper Indian headdresses made at school or little pilgrim caps.

And she wanted to curl up into a ball and cry.

Siobhan would never know a real Thanksgiving, she thought. *It will always be a facsimile of the real thing. Roast squirrel or rabbit during the lean years, a pheasant if we're lucky. Never cranberries but some kind of berry that might serve as a relish.*

God knows they'd always have plenty of mashed potatoes.

She wiped the tears from her eyes. She knew she was being childish. The things that were important, she had.

She noticed movement at the base of the gate tower and saw Mike and Gavin standing and talking with Kevin. They had their horses and their rifles.

Speaking of going turkey hunting, Sarah thought with a bleak smile.

She watched them talk and laugh, although she couldn't hear their words from this distance. Things were much better between her and Mike these days. Almost like before.

Nothing like getting your life handed back to you to make you appreciate the world and everyone in it.

Not surprisingly, Mike turned and looked up to where Sarah was standing. She grinned. He really did have a sort of radar where she was concerned.

"Be safe," she shouted and he nodded. Kevin cranked down the drawbridge and Mike and Gavin rode out. *Whatever* they brought back would be on the Thanksgiving menu, she thought. And that would be fine. Even squirrel.

The plan was for her and Mike to go back to the convent the morning after the big feast. She hoped the nuns had found shelter but just knowing they were alive meant everything.

Funny how the things that matter now are the big things. Life. Death. And everything else was just gravy. As that thought came to her she noticed Frank and Catriona walking across the courtyard. They weren't touching but there was definitely something about the way they moved that said they were together.

Sarah wasn't surprised. There weren't enough men to go around and both Frank and Robby were good-looking guys. It had been two weeks since the army had tried to attack the castle. She was only surprised it took the two of them so long.

As she climbed down to check on Siobhan in the nursery, it occurred to Sarah that people falling in love helped make life feel normal again.

You can't blush and wonder what your beloved is thinking if you're starving or worried about dying.

Yes, people falling in love was definitely a step in the right direction.

And that's what also made this Thanksgiving so special —even if John wasn't here for it. It was a time for the entire castle population to come together and formally celebrate their safety, their new friends, and their new life together.

Just like the first pilgrims.

As Sarah reached the courtyard she saw Ava leaving the dining hall with her daughter Keeva in tow. She waved to her.

"I'm heading to the nursery," Sarah said.

"So are we," Ava said. "Although this one thinks she's too big for it."

"Sure there's just babies there!" Keeva said with a pout.

"Why don't you ask Mrs. O'Connell if you can be her helper with the little ones?" Sarah asked. "I'll bet she'd appreciate it."

"Can I, Mum?" Keeva said.

Ava winked at Sarah. "I think that's a grand idea. Go on ahead. Mrs. Donovan and I will be there in a bit." Keeva grinned and ran across the courtyard to the far stairwell.

"Thank you for that," Ava said as she watched her daughter disappear. "She can be moody, that one."

"Can't they all? To tell you the truth, I've had some problems with Siobhan ever since I had her."

"Postpartum?" Ava frowned but her eyes were kind.

"Possibly. I think it's better now. But there was a time not too long ago when I was the last person Siobhan would even let touch her."

"I'm sure that's not true."

"Oh, ask anyone. They'll tell you. She hated me."

"Sure, I don't believe it." Ava clucked her tongue.

"Well, let's just say it's been a long hard six months and I guess I feel I have a lot to be thankful for. If only…"

"You'll be missing your lad?"

"Honestly, I think I'm only really okay when I *don't* think of him. Do you know what I mean? Otherwise I'm obsessed with worrying about him all of the time."

Ava squeezed Sarah's hand. "Sure that's motherhood, so it is." She slowed their steps and Sarah got the idea that Ava wanted to say something.

"You know I lost me husband right after the first EMP?" Ava said.

"I did hear that," Sarah said. "I did too."

"So maybe you'll know that sometimes—for our children's sake—we've had to do some things. Maybe some things we aren't proud of."

Images of Ava trading her body for food came to mind. She held Ava's hand. "We've all had to do things we could never have imagined before."

Ava looked relieved. She glanced again toward the stairwell where Keeva had gone. "Ye love 'em so much, it's just amazing what you're capable of for their sakes."

"Mike says you never know your true grit until you're under fire."

"Aye, he's a wise man your Mike and no mistake."

They reached the stairwell and stepped in out of the cold. Before they could resume their conversation, Nuala opened the door and a wave of shrieking poured out into the hall.

"Sure I thought you'd never come!" Nuala said as she held Siobhan in her arms. The baby was arching her back in the throes of a tantrum. "Your Siobhan is a monster today, so she is! Take 'er, aye? So I can settle the others down?"

Sarah took the baby in her arms hesitantly. A *calm* Siobhan was no guarantee the child wouldn't start screaming as soon as Sarah was holding her. But Siobhan surprised her by quickly settling in Sarah's arms and while she still wasn't happy, she'd at least stopped howling.

"Shall I find you after dinner tonight then, Sarah?" Ava asked as she stepped into the nursery. "And you can tell me what's needed for this dressing I hear is so necessary for the feast."

Nuala laughed. "Aye, it's taken us four years to get Sarah to stop calling it *stuffing!*"

Both Ava and Nuala laughed. "It has an entirely different meaning here in Ireland, ye ken," Ava said, her eyes sparkling with humor.

"Ha, ha, you two," Sarah said grinning. She waved goodbye and turned to bring Siobhan upstairs to her room. As she turned to go up the stairwell, she was met by Frank and Catriona coming down.

"Oy!" Catriona said. "We were just up there looking for you. A word, Sarah?"

Frank had a sheepish look on his red face and he had trouble looking Sarah in the eye, which she decided didn't bode well for whatever the two needed to tell her.

"What's the problem?" she asked.

"You know Frank here and I've been keeping company, aye?" Catriona said.

"Well, there hasn't been a formal announcement that I know of," Sarah said dryly. "But I think most people have figured it out. Did you want me to talk to Mike about posting banns or something?"

"Oh, you're a wit, Sarah Donovan," Catriona said as she threw her head back and laughed. "And sure there's no mistake." She took Frank's hand in hers. "Nay, we'll handle what's between the two of us, thank ye very much."

"So what's the problem?" Sarah asked again as Siobhan began to fuss.

Catriona took a step closer and lowered her voice. "We've been meeting in a few out of the way places around the castle, ye ken, to...you know."

"Snog," Frank said with a shrug.

"Ah, well put, ye auld romantic," Catriona said slapping him good-naturedly on the arm. "And sure it might be nothing, but we found a place that...well, we thought we should bring it to someone's attention."

"What do you mean?" Sarah was fast losing patience especially as Siobhan began to squirm.

"Can we show you, missus?" Frank asked earnestly. And Sarah noticed that the fun and laughter had drained right out of him.

Patting Siobhan on the back settled her down and since the howls that were coming out of the nursery didn't appear to have abated since Sarah had taken Siobhan out, she decided to keep the baby with her. She followed Catriona and Frank as they made their way down the stone stairwell and back out into the courtyard.

There were a few people walking about outside but not many. It was still snowing and the wind had become sharp. At midday, most people were either working in the kitchen, patrolling the catwalk that spanned the perimeter of the castle, or doing any of a hundred smaller chores like stacking firewood, mending clothing, oiling tack or tending to the horses.

Sarah noticed that Catriona and Frank were holding hands as they walked across the courtyard. Shaun and Saoirse were just coming from the dining hall. Sarah knew Shaun was trying to find a job for Saoirse that didn't involve a lot of contact with other people but also kept her away from sharp implements or weapons in general.

Saoirse scowled at them as they passed in the courtyard. Sarah thought Shaun looked particularly worn. She knew he still grieved for his mother but was keeping busy in helping to organize the running of the castle—and of course as usual he had his hands full with his sister.

Frank and Catriona walked quickly to the stairwell parallel to where the dining hall backed up to the ocean side of the castle. Sarah had never been in here although she knew Mike and Gavin and Tommy had found the ancient weapons and longbows stacked in a room back here. The museum gift shop was in this section too, as was a storage room with a copier machine and some stacked office furniture.

As the two led Sarah down the hall past several doors that used to be administrative offices once upon a time, Sarah felt a chill rake her arms under her wool jacket. She pulled Siobhan inside her coat and rubbed her back, hoping the child wouldn't start to fret. So far, she appeared docile and even sleepy.

"It's freezing in here," Sarah said.

"Aye," Catriona said over her shoulder. "Like what you'd expect from a castle dungeon."

"Is *that* what's down here?" Sarah asked as the hall descended a set of six very slick stone steps into a hallway with a lowered ceiling. Frank had to stoop to pass through it.

"This had better be worth it," Sarah said, hurrying to keep up. A vertical slit window in the hallway gave her a glimpse of the ocean on this side of castle. The window wasn't big enough to get much of a view and there was no glass on it so the cold seaward air slithered into the hallway.

"I can't believe you two really come down here," Sarah grumbled. "It's about as romantic as a bowel blockage."

The hall dead-ended into a stone wall with a small alcove to the right which hid a wooden fairy door with wide brass hinges. They stopped in front of the door. Grasping the door handle, Frank put his shoulder to the door and pushed it open.

At first glance it was too dark to see anything and Sarah felt the first true prickles of unease. She followed them inside. A vertical slit window was in the far corner with just enough light filtering in to give shape to the items in the room.

"Do you see it, Sarah?" Catriona asked in a whisper.

Sarah forced herself to move to where Catriona and Frank stood in front of what looked like a large sculpture. She tightened her hold on Siobhan and waited for her eyes to adjust in the gloom so that she could see what they were looking at.

When the shape became clear, she felt the chill of the room intensify. She reached out and grabbed Frank's arm before she knew she was doing it and a gasp jumped from her throat loud enough to startle the baby.

Dear God...

It was a pile of bones. Human skulls, leg bones, arms and what looked like ribs and backbones.

A pyramid of jumbled human bones of all sizes—large and small—stacked to the ceiling.

Sarah desperately tried to think of any good reason why these could be here.

"What does it mean, Sarah?" Catriona whispered. "It's not good, is it?"

Sarah fought to clear her mind—to try to understand what she was seeing. The sound of the door creaking shut behind her made her dig her nails into Frank's arm. She whirled around.

Shaun stood at the door with a gun in his hands. A gun pointed at them.

"I really wish you hadn't seen this," he said.

Susan Kiernan-Lewis

38.

Shaun stepped into the room and Saoirse was behind him. For someone who wasn't supposed to be allowed near weapons, she looked quite comfortable with the rifle in her hand.

"Shaun," Sarah said. "What is the meaning of this?"

"Good try, Sarah," Shaun said. "But I don't have a good excuse for what you just saw and I'm pretty sure you can't unsee it."

Sarah felt the trembling begin in her legs and she tightened her hold on Siobhan. Both Shaun and Saoirse were pointing their weapons at the three of them. Her mind raced to understand what was happening. But her shaking body already knew.

"I figured you'd find out eventually," Shaun said sadly. "I was actually trying to get rid of the evidence. The last thing I wanted was for things to end like this."

"It doesn't have to end," Sarah said.

"Really? Well, can you tell me what you think the explanation is for the pile of bones behind you?"

Sarah licked her lips. "You…you've been waylaying people who come to the castle?"

"And eating them. Yes, Sarah."

Catriona gasped at Shaun's words and Saoirse snorted in derision.

"It started out an accident," Shaun said. "Ava's husband died that first winter and we were starving. I'm not a hunter. So I did what I had to do to keep my people alive."

Okay, so they ate one of their own who died. They were starving. That's still a far cry from the pile of bones here.

"After that, well, we'd already done it once. It wasn't that hard after that."

"So that's... that's how you survived?" Frank asked. Sarah saw that he'd pulled Catriona into his arms in a protective hold.

"Keep your hands where I can see them," Shaun said to Frank.

"We need to move 'em into the main cages," Saoirse said.

"Will ye force me to take the bairn from ye, Sarah?" Shaun said. "Or will ye come along without trouble?"

"I'll come," she said, her heart pounding in her throat. His gun was pointed at Sarah's heart, which meant it was pointed at Siobhan's back.

"Catriona?" Shaun said. "Come to me, lass."

Catriona hesitated.

"Come to me or I shoot him," Shaun said waving the gun at Frank. Catriona walked to Shaun and he grabbed her by the hair and twisted her around so she was facing away from him. He held the gun to her head.

"Now behave yourself, lad," Shaun said. "Or she dies sooner rather than later. Everyone outside if you please."

Frank and Sarah stepped into the hall. Saoirse quickly patted down Frank and then pressed a hidden lever in a nearby stone wall and a small door cracked open on the wall.

"After you, arsehole," Saoirse said to Frank. He bent over and stepped through the door with Saoirse right behind him, then Sarah, and lastly Shaun and Catriona.

Through the door was a steep and ancient staircase that led two levels downward.

At the bottom of the stairs was another door. Inside was a large cavernous room with three old-fashioned jail cells fixed to the western wall that faced the ocean.

"Inside, genius," Saoirse said as she nudged Frank with her rifle barrel into the first cell. He stepped in, followed by Sarah. Finally Shaun pushed Catriona inside. Saoirse closed and locked the cell door behind them

Sarah tried to think, tried to stall. Tried to appeal to the man she'd lived with every day for the last two weeks.

"And your mother?" she said. "I can't believe she would be a part of this."

"She didn't know about it," Shaun said, frowning. "My mother lived in another world. It wasn't hard to fool her. I'm sorry, Sarah. I genuinely liked you and Mike. But now that you've found evidence of...our history, what choice do I have?"

"We can talk about it together."

"Do you really think after your husband knows what we've done, he'd allow us to stay?"

You'll be lucky not to be branded with the letter C and turned out to starve.

"I can see by your face that my assessment of Himself is correct," Shaun said.

"What about our children?"

"I'm sorry, so I am. You must think us monsters."

Sarah clutched Siobhan so tightly the child began to cry and squirm to free herself.

"And now what?" Frank said. "Someone will notice we're missing."

"Of course they will. Which is why it's time for all of you to become enlightened."

"Mike will never let you get away with this," Sarah said, her chest vibrating with fear.

"Mike and Gavin are both outside the castle at the moment," Shaun said. "Providential for me. The drawbridge will stay up until everyone is secured down here."

He was going to herd the whole castle population into these three jail cells? Sarah's mind was whirling. The window in her cell was small but she might fit through it. But to what end? She could hear the roar of the ocean as it pounded the rocks eighty feet below.

"And then?" she asked, hoping for time, hoping for something. Catriona was in Frank's arms again and was crying.

"Blimey, Sarah. Do you really want to know the details?" Shaun said in frustration. "Once your people are locked up, we'll lower the drawbridge for Mike and Gavin."

"And then you'll kill them as they enter," Frank said with disgust.

"I know you don't believe me," Shaun said, addressing Sarah, "but it kills me to break a trust, so it does. But I have no choice."

"Shaun, listen to me. You don't need to do this to survive now."

"Nay, but Mike wouldn't let us stay and that's a death warrant, so it is. Or do you think he'd still be delivering muffins and rabbit stew to us this time around?"

Saoirse backed out of the opening and disappeared into the hallway. Shaun turned to join her.

"I'm sorry, Sarah. I truly am," he said sadly from the doorway. "No one was more excited about the idea of joining up with you lot but it just won't work now and—what was it your husband said when he tricked us into opening the gate?—the sooner we all come to grips with that the better it'll be for everyone."

****

Fiona folded the cotton diaper and laid it on top of the stack. The squeals of the children in the nursery soothed the wound in her heart. Seeing Ciara laughing and running around—unmindful of the fact that she'd lost her father—helped at the same time it hurt.

"Are ye all right then, Fiona?" Nuala asked from across the room. She held two babies in her arms, both of them squalling but Nuala looked unperturbed.

Everyone is so worried about me, Fiona thought as she forced a smile for Nuala's sake. *And none of their worry can help me. What a useless thing it was, worry. Has it helped Sarah all these months now? Did it once keep anyone alive? Little Maeve? Or Declan?*

She felt her eyes brimming with tears and turned away to focus on the older children. Both Nuala's boys were too big for the nursery but Mary and Kevin O'Malley's lass, Mary Ann, was old enough to be a bit of a help. As Fiona watched her—no more than six years old—she thought she saw a strong maternal streak in the girl.

For all the good it will do you. Take care of them. Love them. And lose them away.

"Penny for them, Fiona?" Liddy said from where she sat by the window with her four-month-old baby in her lap.

Fiona sat down next to Liddy and held her arms out for the child. Liddy handed her over.

"Sure they're a full time job," Fiona said trying to keep her mood light.

"Mary says it's no easier even with Kev helping," Liddy said. "But sure that's a lie."

Fiona looked sadly at Liddy. "You missing Davey?" she asked.

"Missing him? How can I miss someone who loved me so little he'd walk away rather than be the father to our child?"

Fiona knew Liddy's husband Davey didn't exactly walk away voluntarily. When he refused to consider raising the baby Roisin—the result of a rape—as his own, Mike threw him out of the community.

Liddy eyes brimmed with angry tears.

"Sure, he'd have me choose *him*—my dearest sweetheart and husband of eight years—over my rapist's baby?" She wiped her tears away and reached out to take Roisin back. "It wasn't even a contest. So good riddance to bad rubbish."

"I know you don't mean that," Fiona said. "Davey was a good man."

"Aye, he was," Liddy said. "Right up to the moment when he wasn't. And Roisin and I are just fine without him."

So much sadness in the world, Fiona thought as she saw the hurt in Liddy's face. She'd loved Davey and until last summer, Fiona would have bet everything that he'd loved her too.

The door to the nursery swung open and Ava stuck her head inside.

"Ladies?" she said breathlessly. "Sarah's asking for you downstairs. She seems to have found some kind of ancient bathing room."

Nuala turned to look at the other women in the room.

"A bathing room?" Nuala said, but her eyes brightened with interest.

"Aye," Ava said. "She says you're to bring all the bairns."

****

Well, that was a wasted afternoon, Mike thought as he and Gavin trotted down the main road to the castle. Gavin had wanted to lay traps in another patch of woods out on the northern ridge of the deserted village. They'd hoped to find something there a little more exotic than rabbit or squirrel.

No such luck.

"Does it really have to be turkey?" Gavin asked as they rode back. He had four rabbits draped across his saddle. It wouldn't feed the whole castle and it definitely wouldn't rank as the star of a Thanksgiving day feast—at least as far as Sarah was concerned—but it was all they'd scared up.

"She doesn't expect turkey," Mike said. "No more than she expects cranberries."

"But something better than rabbit?"

"I'm not giving up. We have a few days yet. Besides the day is more about coming together and being thankful than it is the food."

"If you say so."

They stopped in front of the castle. The air was cold and while it was still early afternoon, it would be dark in another hour or two.

"I don't see Kev," Gavin said. "He's usually on watch this time of day."

"Halloo, the castle!" Mike called. It would be good to get in out of the wind and have a nice hot cup of tea.

Shaun appeared at the parapet and shouted down to them.

"Having trouble with the trunnion on the door again," he said.

The trunnion was one of the two axles on the door that allowed it to raise. Mike remembered Kev mentioned a couple of days ago that it was sticking.

"How long to fix it?" Mike called up.

"Should be jake within the hour."

Mike looked at Gavin and grinned. "Gives us an excuse to hunt a little longer."

"I've been wanting to try the area on the other side of the parking lot," Gavin said, shrugging.

"Might as well." Mike waved to Shaun and banished the image of the waiting cup of tea as he pointed his horse's nose away from the castle.

39.

One by one Sarah watched the women and children come through the door. Their eyes wide with curiosity until they saw her and Frank and Catriona standing in the jail cell. The new prisoners were shoved into one of the other cells. At first Sarah wanted to scream "Run! Run!" but what would be the point? Where would they run to?

Shaun, Saoirse and another of the castle women, Margo, all had rifles. All the compound women had were crying babies and terrified children.

Eventually Sarah covered her ears as the compound women were escorted into the cells. When they resisted, Saoirse or Margo would point a gun at one of their children's heads. In the end it didn't take long.

Because Shaun was trusted, every one of the compound people was lured to the dungeon without a struggle.

The four compound men were put in cells along with the soldier Robby and six other compound women— including Nuala, Sophia, and Fiona—and their ten children who were all mostly infants.

No castle women were jailed. Did that mean they were all in on it? Even Ava? Sarah felt sick. Of course Ava was in on it. She was Shaun's lover. Sarah felt so stupid. She had trusted her. She had trusted them all.

Shaun refused to catch Sarah's eye. The compound men yelled and made threats but with guns to the heads of their most vulnerable, the threats were empty. Sarah watched Terry, his face dark with shock, as he held his wife Jill and their youngest Darcy between them. She saw the look of disbelief on the face of Nuala in the cell furthest away with her infant in her arms and one hand clutching her older boy Dennis's shoulder.

Fiona had been shoved into Sarah's cell and now sat on the floor with Ciara in her lap as she stared numbly at the crying people standing around her. Sarah didn't bother going to her. There was nothing she could tell her. No way she could comfort her.

"That's all of you then," Shaun said. "I'm sorry about this. I wish there'd been another way. You can thank Sarah Donovan for why you're all here. Margo will be right outside the door so don't try anything foolish."

Margo was the short, heavyset woman who'd helped Sarah get across the drawbridge the day they all fled outside in a panic.

The expression on Margo's round freckled face held no hint of human feeling.

"Why are you doing this?" Sophia screamed. Sarah's stomach tightened to hear the terror in her voice.

"Have you lost your mind?" Terry bellowed. "Open these cells, ye daft fecker!"

After a quick glance at Sarah, Shaun turned and left the room. Margo walked over to Sarah's cell and pointed at the square window in the stone wall.

"You'll notice you have a room with a view," she said with a sneer. "And you're welcome to try it but if you do you'll end up hamburger meat on the rocks below. And hamburger cooks up as easily as anything else."

Margo turned away, slamming the heavy door that led to the hallway behind her.

"Sarah! What does he mean, *you're the reason*?" Sophia called out. "What is happening to us?"

"It's not Mrs. Donovan's fault," Frank said. "Cat and I found evidence that they're all unnatural buggers."

"What are ye talking about?" Kevin shouted. He was holding his infant son in his arms and his wife Mary stood next to him holding the hand of their six-year old daughter.

"They're *cannibals*," Catriona said shrilly. "They've been eating people who come to the castle. That's how they've survived."

For a moment it felt as if all the oxygen had been sucked out of the room at her words. A spasm of stunned silence fell on the group.

"Are ye telling me the crazy bastards intend to eat *us*?" Tommy said. His mouth hung open in astonishment.

Sarah felt her legs weaken and she leaned against the bars of the cell for a moment to steady herself.

When the scream came from Nuala's cell, chills shot up Sarah's back.

"Damian!" Nuala shrieked. "Where is Damian?"

Sarah looked in the cell beside her but couldn't see him.

Was this an accident? Was Damian hiding somewhere in the castle? Had the bastards rounded up everyone but missed him?

Sarah noticed the door to the hallway was open just enough for her to see Margo standing there. Hearing Nuala's scream, Margo stuck her head in. There was a malicious grin on her face as she caught Sarah's eye. Margo winked at Sarah then closed the door as Nuala continued to scream.

It was then Sarah knew. It wasn't an accident.

They have Damian.

Susan Kiernan-Lewis

40.

"They've got him!" Nuala said, shaking her head in horror as tears coursed down her cheeks. "Somebody has to do something! That bitch Saoirse! She blamed Damian for why she was thrown out of the castle! Sarah! We need to do something! *She has Damian!*"

Helplessly, Sarah watched Nuala. All the babies were crying now, Siobhan included, and most of the women too.

They have Damian. They're going to kill Mike and Gavin. They're going to kill all of us. The babies, the men, all of us...

"Sarah, do you hear me?" Nuala screamed. "*Do* something!"

Damian is her dearest boy, just like John is mine. She's out of her mind with fear for him. Of course she is.

Sarah looked at Siobhan. *She's in my arms but she's in just as much danger as Damian. In the end, her turn will come too.*

Sarah turned away as others tried to soothe Nuala, tried to tell her it would be all right, tried to assure her that Damian would be all right. Sarah walked over and looked out the window. She could see ocean and gray sky.

Just yesterday she and Nuala had taken the children to the beach to find sand dollars and run in the sand. She'd stared across the sea and tried to imagine what part of Newfoundland or Canada they were parallel to—silly daydreaming with children's laughter and voices in the background.

Now she leaned into the window and peered over the edge. Eighty or ninety feet below there was nothing but large jagged rocks. Hopeless. She tried to focus on the ocean and to will herself mentally to leave this hellhole. But she couldn't. The ocean's roar wasn't loud enough to drown out the cries of despair that surrounded her.

As she watched the gray and green ocean under the dark Irish clouds, the sight of the ever moving waves could not blot out the image—or the moment—when Shaun had aimed his gun at Siobhan's back as Sarah held her. Sarah thought of that moment, and was surprised to realize that all her anxieties and fears—all the ones she'd harbored for so many months—all her anxieties about what *might* happen just got trumped by a single promise from Shaun of what was *going* to happen.

As she stood and looked out the window, a heavy pressure began to slowly lift from her shoulders when she realized her worry about what was coming wasn't going to stop it. Not one bit.

It was coming.

Her lungs expanded as she took in and let out a long breath. It was the first real breath she'd taken in months and she felt the tension ease from her mind as it gathered and coiled in her shoulders.

One way or another, it's over. Either we all die— Siobhan and Mike and all of us—or we don't. And fearing it or hiding from it won't affect what happens now.

There was a relief in that.

Sarah looked out the window again and down. There was a narrow crumbling ledge barely four inches wide situated five feet below the windowsill. She craned her head out the window but couldn't see how far the shelf went around the exterior castle wall.

She wouldn't know that until she was on it.

The minute the thought came to her, she realized she'd known all along what she had to do. She turned and handed Siobhan to Catriona.

"Be a good girl for Mommy, okay, sweetie?" Sarah said, her voice shaky as she kicked off her shoes and shrugged out of her jacket.

"What are you doing?" Catriona said. "You can't seriously be thinking of going out there."

Terry came to the bars that adjoined their cell.

"Sarah, don't be daft. You heard what that hag said. You'll kill yourself."

"It's true," Frank said. "You can't get down from here."

"I'm not trying to get down," Sarah said as she peeled off her socks. "Tommy, there's another window twenty feet to my right, isn't there? Just like on the other side of the castle? What is that room?"

"I...I'm not sure..."

"Think!"

"A store room maybe or more dungeons."

"Sarah, you can't. You'll fall," Catriona said weakly.

"If you have a better idea I'd love to hear it," Sarah said. She walked over to Fiona and knelt down. "Be brave, Fi," she whispered. "Take strength from Declan. You know he's near." She kissed Ciara and stood up and nodded grimly at both Frank and Catriona as they gaped at her.

"And meanwhile, just in case I do fall, I need you to be thinking of a Plan B."

Then Sarah kissed her baby and climbed out the window.

****

Fiona blinked in astonishment as Sarah crawled out the cell window and dropped out of view.

Is she mental? Has she finally gone round the bend?

Nuala's screaming was hysterical now and Fiona could see that Robby was holding Nuala's baby and patting Dennis on the shoulder while Nuala pounded the cell bars.

"What did Sarah say?" Nuala screamed. "Where is she? What's happening?"

"Plan B!" Frank shouted to her and everyone else in the cages. "She said to come up with a Plan B!"

"Where's Mike?" Nuala screamed. "He and Gavin aren't here! They'll rescue us!"

Fiona realized she'd been thinking the same thing. Her brother wouldn't let this happen. Mike would sort this out.

But Frank shook his head.

"What do you know?" she asked Frank. He turned to look at her and hesitated.

"Don't tell her, Frank," Catriona said. "There's no point."

"Don't tell me what?" Fiona said. But she didn't want to know. A part of her prayed he would listen to Catriona and not tell her.

"They're waiting for Mike and Gavin once we're all in here. They intend to kill them as soon as they come back into the castle."

Fiona felt as if she'd been punched in the stomach. Mike was out there, hunting for food, enjoying the day, and laughing and talking with Gavin. He was unaware that he was walking back into a death trap.

Nuala's howls crested and bounced off the stone walls until only her wails of agony filled the room.

Plan B she says as she hops out the window like she's going to the market for milk.

Like she wasn't going to her death as sure as summer follows spring.

Which any sane person knew she was.

Fiona stared out the window, her eyes filling with tears.

That was just so Sarah.

*****

Sarah's adrenalin took her as far as getting out the window. She hung from the windowsill by her fingertips, knowing the ledge was just inches from her feet—and let go. As she gripped the lip of the window and steadied herself on the ledge, she realized she didn't have too much more of that kind of nerve in her.

She took a full moment to steady herself on the ledge, her stomach and chest pressed to the castle wall and her fingers gripping into small crevices in the rock face.

Don't look down. Don't look down.

She pressed the side of her face against the wall, and while planting her left foot took a tiny tentative step forward with her right, then stopped. She felt solidly centered, although a sparrow or crow could easily unbalance her—and God knows a sneeze—if she didn't think too much about the rocks below, or the cold, the wind, and the sounds of Nuala's screaming still audible through the window—she would be okay. From her vantage point she could now see the ledge curved along the castle rock face to where it continued beneath another window twenty feet away.

Twenty feet. That's all. I can make that. She crept along with several more tentative, short sliding steps. Slowly. Inches at a time. Forcing herself not to think about anything. Not to think of Siobhan or John or Mike— somewhere out there—*had he come back yet?* Had Shaun already killed him?

She grimaced. *Stop! Just move. Don't think. Tiny steps. No hurry. Just get there.*

A gust of wind hit her full force but she held on. She was glad she'd removed her shoes and socks because she was able to grip the ledge with her toes. But the cold was numbing her feet.

With her next step she felt the ledge crumble away. For a split second she lost her balance, but immediately leaned back on the secure foot and dug her fingernails deeper into the rock face. She recovered her balance, her heart pounding in her ears.

She was okay. She was still on the ledge. But the piece that had fallen was big. It created at least a two foot gap in the shelf. Sarah stared at the break and tried not to focus on the rocks on the distant ground below.

She looked at the ledge on the other side of the gap. Would it crumble too? Should she try to step beyond the edge of it? Could she do that? Even in the cold, she felt the sweat dripping off her face and into her eyes. She didn't dare move from her handholds long enough to wipe it away.

Sarah closed her eyes and blocked out the sound of the ocean and her own heartbeat drumming in her ears. She took a deep breath and then another to try to slow down her pulse. She could only pray the ledge wouldn't break more.

It wasn't stepping over the gap that worried her so much as her hands. She needed secure handholds above and across the gap to allow her to take the first big step without falling. Wishing she could wipe her hands on her jeans and knowing she absolutely had to resist the impulse, Sarah felt the muscles in her calves tighten—heralding the start to cramping. Slowly, she moved both feet close together by the ledge, and groped until she found two handholds above the gap.

Now or never.

She lifted her right foot and stepped across the gap, holding her breath as the ledge lip held. As she stood there straddling the break, she glanced down between her feet at the rocks far below and instantly felt a wave of dizziness. She quickly looked up again before bringing her trailing foot across to the other side of the ledge. The sweat was pouring down her face now. But the ledge held.

The window was close now—only five feet away. And yet she felt terror riding on her shoulders like a malevolent imp. The urge to look down was intense. She bit a hole in her lip as she turned her head—the first step to upsetting her balance—and forced herself to keep her eyes forward. On the window.

It was right *there*.

The desire to end the trial, to have it be over was so strong that she found herself rushing to get there faster. Her mind was whirling with warnings but her body wasn't listening. She took three more quick sliding steps and reached for the sill before she even knew there was something to grab onto. She knew that was a mistake but by that time she was already committed.

With a grunt of surprise, her fingers fumbled at the sill, and found nothing to hold onto. Her knee moved upward in premature anticipation of the climb to the window when her center of gravity shifted. With a fierce intake of breath, she felt her balance shifting away from the wall.

****

Fiona held Ciara tightly in her arms and felt the child shiver.

"Are ye hungry, lass?" Fiona whispered. Ciara shook her head.

It had only been a few minutes since Sarah left the cell and since then Nuala had collapsed into muted sobs. Frank and Catriona held each other with the baby Siobhan between them.

"I'm going to look," Catriona said.

"Nay, don't!" Fiona said.

Catriona looked at her in surprise.

"You might distract her," Fiona said. But that was a lie. The truth was, Fiona couldn't bear to hear that Sarah had fallen. She needed just a few more moments where she could pretend that the world wasn't ending in the most horrible, excruciatingly way possible, with every single person she loved in this world dying within hours of each other.

Suddenly Margo pulled open the dungeon door, and stood in the doorway a rifle slung over her shoulder.

"Tell that bitch to shut up," she said nodding, toward Nuala, "if she knows what's good for her."

"You monster!" Nuala shrieked as she wrapped her fingers around the bars of the cell. "For harming a child you should burn in the lowest level of hell!"

"Mrs. O'Connell," Robby said, trying to pull her away from the bars, "Nuala, please."

"Aye, *Mrs. O'Connell*," Margot said tauntingly. "Keep it down in here. You're giving me a headache. It's no picnic standing out in that drafty hallway if you think it is."

Margot glared at the faces staring back at her. When she turned to leave, she glanced into Fiona's cell and grinned. "So she tried it anyway, did she? She's got guts, I'll give her that. Mind you that's all she has about now."

With a nasty laugh, she turned and left the room.

The minute she was gone Catriona walked to the window.

"Catriona, no!" Fiona said, scrambling to her feet.

But everyone in the adjoining cells pressed close to the bars to hear.

"Well?" Tommy said.

Catriona pulled back from the window, her face stricken. "I...I can't see her."

There was a terrible silence and then Frank went to the window and looked out. Finally he turned away and spoke to everyone waiting.

"Aye, then. Time for Plan B."

Susan Kiernan-Lewis

41.

Sarah lunged at the windowsill in terror and desperation. Both hands clawed at the stone, trying to correct the imbalance of her body's momentum outward. With no time to think, she fought to find even a half handhold to keep her from falling. Her fingers scrambled across the rock and her toes clenched in knots on the ledge.

Suddenly her hands felt the stone at the front of the windowsill. It was slightly raised all the way across. It was enough. She sheared off the skin on her fingertips clinging to it while halting the backward momentum of her body. Gently, slowly, she pulled herself forward to the front of the window.

No time for prayers of thanks. Her knees were shaking. She needed to get inside *now*.

In one swift motion, she pulled at the lip of the windowsill and felt her toes lift off the shelf and dig into the wall. Hand over hand, grabbing at whatever stone or piece of unfiled mortar there was in the vertical window, she felt her jeans rip at the knee as she crawled and hauled her body up and then over the windowsill.

She lay half in and half out of the window, her chest heaving with fear and disbelief. It took several long seconds before she could pull herself all the way in and look around. She was in some kind of storage room. But there were no copiers or stacks of toilet paper here. Clearly it was a room that hadn't been used in centuries and probably not visited in decades.

Sarah jumped to the floor and began looking through the piles of rubbish and useless office supplies in the room. She found something in a box that looked like a mace. It was clearly a reproduction with a blunt heavy head and a slender handle. Good for bashing over the head if she got close enough. Useless for stabbing or anything else but it would have to do. She jammed it into her belt.

She opened the room's heavy door and peered out into the hallway.

She had no idea where she was. This was not a part of the castle she'd ever visited. Thankful that she was barefoot against the floor of the stone hallway, she stepped out and held her breath to listen.

It was absolutely quiet.

Where would they take Damian? *Would they kill him in the kitchen like we do the chickens?* Just the thought made her want to vomit, but she turned in the direction of where she knew a stairwell must be. At least there would be people in the kitchen. She could hold one of them—threaten them with a knife to their throat—and force them to…now wasn't the time to think of all that.

Because when she thought it out, it all felt pretty hopeless.

She ran silently to the end of the hall to the stairs. She hesitated at the foot of the steps, hating the time it took and knowing it was necessary. She didn't hear any voices. She ran quickly up the stairs with her heart pounding so hard in her ears she was practically deaf.

At the top she recognized where she must be although she'd never been here. It looked just like the front of the castle only in reverse. This was where the castle people had lived before Mike and Sarah had come. This was where their bedrooms were.

That meant that down this hallway and down another set of stairs would take her to the courtyard—the only way to get to the great dining hall and the kitchen.

She had no idea how long she'd been gone. She only knew she couldn't waste time. She walked down the second level hallway mindful of the doors that led from it. They were all closed and no noises came from within.

Suddenly, she heard voices. She stopped in the hall and looked at the door next to her. Should she hide? She pulled out the mace and slowed but didn't stop.

Anybody I meet is an enemy. That's all I need to know.

Ava appeared from around the corner of the far stairwell and stepped into the hallway. She had been laughing. She held her daughter Keeva's hand. The minute Ava saw Sarah, her face froze in horror.

"No!" Ava gasped. She swiveled and dragged her daughter back down the hall toward the stairwell.

Sarah bolted after them with visions of holding the mace over Keeva's head unfolding vividly in her mind. Could she really threaten the child in order to get Ava to unlock the dungeon cells?

Hell yes.

The two had disappeared in the stairwell before Sarah reached it. Before she could race after them, an unholy scream erupted from the stairwell and echoed down the hallway.

A child's scream of unmitigated terror.

Damian.

*****

Fiona stood by the window, numb with horror.

Everyone was talking at once, crying at once, screaming at once. All three cells were a roiling cacophony of terror.

The door flew open again and Margot stormed into the room. This time she aimed her rifle at the cells.

Nuala continued to scream.

"I told you lot to shut up!" Margo said, running from cell to cell and pointing her rifle. "And now you'll bloody well have something to cry about!"

"No, missus!" Frank yelled. "Robby, get her under control, can't you? Everyone stop and think of the children!"

Margo nodded at Frank.

"Keep this up and we might make an exception for you. It would do Shaun good to have a little competition around here. What do ye say, handsome? Think you could handle this many hens?"

Frank opened his mouth to speak and Catriona set her foot down heavily on his instep. He swallowed.

Good girl, Cat, Fiona thought. *No sense in letting your man get himself killed. Sure that's all any of them are keen to do at the end of the day. No matter how old, they're all the same that way.*

In many ways, Fiona thought, the drama inside the cells —the people crying and railing, the threats by the sociopath Margo, the weeping terrified children, and the guarantee of imminent death—it all felt like it was happening a long way away and to different people.

When Fiona looked out the window she couldn't see the ocean from where she stood but she could see the clouds over the sea.

And she could imagine that somewhere in the world it was a beautiful day that anyone would be grateful for.

******

The scream came from the first room off the hall closest to the stairwell. Sarah was at the door in three strides. She wrenched the door open.

Inside Saoirse was kneeling on a bed with an hysterical Damian cowering beneath her his hands covering his face.

Saoirse turned to face Sarah. In her hand she held a large field dressing knife. Her mouth was open in surprise.

If Sarah knew one thing about Saoirse, she knew talking was a waste of time. She ran into the room swinging the mace over her head and screaming the most ear-splitting rebel yell she could manage.

Saoirse watched her come in apparent shock until Sarah hit the bed and slashed out with the mace. Saoirse ducked and the top of the mace swung past her head. Damian tumbled to the floor as Saoirse leapt to her feet with her knife held high in the air.

"How the feck did you get out?" Saoirse snarled. Without waiting for an answer, she lunged at Sarah. Sarah staggered backward and felt the blade slice through her shirt and the top layer of skin on her stomach in one agonizing swipe.

Sarah punched out hard with her own weapon, and again Saoirse twisted away from contact with it before bringing her arm up in a wicked arc heading straight down onto Sarah's chest. At that moment, a clap of thunder boomed and lightning flashed outside the bedroom window.

Using the split second of distraction Sarah brought her mace up in front of her to deflect the oncoming blow. Saoirse hit the mace's handle, snapping it into two pieces in Sarah's hands. The look of triumph on Saoirse's face vanished as Sarah dropped one piece and drove the jagged end of the other as hard as she could into Saoirse's stomach.

Another lighting flash coincided with the sound of Saoirse's butcher knife clattering to the stone floor. Saoirse's eyes bulged as she clawed at the handle embedded deep in her midriff.

A third lightning flash made Saoirse's fall from the bed look like an old-time movie reel stuttering and stopping as she toppled to the floor. Her life's blood gushed out of her in a steady stream.

Damian sat on the floor in shock,

"Hey, buddy," Sarah said, as she wiped a spattering of Saoirse's blood from her face. "Let's get out of here, okay?"

She watched the boy's eyes turn to terror as he looked over her shoulder at the doorway.

"*What have you done?*" an agonized voice croaked.

Sarah turned to see Shaun standing in the room, a gun in his hand, staring at his sister's bloody body.

*****

"I'm waiting, handsome," Margo said. She stood with her rifle resting in her arms, smiling at Frank where he stood next to Catriona. "Just say the word and you're outta there. I'll keep you well fed and well ridden."

"Sorry, love," Frank said sadly to Catriona before turning to Margo, "but I'd rather screw a greased pig."

Fiona's heart squeezed at the expression on Margo's face as she hoisted the gun to her shoulder.

"Wrong answer, arsehole," she said, her voice dripping venom.

"You're a monster!" Nuala screamed. "You'll burn for all eternity for killing children! *Eternity!*"

"Shut up!" Margo screamed over her shoulder and focused back on Frank.

Robby and Kevin began shouting. Fiona saw Robby grab the top bar of his cell ceiling and pull himself up to slam his feet against the lock. The impact jarred all three cages.

Tommy was in the middle cell and did likewise while the women screamed and the children cried.

"Stop it! Stop it all of ye," Margo screamed, running back to the cell with Nuala in it. "I swear I'll fecking mow all of ye down!"

"I've got mine loose!" Tommy screamed and Margo turned to him.

Now Frank was kicking at the lock on his cell while Catriona hugged Siobhan and covered the child's face with her hand at the back of the cell.

Margo ran to Nuala's cell, and shot into it, once, twice, three times. The women screamed and Margo pivoted, her eyes glazed with madness, to the middle cell and opened fire on that one too.

Blood exploded into the air as people screamed.

Susan Kiernan-Lewis

42.

Shaun came into the room like a robot, stiff legged and dull. He knelt by Saoirse's body. His face was white with shock and disbelief.

He crouched between the door and Sarah and Damian.

No way out but through him.

Sarah licked her lips. Should she tell Damian to run? Or to hide under the bed?

Shaun had a gun. That trumped Sarah's nothing. By a lot.

She scanned the room but the only weapon was Saoirse's knife and she was laying on that.

"I'll make you pay for this," Shaun said in a soft voice. "You've now killed everyone I love, you filthy, Yank bitch."

"Not quite everyone," Sarah said. "There's still Ava."

He looked at her, his eyes hooded. "You're not fit to say her name."

I have no weapon. No avenue of escape. No shoes...

And saving Damian only counts if he lives to walk out of this room.

She had to get Shaun to put the gun down or at least exchange it.

"Your sister was crazy, Shaun. Everyone knows that. *You* know that."

He turned his head toward her and his eyes were wet.

"Don't talk about her!" he snarled.

"She said shooting was too good for me. She was going to cut me up like some psycho bitch from a bad horror flick."

He hesitated and glanced back at Saoirse. And then his gun.

That's right, Shaun. Connect the dots. Put the gun down.

"I was going to save you for last," he said as if speaking to Saoirse. "But circumstances change."

Sarah watched him and for a moment she wondered why she thought an attack by a hundred and sixty pound man with a knife was any better than being shot at close range.

But she had *no* chance with the gun.

"Damian," she said calmly. "Listen to me." She didn't dare take her eyes off Shaun to look at the boy.

"Do you hear me?"

"Aye," the boy whispered.

"When the bad man attacks me I need you to run, do you hear? Don't wait to see what happens. Just *run*."

"Where?" Damian asked breathlessly.

The fifty million dollar question.

"What a clever lad you are," Shaun said as he put the gun down on Saoirse's dresser and picked up the butcher knife from the floor. "You're smart enough to know there is nowhere to go. And you mind well too, which is why I know you won't make me chase you, eh?"

Without any further warning, Shaun flung himself at Sarah, slashing the air in front of him with the carving knife. Although she was waiting for it, she wasn't ready. She fell from the bed, twisting fiercely away, trying to avoid the deadly slashing blade.

"I'll eat your baby first, you malicious bitch!" Shaun screamed, his teeth bared like a wild animal. His breath was rancid. He smelled like he'd recently eaten.

She battered him with her hands, and desperately tried to bring her knees up under her.

"Hold still, you fecking bitch," Shaun screeched as he grabbed her hair with one hand and yanked her to a sitting position on the floor. "This is for Saoirse, do ye hear me?"

Sarah jabbed him hard in the eye with two fingers.

He roared with fury and she raised her head and slammed it against his face as hard as she could, twice in fast succession.

"Goddamn you!" he screamed. He pulled the knife back like he would throw a punch. Sarah was pinned under him, gripped in place by his knees, nowhere to go, nowhere to maneuver.

An image of John came into her head. She closed her eyes. *I love you...*

Shaun grunted and his head fell forward onto her chest. Standing behind him Sarah saw Damian holding the handgun by the barrel, ready to hit him again. Shaun moaned and put a hand to his head.

His other hand still held the knife.

Sarah tried to scramble out from under him but he was too heavy.

"Give it to me!" she screamed.

Damian pushed the gun over Shaun's shoulder, handle side toward her. She slipped her fingers into the trigger guard, and pressed it against Shaun's chest just as he brought his knife up again. She pulled the trigger.

Shaun jerked once. His eyes flew open in surprise. Sarah shot him again. And again.

By the time she got to her feet, holding the gun in both hands, Shaun was face down on the floor next to his sister.

She looked at Damian. His eyes were wide.

"Someone's coming!" he said.

"Get behind me," Sarah said and pointed the gun at the doorway. "If we have to shoot every mother…person in this castle—"

The door burst open and Mike filled the opening with Gavin right behind him. Mike's eyes went from Sarah to the two bodies on the ground.

"Holy Mother of…Sarah!"

"They're holding the others in the dungeon," she said, gasping. "You have to hurry…"

"The dungeon?"

"I know where they are!" Gavin said and disappeared out the door.

Mike pulled the gun from her hands and she sagged to her knees. He wrapped one arm around her and pulled Damian into a hug with the other.

"You did well, lad," he said in a hoarse whisper with his eyes on Sarah. "Ye both did."

****

Fiona watched as Margo turned the gun onto her cell. People were dying. Everyone was screaming and still the relentless noise of the men smashing the locks with their boots resounded over all else.

She tucked Ciara behind her and crossed herself, thinking only of Declan and how she would see him soon. She straightened to her full height as Margo lined her up in her scope and then pulled the trigger.

It clicked empty. Margo cursed and pulled another cartridge from her jeans pocket and slammed it into the rifle just as Robby smashed open the far cell door. Margo turned her rifle on him and shot him as he was coming out the door. But there was another one right behind him.

Fiona watched with a sickening feeling of mounting hope and she tried to push it away.

No, it's a trick. We can't win. We can't get away!

The gunshots came one after another now, *boom-boom-boom* like a repeating rifle. It wasn't until Fiona watched Margo jerk rudely as if pantomiming a grand mal seizure that she realized the shots weren't coming from Margo's gun.

Margo fell onto her face, her body drilled with bullets, as Gavin stepped into the room.

"Gavin…" She spoke so softly that he didn't hear her.

Nuala rushed out of her cell. "My Damian—"

"He's okay. Sarah got to him in time," Gavin said.

Nuala let out a long moan and crumpled to the floor. Her boy Dennis was behind her with a hand on her shoulder and the baby in his arms. Robby sat up, his face streaked with blood.

A gasp of horror made Fiona turn to see Frank kneeling on the floor with Catriona's body in his arms. Siobhan was crawling toward Fiona.

Fiona scooped her up and knelt to draw Ciara into her trembling arms.

The room was filled with cries of relief and cries of grief. Gavin's voice was deep and questioning under it all. The babies howling was louder than anyone else's.

Ciara tugged on Fiona's sweater. "Hungry, Mummy," she said. "Now, please?"

Fiona stared into the petulant face of her tired and hungry child and bit back the irrational bubble of laughter that threatened to escape.

A sound she was sure would echo unmercifully against the stone walls of a castle dungeon.

Susan Kiernan-Lewis

43.

That night the men of the castle moved the four bodies to the room where Fiona had sat with Beryl and Declan's body two weeks earlier. Four bodies. Saoirse, Shaun, Margo and Catriona.

Kevin had taken a bullet in the leg which had needed to be dealt with immediately, and Robby was shot in the hand although the bullet had gone straight through. Liddy's forehead was creased by a ricochet but otherwise there were no other serious injuries.

Mary stayed in the clinic with Kevin nursing him after the bullet was removed. Everyone else ate a meal of wine and leftover cold rabbit because nobody was up for cooking. Then they all retired for the evening.

The remaining members of Shaun's group—eleven women and two children—were easily locked in their rooms for the night.

Sarah sat in her room, Siobhan asleep in her arms, and watched Mike undress with all the exhaustion of a man who'd just run a marathon. His initial plan had been to turn the women out immediately into the night but temperatures had dropped and it had begun to rain.

Sarah wasn't sure they should be turned out at all. Their crime was really one of passive acceptance of the horrors of their leader. But they'd all known what was going on.

So there was that.

Sarah thought back to the evening meal—how loud the room had been with everyone laughing and talking at once.

There were tears, too. They had lost dear Catriona after all, who left behind a four-month-old baby daughter. Nuala's boys were quiet too. Especially Damian who'd spent most of the evening sitting at Nuala's feet with his arms wrapped around one of the dogs. Sarah noticed Mike talking to him at one point. She knew he'd keep an eye on him going forward.

And then there was Fiona.

As terrifying as the day was, it somehow served as a catalyst to push Fiona out of her malaise. For the first time since they buried Declan, she showed signs of coming back to them. To lose a husband was a terrible thing and nobody knew that better than Sarah. But the day would come when Fiona would love again and laugh again. And her memories of Declan would be bittersweet. But mostly sweet.

Mike groaned as he sat down on the bed. It was well past midnight. He had bathed before coming to bed.

"You never told me why you didn't wait for Shaun to let down the drawbridge for you. What made you suspicious?"

Mike rubbed his face with both hands and leaned back on their bed as Sarah settled the baby in her cot and tucked her in.

"His reason for why we couldn't come inside didn't ring true," Mike said. "I mean I could well believe something was the matter with the fecking door but when you added it up with all the other things that didn't make sense, it set off alarm bells."

"What other things?"

"Like the fact that everyone in the castle was malnourished but not underweight. And how they said the area was hunted out but Gav and I always found plenty to trap. Plus they never planted a garden. And then there were the dogs. Most people nowadays have trouble feeding themselves, but this lot had *pets*. So how were they all eating?"

"So you always thought they might be cannibals?"

"Let's just say it crossed me mind."

"You acted like he was your long lost brother the way the two of you celebrated after the battle."

"Aye, well, to an American I can imagine it looked exactly as it was supposed to."

She sat down next to him on the bed. "Tricky Irish bastard."

He kissed her on the mouth. "And don't you forget it."

"So once you knew there was something fishy going on, *how* exactly did you get in?"

"Beryl knew all the castle's secrets and she'd never had a more eager audience than Tommy and Gavin."

"So there was *another* way in besides the secret tunnel?"

"Not a very pleasant way. It has to do with the castle sewer system but aye. I figured if I was wrong the worst that would happen was I'd be little embarrassed. When we got inside and I heard the gunshots, I knew I wasn't wrong."

"You came just in time."

"Nay, lass. We came too late for Damian. If you hadn't gotten to him when you did the lad would have died. Until I heard the gunshots, I had no clue which way to go."

Sarah's eyes closed sleepily as she snuggled next to him in the bed, trying to stay awake long enough to focus on the warmth and comfort of the moment.

"You know what's weird, Mike? After all that's happened, I think you were right after all."

"Now those are words a husband doesn't hear very often. How so?"

"I think we're safe here. In fact I think it would take a miracle to get in and most people aren't like us. They're not so stubborn that they'll cling to a wall like a human fly with a nest of jagged rocks below or swim through human waste to get inside or continue to kick at a locked door while some maniac shoots at them. You know?"

"By God, I think you're right.

And even though it hurt like fire because of the cut on her stomach, Sarah laughed and laughed. And the feeling of being safe—and even a little invincible—drifted over like the best drugs money could buy, and with her husband's strong, loving arms around her, she fell asleep without a care in the world.

******

The next morning the snow had stopped. Mike had approved a hearty breakfast for everyone—castle women included—but it was a somber affair. All of the women ate staring at their plates and Sarah could well imagine most of them were wondering where their next meal would come from.

At one point in the morning she debated trying to talk Mike into letting them stay but decided against it. There was only room for one hundred people in the castle to be sustained comfortably, and while it was true they didn't have nearly that many yet, it did occur to Sarah they might hand pick their community going forward.

And those people with a history of eating their neighbors would probably not make the cut.

The plan this morning was that *all* the people in the castle would join together to bury their dead. After that, the eleven castle women and their children would begin their walk down the road—never to return.

Sarah held Siobhan in her arms as they walked out of the castle heading toward the garden cemetery that they were quickly filling up. She saw Ava in the group ahead of her. Her eyes were downcast and her little girl's hand was tightly in hers. Both were dressed warmly. Sarah had given instructions for the women to have a bundle of whatever meat, bread and ibuprofen they could spare.

Isn't this what I was afraid would happen? That we'd invade a castle and throw the people out to starve or be murdered? But the thought wouldn't gel. *These* people were the murderers, Sarah reminded herself. Better that the people they meet should be mindful of *them*.

"All right, love?" Mike came up behind Sarah and put an arm around her.

"I'm good," Sarah said. "Sick of funerals though."

"Aye. This should last us awhile."

Nuala spotted Sarah in the crowd and waved. Sarah grinned.

"Nuala's so happy," Sarah said.

"There's nothing like nearly losing your most precious treasure to help you focus on what's important."

Sarah looked into Siobhan's sleepy face. "You're exactly right," she said. Mike had promised her last night that they would go back to the convent first thing in the morning. The thought that every step was now taking her closer to John buoyed her heart like nothing she could ever remember feeling.

She was so sure she would see him. She couldn't even entertain the possibility that he wouldn't be there.

"I'll go help the lads," Mike said, "if you're sure you're okay."

"I'm fine," Sarah said.

"Aye, ye are," he said, kissing her before turning away.

Sarah watched as the group arranged themselves near where the bodies would be lowered into the ground. She could see Mike standing heads and shoulders above the other men and giving directions. She couldn't help but grin.

"Sarah," a small voice said and Sarah turned to see Ava standing at her elbow. "I wanted to say sorry."

Ava's face was white with dark circles under her eyes. Sarah felt a twinge of guilt for what she and Mike were doing to her. And then she remembered...

"You ran to get Shaun when you saw me in the hall, didn't you?"

Ava looked beyond the group toward where the bodies waited to go in the ground.

"I have no defense. I loved him."

Sarah rearranged Siobhan in her sling and winced as she shifted the baby across the shallow cut Saoirse had scored on her stomach. Not enough for stitches, but still painful.

"Did Mike tell you Keeva and the other children could stay?"

"He did and I thanked him. But a child needs her mother. She'll be better off with me."

Some people can convince themselves of anything.

"Catriona died last night partly because of you. She leaves a baby not four months old. So I agree with you, Ava, that a child needs her mother but thanks to you, Teagan doesn't have one. "

"You have every reason to hate me."

"I don't need you to tell me that."

Ava turned and gazed back at the castle walls and her eyes filled with tears.

"This castle has been my home for nearly five years."

"It's my castle now," Sarah said coldly.

Ava nodded. "I know," she said as she turned away. "I just wanted to say sorry."

Sarah watched her move to the front of the group. She knew Ava mourned Shaun maybe even more than she mourned the loss of a warm, safe home.

But when Sarah tried to feel regret or guilt over throwing Ava and the rest of them out into the cold, the image of that mountain of bones in the castle basement—some as small as Siobhan's—jumped to her mind. And then she couldn't feel anything at all.

The day after the castle folk left broke sunny and cold. It was early December and already the women were planning Christmas and the spring garden. Work details were created to remove the branches, debris and weeds in the garden that five years of neglect had generated. There would also be a second garden inside the castle walls where the lawn and courtyard were now. They had the seeds that Sarah had brought back from the States the year before and Mike and Sarah would bring back more from the compound.

Nuala stood in the courtyard with Siobhan in one arm and little Darcy in the other. The boys Damian and Dennis, who were deemed old enough to help Gavin with the horses, were in the stables working with him.

Mike checked and double-checked the harness on the two horses attached to their biggest wagon. Sarah knew he didn't like traveling just the two of them. He would have preferred to bring Gavin or someone to ride shotgun—literally. But there was so much work to do at the castle to get ready for winter that they couldn't spare even one man to come with them.

"I'll take good care of her, Sarah," Nuala said, giving Siobhan a squeeze. "You're not to worry while you're gone."

"I know," Sarah said. "I'm not worried." Sarah tweaked Siobhan's cheek and ran her hands down her jeans as if she could rub off her extra energy. She was so excited to finally be going that it was all she could do not to jump in the wagon and grab the reins and race out the front gate.

"Mike says it'll take us at least five days to get there."

"That'll be hard going after four weeks sleeping in a warm bed with a fireplace at your feet, I'll wager," Nuala said.

"Nothing feels warmer to me than knowing I'll see John soon," Sarah said. "Not even a fireplace as big as the ones in the grand dining hall." Nuala nodded but didn't smile. Sarah knew Nuala worried about how Sarah might react if John wasn't at the convent.

She shouldn't worry about that.

He'll be there. He has to be.

Fiona came out to the wagon with her hands holding a basket.

"You know we're trying to travel light," Mike said to his sister, "so that we have room to cart stuff back."

"This is for the road," Fiona said. "Blankets and water and the like. Do you have a lighter? A lot easier to build a fire if you have a lighter."

"Thank you, Fiona," Mike said with exaggerated patience. "We have everything we need. Ready, Sarah?"

"You never said what you'll do after that," Nuala said as she walked with them to the wagon.

"After the convent," Mike said, "we'll go to the compound and pack up as much as we can carry."

"What about the nuns?" Fiona said. "Won't you bring them back too?"

"If we find them," Sarah said. "And they want to come." She climbed up to the wagon seat and nodded to Terry standing by the crank on the drawbridge even before Mike was seated.

Fiona reached up and touched Sarah's shoe to get her attention.

"Today's the day, isn't it? The day he said he'd come?"

Tears sprang to Sarah's eyes that Fiona remembered. December first. It was the day John had told Sarah he'd come back.

And miracle or not, Sarah had no doubt he'd be there —waiting for her. She had an image of him, six years old, his little backpack at his feet, as he waited for her to pick him up from carpool all those many years ago—his face searching for each car to see if it was her, his eyes brightening when he found her.

He had to be there.

"Oy! Mike!" Tommy called down from the top parapet where he was scanning the environs before the door opened. "There's people coming!"

Mike frowned and Sarah grabbed his arm. "Mike, we're still going," she said.

"Aye, Sarah. Let's just see who's come calling first though, do ye mind?"

Frustration welled up inside Sarah to see her journey delayed even an hour. It was probably nothing. People came down the road from time to time. Half the time they didn't even call up to the castle. It occurred to Sarah that it might be one of the castle women coming to beg to be taken back in.

She squinted up at Tommy. He had the pair of binoculars they'd taken off Hurley.

"Can you see who it is?" she called up to him.

Suddenly, Tommy turned away and disappeared down the stairwell. When he emerged, in the courtyard he ran to where Terry stood by the drawbridge handle.

"Raise the drawbridge! Raise it!" he shouted. "It's John! He's come home!"

Epilogue

The grand hall was festooned with pine boughs along all three of the ten foot high stone fireplaces. Many white candles created a glow that illuminated the whole room.

The full week before Christmas had been like that. Like a step back in time before the EMP. Like magic had returned to the world.

Sarah tucked her feet up under her in the big chair by the fireplace. A glass of Irish whiskey was on the table before her and a warm wool blanket was across her knees. They'd been hard pressed to find a Christmas tree of any size in this part of Ireland so in the end they'd settled on quantity. Four short, fat Christmas trees anchored each corner of the grand room, decorated with whatever piece of brightly colored fabric, plastic or metal that anyone could find.

Mike had vetoed the idea of candles on the trees but Sarah thought they were still beautiful.

But nothing was more beautiful than the sight and sound of John, Gavin, Robby, Tommy, Sophia and Regan playing Monopoly at the end of the grand dining table.

Not only had John come home—all the way from Oxford where he set out from the day after the second EMP went off—but he came home with every one of the Sisters from the order and with dear Regan, too.

Regan had indeed survived her run-in with the army and melted away into the woods. She'd made her way back to the convent where she and the nuns created a temporary tent encampment while they waited for John. Regan knew John would come to the convent first if he made it back to Ireland.

And he had.

Literally two days before Regan decided they had to leave for the castle or risk freezing to death on the road, John had walked through the woods and into the convent garden in front of the burnt remnants of the convent.

They left for Henredon Castle the next morning.

As Sarah listened to the young people laugh, she thought she noticed a special affinity between Tommy and Regan. Regan was determined to continue her plan to help the raped women of the compound reunite with their families—those that still wanted to go. Tommy had volunteered to go with her—in memory of Jaz—but as Sarah watched him look at Regan, she thought it likely that something else was driving him too.

Sarah looked into the fire as the whiskey warmed her through to her toes. Nuala would bring the little ones in as soon as the feast was ready to be served and then peace would be gone. Sarah grinned at the thought.

Christmas Day. A castle full of babies and nuns and people grateful to God to be alive.

A motion out of the corner of her eye made her turn in time to see Mike enter the room. He was talking to Davey —Liddy's disgraced husband. He'd been living in the woods for the past eight months and met up with John and the nuns on the road to Henredon Castle. Sarah already knew Davey had thrown himself on Liddy's mercy and begged her forgiveness with promises to be a good dad to little Roice. Now it looked like he was clearing it with Mike too.

Sarah watched Mike clap Davey on the shoulder and she found herself relaxing.

You never know what you can live without until you're forced to.

Mike made his way over to her by the fire. The young people called to him to get him to play but he just grinned and shook his head. He took a seat next to Sarah and relaxed with a heavy sigh.

"Merry Christmas," she said.

"And to you, darlin'. Happy?"

"I am."

"Young John coming home like that..." Mike shook his head as if he still couldn't believe it.

"I know. And Regan."

"I hate letting her out the door again."

"Plenty of time to worry about that later," Sarah said.

He turned to look at her and smiled. "Isn't that what I'm always telling you?"

She laughed and leaned toward him. They kissed and she could taste the whiskey on his breath. Obviously the men had been celebrating Christmas by the outdoor fire pit in the courtyard.

"You did it, Mike. You said you'd get us somewhere safe. And you did."

"Aye, well. *We* did. But like everything you and I do, nothing is ever as easy as it sounds."

"I'm sorry I doubted you."

"Pssht! None of that," he said. "Blimey. Looks like it's time. No rest for the weary."

She turned to follow his eyes and saw Nuala, Fiona and Liddy coming into the grand hall with babies in their arms and children squealing and running around them.

The sight of the delighted children combined with the aroma of evergreen pine boughs and the roasted meats made Sarah turn again to Mike. He reached for her hand.

"You're not going to believe this," she said, her eyes brimming with tears, "but I think this might be the best Christmas ever."

"Funny," he said, kissing her hand, his eyes twinkling. "I was just thinking the same thing."

ABOUT THE AUTHOR

Susan Kiernan-Lewis lives in North Florida and writes mysteries and dystopian adventure. Like many authors, Susan depends on the reviews and word of mouth referrals of her readers. If you enjoyed *Never Never*, please leave a review saying so on Amazon.com, Barnesandnoble.com or Goodreads.com.

Check out Susan's blog at susankiernanlewis.com and feel free to contact her at sanmarcopress@me.com.

Susan Kiernan-Lewis